MURDER IN THE ETERNAL CITY

CAPTAIN LACEY REGENCY MYSTERIES
BOOK SIXTEEN

ASHLEY GARDNER

JA / AG PUBLISHING

CHAPTER 1

The first English person I encountered as I wandered the vast city of Rome in February of 1820 was a man I already knew.

Or at least, I thought I knew him. I spied him outside the great church of Sant'Agnese en Agone in the Piazza Navona, that plaza that glides its wondrous length where an ancient stadium once stood. I'd paused to admire the fountain designed by Bernini with its vast marble figures that represented the great rivers of the world. An obelisk—purloined from Egypt—filled with mysterious hieroglyphs, rose from its center.

I had been contemplating these hieroglyphs, which I'd grown interested in during my sojourn along the Nile, when the gentleman in question ambled from the interior of the church and into a tiny passageway that led from the piazza to narrower streets behind it.

I called out, but over the fountain's rushing water, a sudden wind, and a group of tourists that had come to see the piazza, he had no hope of hearing me.

Curious, I left my post and followed him, wondering if I had indeed recognized the fellow. I did not know him well, but I'd been introduced to him at one of the many gatherings in England I'd attended as the guest of my friend Lucius Grenville.

My quarry seemed to be in no hurry, and I thought I'd quickly catch up to him. However, as I emerged from the passageway, the walls next to me grimy and flaking, I found myself in another narrow street crossways to mine but empty.

The fellow must have picked up his pace and plunged down yet another lane that led from this one. I heard a step and turned that direction, following an artery that ran between tall houses on one side and the bulk of a church wall on the other. I rounded the front of the church, which was shut this early in the day, and continued.

My confidence that I knew my way around these back streets began to evaporate as I turned another corner, and then another. When I'd arrived in the city a few days ago, I'd spent hours exploring it, with an entire afternoon at the ancient Forum Romano and the wreck of the Colosseum. Brewster had poked about with me, and I had thought I'd learned Rome quite well.

But at present, I had to admit I was hopelessly lost.

No sign of my gentleman either. Presumably he lodged somewhere nearby and had entered his abode when I'd been in another lane.

As I had no compelling need to speak to him and no reason to pursue him other than curiosity, I abandoned the chase. Now to find my own lodgings.

The passageway I stood in was quiet. I could hear the distant rumble of a cart, the shout of a vendor in a market hidden from me, and the clang of a bell from a watercraft on the Tiber. This small lane of private houses was deserted, shutters above me closed tightly.

I made my way back around the church, in which, if I recalled correctly, Grenville had last evening showed me a fresco by Rafael painted on its wall. The art had been dim with age but arched grandly above an alcove in a side chapel.

Then again, that might have been another church entirely. Every street in Rome had two or three churches springing up from the pavement, distinct places of worship for different guilds, great families, and foreign residents.

Grenville had hired a house near the Piazza Navona for a few days so we could see the sights before a short journey south to Napoli where I would visit the ruins of Pompeii and Herculaneum. Our wives had remained at Grenville's villa north of the city, those ladies preferring walks in manicured parks to stumbling over muddy ruins.

I'd convinced myself another turn through an alley, empty and dark between soaring walls, would take me back to a wider road that led to the piazza, but I was wrong. I emerged instead on the bank of the river, with a finely arched bridge to my left. At the end of the bridge to my right rose the squat tower of the Castle Sant'Angelo.

That, at least, was a familiar landmark. I could stroll along this side of the Tiber and find another street to take me to my lodgings.

A few more turns into the maze showed me I was again mistaken. I rounded another corner, the fetid smell of the river fading behind me, and collided directly into a man coming the other way.

I took an instant step back, leaning on my walking stick to keep myself upright.

"I do beg your pardon, sir," I said as politely as I could,

though he had rushed into *me*, not paying attention to where he was going.

The fellow was Italian, as tall as I was, with a thick head of dark hair. He appeared to be about my age—a few years past forty—and dressed in a subdued dark suit made of fine material which contrasted his muddy and worn boots.

A scowl marred his face, and a pair of dark brown eyes glared at me. I tried to apologize in my faulty Italian, which only made his scowl deepen.

"Ah, you are English," he snapped in that language. "Wandering about, getting in the way."

"Lost, I am afraid, sir. Can you direct me—?"

"Do you not carry a map?"

His churlishness began to annoy me. I put a sterner note into my voice. "I had not planned to stray from the Piazza Navona. If you will point me in its direction, I will endeavor to keep to my allotted place before I depart your fair city, and cease disturbing you. Your errand is apparently an urgent one."

The fact that the man remained in place during this speech instead of scoffing and striding off was encouraging. By the end, his demeanor had softened, though he had not entirely unbent.

"Forgive my temper," he said. "My errand, as you say, is urgent. Go through this street, then around to the next one over, and another jog ..." He let out an exasperated breath. "With me, sir."

He spoke like a soldier. I fell into step behind him as we quick-marched up the lanes, my walking stick tapping, and back to the wide expanse of the piazza.

"Thank you," I said with sincerity as we reached the open vista under a gray sky. "Captain Lacey, at your service, sir. My lodgings are there." I pointed with my walking stick to another opening across the square that led in the direction of the Pantheon. The house Grenville had taken backed onto those that lined the piazza. "If ever you have need of a bumbling Englishman, you may call on me."

I was trying to be amusing, having no idea what sort of service I could offer him when I lost myself within a few streets of home.

The man looked me up and down. "Not bumbling. And, in fact ..." Another once-over. "At present I could use the assistance of what you English term a *stout fellow.*"

"Oh?" I was not certain how robust I would be if he had need of strength. My leg, injured during the war, had already begun to ache from our rapid pace.

Red stained the fellow's cheekbones. "It is my daughter. She ... If I do not retrieve her, she—" He broke off, shaking his head. "I will understand if you want nothing to do with my family and our troubles."

"Not at all. I have two daughters myself." One was a grown young lady, and I had a notion of what sort of troubles he meant.

His flush cleared when he saw that I'd grasped his inference. "Excellent. My name is Proietti, Alessandro Proietti. I was once a colonel, but no longer, although I cannot seem to leave off the habit of giving orders."

"Indeed? What regiment?" I asked with interest. Bonaparte had recruited and conscripted plenty of Italians when he'd invaded, especially in the northern states, though many had joined the Austrians to oppose him.

"I was in an infantry regiment under the Holy Roman Emperor against the Corsican upstart. Retired as soon as we rid ourselves of him. Now the Austrians have walked into places where the French were, and I'm not certain we're better off." His bitterness reflected what I'd heard from many as we'd traveled south from the Alps.

"I too, have retired. Wounded on the Peninsula." I tapped my left leg with my walking stick, and Proietti sent it a look of sympathy. "Now, as to this errand."

Proietti's clouded countenance returned. "A blackguard, as you say in your language, has convinced my daughter he would be a far better husband to her than I am a father. Husband." He spat the word. "He has no intention of being honorable. Blackguard is a very good word for him."

As an outsider, I could not judge whether the abductor was right to spirit the daughter from the heavy hand of her father, but the worry on Proietti's face told me differently. A brutal father would be obsessively enraged and would never have stopped, however reluctantly, to assist a stranger.

I would accompany him and see whether I could help. If it became clear that I was wrong about Proietti, I'd take myself from the fray and hunt up a watchman.

"Very well," I said. "Lead on, Colonel."

Proietti's expression became one of gratitude. "It is not far, I assure you." He turned toward the alleys.

A heavy tread behind us stopped me before I could follow. "Who's this then?" Thomas Brewster asked as he reached me, sending a surly glance to Proietti.

Brewster was my bodyguard, tasked to keep me safe in the streets of Rome. I had neatly evaded him this morning, though it had not been on purpose. I'd wakened early and decided to stroll the piazza on my own, never thinking I'd run into mishap on so short a walk.

"Just the man," I said. "This is Mr. Brewster, Signor Proietti. Another stout fellow."

Indeed, Brewster, formerly a pugilist, had a fighter's build and girth, massive hands, a nose that had been broken more than once, and a gaze that would wilt the most resilient opponent.

Brewster turned those hard eyes on me. "What you on about, guv?"

"An important mission, to assist this gentleman," I said by way of explanation. "Your presence would be welcome."

Brewster regarded me stonily a moment then heaved a long sigh. "Here we go."

Proietti, once we finished our exchange, strode from the piazza into the passageway from which we'd emerged. I followed him quietly, and Brewster came behind me, his steps far less muffled than mine.

PROIETTI TOOK US THROUGH A BEWILDERING ARRAY OF SMALL streets with tall houses on either side. An occasional fountain burbled in unexpected courtyards that were quickly lost behind us. Grenville had explained that I could drink from any of these fountains and find pure, clean water that had flowed from faraway springs since ancient times.

Signor Proietti finally halted before a six-story house that was a faded shade of green, topped by a mansard roof with dormer windows. He stepped to the black-painted front door and pounded on it with his fist.

The door was opened almost immediately, not by an angry young man or an annoyed landlady, but by a stiff servant with gray hair who stared coldly out at Proietti in obvious recognition. They exchanged no words, and at last the servant stepped aside and admitted us.

Proietti charged in without pleasantries. Brewster and I followed at a more discreet pace.

I'd half expected to find a dilapidated boarding house with a wild and handsome young man declaring he'd never send his beautiful and weeping young lady back to her family, as happened in poorly written melodramas.

Instead, I stepped into grandeur—though one that was waning. The high ceiling, decorated with gilded vaulted arches, framed ceiling paintings that rivaled any I'd seen in nearby churches. A staircase rose in magnificence before us, winding its way to the top of the house.

Proietti ran up this staircase without waiting for the servant. Brewster, who was wont to duck below stairs the moment we entered a grand house, came behind me as I more slowly mounted the stairs. Brewster studied the artwork and small trinkets strewn about the place with a professional eye as we went. He had once been a thief, a good one, and sometimes still was.

Proietti gained the next floor and banged open a door. I followed him, my walking stick ringing on terrazzo tile, to double doors leading to a large sitting room, one door swaying on its hinge.

As I entered, my lingering imaginings of a melodrama fled. The chamber was well furnished with lush chairs and settees similar to what Grenville had placed into his tastefully decorated villa. Long windows gave a view of the Tiber, over which rose the dome of St. Peter's Basilica.

The man who'd moved to meet Proietti in the middle of the room was quiet and respectable, older than I'd envisioned, with gray in his hair. He might be in his early fifties, nearer my age and Proietti's than my daughter's.

The young lady who'd risen from a divan when Proietti had

stormed in was comely, though not of overblown beauty. Her blue gown of fine cotton, without many frills, was what any young lady might wear on a given morning. She'd pulled her dark hair into a simple knot, two curls dangling to her cheeks.

She was about Gabriella's age, which again made me understand Proietti's concern. If circumstances had been different, this might be my daughter attempting to elope with an older, likely wealthy man. Gabriella seemed to have been raised with good sense, but the allure of wealth could turn an impressionable girl's head.

An older woman remained on a chair next to the divan, her back ramrod straight, her plain lavender gown a good canvas for the diamonds that glittered on her chest. More winked in her ears behind her iron gray hair. She bathed Proietti and then Brewster and me with a look of profound disapproval.

The conversation proceeded in Italian, a language of which I knew only the rudiments. I'd learned much Spanish and Portuguese during my time in the Peninsula Wars, but Italian was different enough from those to cause me to lose the thread.

I heard the words, *her father* from Proietti, and *incapable* and *inefficient*—at least I believed—from the other man. The daughter, with much spirit, moved immediately to the two men and joined the argument. The older woman, by resemblance the gentleman's mother, planted her hands on her walking stick and glowered at us all. Occasionally she interjected a word or two, and the shouting would pause, only to resume when she fell silent, her mouth in a hard line.

I concluded, as the voices rose, that this was a private house, owned or leased by the gentleman. No landlord came rushing in to complain, and no neighbors in other rooms shouted about the noise.

The gentleman eventually swung to me, a frown on his face. Proietti's daughter also shot a puzzled glance at me, clearly wondering who I was and why I'd brought along a ruffian.

The man directed a string of words at me. He didn't snarl or behave like a boor—he was angry but held himself more in check than did Proietti.

Proietti barked something at him, and the older gentleman's words slid smoothly into English.

"Why have you come here?" he demanded of me.

I gave him a polite bow but kept my tones cool. "A gentleman asked my assistance to retrieve his daughter. I could hardly decline."

The man's face creased with displeasure. "You know nothing of this. I have not stolen her away, and my mother, a worthy chaperone, lives here with me." He gestured to the woman on the chair, who by her expression understood every word.

"He is married to another," Proietti snapped. "A blackguard, as I told you."

The gentleman's chilly demeanor reminded me of James Denis—Denis being a criminal overlord in London. Could this man be as dangerous?

The gentleman lifted his hand. "My marriage is nothing to concern you."

I wondered if he planned to divorce his wife for this lively young woman. I wasn't certain of the laws regarding marriage in the Papal States, where Rome was located, but I was certain they'd be strict. I'd read that during Bonaparte's occupation he'd instigated many reforms over the whole of the Italian peninsula, including legalizing divorce. But once he was gone,

I believed laws had returned to what they'd been prior to his invasion.

However, this gentleman could be inferring that his wife was at death's door—if so, he was rather callously choosing her successor.

"You have no right to keep my daughter," Proietti snarled.

The older woman spoke from the sofa, her English even better than her son's. "She is a guest. *My* guest."

The gentleman's voice grew stern, its iciness deepening. "My mother has invited Signorina Proietti to stay in my home, and Signorina Proietti has made the choice to do so."

Proietti switched to Italian to appeal to his daughter. I did not understand much, but I knew he was asking her to come home with him.

The daughter lifted her chin. "No, Papa." The words were clear in any language.

A discreet cough at the door announced the haughty servant who'd admitted us. Several larger young men dressed in livery, likely the household's footmen, followed him. Brewster stiffened behind me, ready and willing to fight if need be.

The older gentleman turned to me. "Forgive my manners, sir, but you are not welcome here. Colonel Proietti is also no longer welcome. Please leave at once, Proietti. You will not be admitted again."

Signorina Proietti's eyes constricted, tears moistening them, as though she'd not meant to have her father banished from the house. Her infatuation for the cool gentleman beside her was clear, but I could see she preferred that her gentleman and her father be friends.

Proietti opened his mouth to argue, but I stepped forward. None of my business, I knew, but I did not want to see Proietti thrown down the stairs. Nor did I need Brewster to be arrested for bashing his fists into the man's servants.

"Perhaps this can be discussed later," I said. "At a set time and place, on neutral ground. You can understand, Signor, why a father wishes reassurance that his daughter will be taken care of? And you, Colonel Proietti, want your daughter's happiness above all things."

Proietti turned a look of irritation upon me, but the older gentleman, to my surprise, nodded in agreement. He and his mother had kept their tempers best out of anyone in this argument.

"I agree," he said to Proietti. "I will meet you with my men of business and explain things to you."

"Will you indeed?" Proietti demanded, clearly not believing him.

"He has said so," the older woman stated in disdain.

"Papa, please," Signorina Proietti said in Italian—I understood the simple phrase. "I wish this."

"Return home and take your retainers with you." The gentleman's words were in English, for my benefit. "I will send word when I can meet."

"Very well." Proietti growled the assent, but I could see he thought nothing would come of this meeting. He turned to his daughter, imploring her with a long look one more time, but she shook her head. She didn't like to turn her father away, but the pull to the rich gentleman was, at the moment, too strong.

The footmen were ready to advance. Proietti at last snapped off a curt nod to the gentleman, a slightly more polite one to his mother, and strode from the room, the servants parting to let him pass.

I gave the gentleman, Signorina Proietti, and the older

woman another bow. "I beg your pardon for disturbing you. Please make certain you have this meeting, Signor."

"It will be done."

The gentleman spoke without a qualm, and I suspected he'd win this war. I recognized a person of strong will and influence when I met him.

The daughter now seemed less certain, yet she sent me a regal nod, already practicing to be mistress of this house. The older woman did nothing, said nothing, but it was plain she was finished with us.

I started after Proietti, Brewster's heavy tread behind me. The footmen melted from Brewster's path, and I noted their obvious relief that they wouldn't have to test themselves against him.

Downstairs, we emerged into the narrow street and the cool February air, the sky still cloudy. I smelled moisture—rain was coming.

Proietti waited for us at the end of the lane. I'd half expected him to disappear and leave me behind in his frustration, but he lingered, if restlessly.

"I will see you back to your lodgings," he said when we reached him. "I do not need you wandering all over again."

We set off at a quick pace, my knee now truly aching from all the activity.

"Who is he?" I asked as we went.

"Aristocrat," Proietti said, the word clipped. "A bloody conte. Trevisan is his name. From Milan." His sneer spoke volumes. A wealthy man, not even from Rome, who'd moved in and ensnared Proietti's daughter, was not to be borne.

Brewster shot a glance at me, and I returned a minute nod. James Denis had asked a favor of me before I'd set off from London—to seek a count who resided in Rome and arrange for Denis to purchase a small statue from him. That count was not called Trevisan, but the coincidence startled me.

Proietti proceeded at a rapid march, and I hurried to catch up to him.

———

PROIETTI SAID NOTHING MORE AS HE LED US TO THE PIAZZA Navona, where he tipped his hat. "Thank you, Captain Lacey," he said. "I am sorry you had to witness such a scene."

"Not at all," I assured him. "I suppose the conte will keep his word to a meeting?"

"Oh, he will." Proietti's words held disgust. "He prides himself on his correctness. He will bring men of business and lawyers with him." He let out a heavy breath. "I suppose I'd better do the same. Good day, Captain."

He held out his hand, and I shook it.

"Good day," I returned. "If you have need of me again, please do call. I am lodging in a house near the Palazzo Giustiniani, though we depart in the morning for Pompeii for a few weeks. A letter to the Villa Bella in Napoli will reach me."

"Thank you, Captain," Proietti said with true gratitude. "I hope it will not be necessary. *Buon viaggio*—have a fine journey."

We parted after this cordial exchange, and Brewster and I made for the far side of the square.

"Shouldn't have promised him that," Brewster warned as we went. "Who knows what sort of muck he'll drag you into?"

"I sympathize with him, is all," I said, a bit defensively. "Gabriella is about his daughter's age, perhaps only a year younger at most."

"But Miss Lacey has a good head on her shoulders. Not

flighty, prancing after the first bloke she meets with money and a fancy title."

I agreed with Brewster, and was pleased he said so, but I always held a father's worry. "I do wonder what Conte Trevisan was hinting about his marriage. Does he mean to divorce and remarry? Or simply have Proietti's daughter as his mistress?"

Brewster shrugged. "Who knows? Rich blokes can do anything they like, can't they? Or maybe he didn't know the right words in English."

"He spoke very well. I'll wager he's fluent in several languages."

"Aye, well. None of our business, is it?" Brewster's tone held annoyance. He was here to keep me out of mischief, which I'd proved in the past too apt to dig myself into.

I said nothing more as we crossed the piazza, weaving our way through vendors, beggars, tourists, and others who were emerging to begin their morning. Brewster sent me a chary glance but fell silent.

The house Grenville had hired lay across a narrow street from the church of San Luigi dei Francesi. Beautiful paintings by Caravaggio adorned that church, which I'd gazed at for a long while the day of our arrival. Such stark realism in Caravaggio's works, at the same time depicting the mystical and sublime.

Grenville had risen while I'd had my morning walk, and he breakfasted in a small room on the second floor of this narrow house.

Lucius Grenville had enough wealth, I suspected, to buy the conte I'd met this hour twice over, but one would never know it by the modest home he'd let and the subdued suit he wore.

He had, however, immediately employed a chef so we would eat the finest meals possible during our sojourn.

Brewster had absented himself to the kitchen, and I seated myself at the table in Grenville's breakfast room, accepting coffee in a small cup from Grenville's valet, Gautier.

"Had an adventure this morning," I began.

Grenville had patted his mouth with a napkin after he greeted me, and now the eyes above the white cloth filled with irritation. "Of course, you did." Grenville lowered the napkin. "Because I lingered in bed and then decided to sit down to a lavish breakfast."

"It was not as exciting as all that." I had to be amused, Grenville always adamant that my life was far more interesting than his. I took a sip of coffee, which was quite rich and good. I had already decided that the best thing about Rome was its coffee. "I will start with catching sight of an Englishman. I have been trying to remember his name— Ah, I have it. Broadhurst. His given name ... Norris, I believe? Yes, it was. Was introduced to him at a racing meet, or some such, that I attended with you."

Grenville had gone very still. "Norris Broadhurst?" he repeated, an odd note in his voice. "You could not possibly have seen him, Lacey."

I raised my brows. "I am willing to wager he was the man I spied coming out of that church. I tried to greet him, but he vanished."

"Well he might have, my friend." Grenville regarded me gravely. "Norris Broadhurst is dead. Has been this past twelvemonth."

CHAPTER 2

*D*ead?" I repeated in astonishment.

"Quite." Grenville reached for his own cup, which Gautier had instantly refilled the moment he'd set it down. "Sadly, unlamented. He swindled many before his demise. I escaped his machinations, fortunately, because my man of business is astute."

I listened in surprise. I was good at remembering faces, and I was certain I'd seen Broadhurst's. His countenance was round and somewhat plump, his hair going to gray and close-cropped. Today he'd dressed in old-fashioned breeches and boots topped by a rich brown greatcoat, an ensemble for tramping through streets on a February morning. He'd been clapping on a hat as he'd emerged from the church, a broad back turning to me as he'd made for the lanes behind it.

"Was he a religious man?" I asked. "Catholic?"

Grenville blinked. "Good Lord, no. Did his churchgoing on occasion for the show of it, I believe, but I'd not say he was devout. And he was firmly C of E. He'd not have schemed so much money out of his friends if he hadn't been."

True, much of the *haut ton* regarded anyone not of the
Church of England with grave suspicion. However, a person
visiting a church in Rome did not mean he'd converted to that
faith. He, like me, might be viewing paintings, friezes, ceilings,
and tombs of notables long dead.

Grenville studied me, intrigued. "You are convinced you
saw him. Was this the whole of your adventure?"

"Not at all, but now I am curious. Did Broadhurst have a
brother?"

"He might have. He was not in my circle, and attended
Oxford, while I'm a Cambridge man. Gautier?"

Grenville directed the question at the valet who had gone
to the door to retrieve another coffee pot from a footman.

"Mr. Norris Broadhurst indeed had a younger brother,"
Gautier informed us, setting the silver pot on its warmer. "I
believe his Christian name is Alistair. Whether he resembles
the late Mr. Broadhurst, I cannot say."

"There you are." Grenville opened his hand. "You saw the
brother who has come to Rome to see the sights, perhaps to
console himself for his loss."

"That will be it." I sipped more coffee, glad the minor
mystery had been cleared up. I wondered, though, where the
man had been hastening off to on the back streets of Rome so
early, and if he'd had anything to do with his brother's
swindling.

I then turned to my meeting with Proietti and his troubles
with his daughter, telling the story while it was fresh in my
memory.

Grenville listened with flattering attention, but he frowned
as I concluded. "Tricky to be drawn into another man's affairs.
I hope this Proietti does not call upon you to extricate him

from prison when the conte objects to his home being stormed. And that you are not taken to prison with him."

"I am certain it will not come to that." I spoke confidently, but truth to tell, I was not certain. What I knew of Proietti was only that he'd been an officer under the Austrians and that he was concerned about his daughter.

"I will not ask you why you chose to help him," Grenville said, eyes twinkling. "I know it is difficult for you to keep yourself to yourself."

He meant that I was too curious by half and could not mind my own business. "I know how I'd feel if my daughter had run off with a questionable gentleman. I am happy Gabriella has fallen for a staid young Frenchman her stepfather and step-uncle approve of, but even then, I am uneasy."

"From what I have heard, young Monsieur Devere is a good lad." Grenville's tone was meant to be soothing, I supposed.

"That remains to be seen," I answered with caution.

I'd been told the young man's name—Emile Devere—and that he worked for his family—I was vague on the nature of their business. He and Gabriella had been acquainted with each other from childhood, but I knew little more about him.

"We will meet him soon enough." Grenville's answer was breezy. Emile would be joining us at the villa after Grenville and I made our trip south to Napoli and Pompeii. "This aristocrat you met this morning interests me at bit. Who is he?"

"He's called Trevisan and apparently is from Milan, which seemed to be a terrible thing in Proietti's eyes."

Grenville pondered this, then shook his head. "I have not heard of him, though I imagine my cronies here have. Gossip is rife among the British ex-patriates."

"It is none of my affair, as you have pointed out." I waited for Grenville to agree with me, to tell me to put the incident behind me and concentrate on our upcoming journey.

"This has never stopped you before," Grenville concluded. "Or me. And if this daughter is in a dire place, I could not turn my back and leave her there."

I relaxed in some relief, pleased he understood—but then Grenville had a daughter of his own. There had been something I hadn't liked about Trevisan, though whether it was simply because he'd stubbornly refused to let Proietti leave with his daughter, or something more sinister I could not tell. Trevisan's mother had been an enigma as well.

"Proietti showed remarkable restraint," I observed. "I'd have throttled the man and dragged Gabriella away. Or even better, have Brewster escort Gabriella out while I let Conte Trevisan know what I thought of him absconding with respectable young ladies."

"And been arrested for your pains," Grenville pointed out. "We are strangers here. I do not know the exact penalties for attacking such a man, or even for challenging him to a duel, but I imagine they are dire. Perhaps Proietti decided it prudent to live to fight another day."

"Yes, he might be more level-headed than I am." I drained the rest of the rich brew and set the cup back into its saucer. "Or there could be more to this situation than I comprehend."

"If we are wrong, and it is a family squabble the two men and the daughter will work out, then ..." Grenville shrugged his well-clad shoulders. "So be it."

We each gave the other a nod, in agreement.

"Also do not forget I must at some time locate the man from whom Mr. Denis wishes to purchase a piece of artwork," I said. "He assures me it is a perfectly legal transaction, a simple matter of negotiating a price and carrying the statue to him."

Grenville's brows rose. "Are you certain there is nothing important concealed in this statue? It does not convey a secret message? It is not being pursued by the crowned heads of Europe?"

Denis had sent me on such errands before. However, after our last adventure that had nearly ended in disaster, Denis had declared he was in *my* debt. His rivalry with another man had put my family in grave danger, and he'd acknowledged his regret they'd been dragged into it.

I sat back in my chair, observing a sunbeam that had escaped the clouds and filtered through the window. Even the drabbest days here could brighten unexpectedly. "Denis gave me his word there is nothing to it. Before you argue, I am inclined to believe him. I am to give the owner the sum he asks, provided to me by Denis's man of business in Rome, and then take the statue to him."

"Why cannot the man of business make the transaction?" Grenville asked. "Bundle it up and send it to Denis himself?"

I had considered this. "I rather think Denis doesn't trust anyone to keep their hands off it, and I must say, I don't blame him. Possible for a man of business to switch it for a fake, or for a lad sent to deliver it to keep it and pretend it is lost. Denis knows I will do everything in my power to transport it safely from the seller's house to his."

"I concede the point." Grenville signaled to Matthias, his head footman, that he could begin clearing the table. "I will keep my objections to myself, as long as you take me with you for this transaction."

"I would welcome the company, of course. As well as your expertise in antiquities."

"Done," Grenville said, and raised his empty coffee cup in salute. "We will do all and regale our ladies with the tale."

I lifted my cup in return and agreed.

———

WE HAD ALREADY DECIDED TO EXPLORE ROME A BIT MORE before we left it behind. Not long after we finished breakfast, I took up my hat and walking stick and followed Grenville out. Brewster came with us, as usual, and as usual grumbled about looking after us both, but I did not miss the glint of interest in his eye as we walked. He was as intrigued by antiquities as we were.

We began by traversing a narrow street around the corner from our house that quickly widened into the piazza surrounding the great Pantheon. A fountain with another obelisk, one of many looted from Egypt over the centuries, rested in the piazza's center. Beyond the fountain rose the massive edifice of the Pantheon, once a temple to the old gods and now a church.

I admired the facade with its huge granite columns, triangular pediment, and inscription. When I'd traveled to Egypt, I'd been frustrated by the hieroglyphs, whose meaning I'd longed to decipher. At least here in Rome, I could read the Latin, beaten into me as a boy by a tutor too afraid of my father to risk me not learning my lessons.

"*M. Agrippa L F Cos Tertium Fecit*," Grenville pronounced, skimming his walking stick through the air as though underlining the words. "Marcus Agrippa, son of Lucius, during his third term as consul, made this. Except he didn't, you know."

I had read the guidebooks Grenville had pressed on me before our journey. "Because the first temple Agrippa erected on this spot was destroyed," I continued dutifully. "Rebuilt by the emperor Hadrian, inscribed to honor Agrippa, the close friend of Augustus Caesar."

"Kind of Hadrian," Grenville said. "But likely also done to forge a connection between himself and the great Augustus. An emperor ever had to remind lesser men of his grandeur."

I'd also re-read my Gibbon before we'd come and knew that most emperors had spent so much effort on their grandeur that they'd fallen from power, usually violently, before they'd had time to grow comfortable in their purple robes.

Once we'd boasted of our knowledge of the ancients, we wandered through the porch and its breathtaking columns and onto the marble floor of the interior.

The dome was the marvel of the place, made of concrete, arching overhead to its oculus, open to the gray sky above. Largest of its kind in the world, the dome was worth the long journey from England to stand beneath and admire.

After we'd gaped upward for a while, we wandered to the tomb of Raphael. A Madonna with child, her face serene, the child's very adult, stood in a shielded niche adorned with columns of purple stone. Epitaphs praising the artist rested below them. Grenville and I read the Latin inscriptions, which stated that Nature herself feared she would die once Raphael was gone.

As I turned from this effusion of praise, I again caught sight of the gentleman I'd pursued this morning. Broadhurst—or if Grenville was correct, his brother.

The man lingered near a chapel on the other side of the rotunda, on the edge of a small group who had entered, as had Grenville and I, to observe the Pantheon's magnificence. The moment I set my eyes on the fellow he vanished behind a clump of gentlemen in greatcoats, leaving me to doubt myself once more.

"Did you see?" I gestured with my walking stick, pulling Grenville's attention from the tomb of the great artist. "Broadhurst. I vow to you."

"Mmm?" Grenville peered at where I pointed, straining a bit, as he did not have my height. "Beg pardon, my dear chap, I did not. Where?"

I could only wave my hand in the direction, but Broadhurst, or whoever he was, did not reappear.

Brewster, however, made a sharp gesture to me from the other side of the Pantheon. He'd halted inside the doorway, studying a side altar that sported beautiful gilded candlesticks and a gold crucifix. He'd had his hands stiffly at his sides, as though keeping himself from temptation. He'd not seen Broadhurst this morning, but he'd noted my interest in the man now and had fixed his sharp eyes on him.

He pointed to the entrance with an inquiring look. *Want me to nab him?* I surmised he was asking.

I shook my head—the gentleman had done nothing to deserve Brewster laying hold of him—but I moved quickly that way and out the door.

The clouds had thickened again while we'd been inside, and rain began to patter down. I caught sight of a brown-coated back that I believed belonged to my quarry and followed him as rapidly as I could around the Pantheon to the narrow street beside it.

The thick walls of the round building squeezed out the space, making me slow my steps. Other tourists lingered in the narrow passageway, gaping at the architecture, and I was obliged to push my way through them.

I'd feared I'd lost the man again, but when I reached the

rear of the Pantheon, the rotunda giving way to a squarer wall behind it, I found him waiting for me. He stepped out from a niche behind the building and faced me squarely.

If Grenville had not suggested that the gentleman I'd glimpsed this morning had been his brother, I'd swear he was Norris Broadhurst himself. Same round face, same short graying hair, same broad build.

"Captain Lacey?" he inquired.

"Indeed." I halted, out of breath, and tipped my hat. "You are Mr. Broadhurst?"

"No." The word was abrupt. "My name is Mr. Cockburn." He spoke loudly and carefully, gazing behind me as though making certain that if anyone overheard, they'd overhear correctly.

He needn't have worried, because we were quite alone in this place. The crumbling bricks behind the Pantheon were of no interest to those who wished to gaze upon its remarkable facade and interior. Grenville and Brewster, if they had followed, had either lost me or not yet caught up.

The man leaned closer, lowering his voice to a near whisper. "Truth to tell, you have the right of it." He drew a long breath. "I have heard of your reputation, Captain Lacey, and I spied you this morning in the piazza. I apologize for fleeing— your presence startled me, but I made up my mind later to speak to you, and hence followed you here."

"And dashed out again the moment I saw you?" I asked in irritation. "You could have called on me or written, to save my injured leg while I chased you about."

"I do beg your pardon." Mr. Broadhurst wore an expression of chagrin, but also one of fear. "I could not risk approaching you where others could see."

"Well, here I am before you," I stated.

"Indeed." Broadhurst passed a pale tongue over his lips. "I wish to ask you to look into a murder, sir. I have been told you do such things for the Runners."

What I mostly did was inquire into problems I'd found myself in the middle of. I had in the past given several criminals to Mr. Pomeroy, my former sergeant turned Bow Street Runner, but gossip likely amplified my deeds.

"A murder?" I echoed. "That is dire. Who has been killed?"

The man flung out his arms dramatically. "*I* have."

CHAPTER 3

I stared at the man in perplexity, wondering if he were slightly mad. His eyes were moist, his cheeks flushed, his large body quivering. I read panic in him, and also despair.

"Look here," I said. "You need to be clear with me. Are you saying you are indeed Norris Broadhurst? If you are, who is the poor fellow dead in England with your name?"

Before the man could answer, Grenville's voice came around the corner. "Lacey, where have you got to?"

The man shrank into the wall. "Tell no one. Please, sir, I beg of you."

I studied Broadhurst for a fleeting moment. He looked harmless enough, possessing the softness of a City gent, a person who'd worked indoors most of his life. The slight hump in his back, from bending over a desk for years, was another indication of his profession. He truly was afraid and not, in my opinion, likely to pull out a knife and try to gut me.

I motioned for him to keep still and trudged back to the narrow lane that ran beside the Pantheon.

Grenville and Brewster had not yet reached this alley and were calling into other passageways. At least Grenville was shouting for me—Brewster moved in silence, glowering at the bricks as though he'd beat on them until they disgorged me.

I hailed them, and they turned to wait for me in both annoyance and worry. When I reached the pair, I confessed I'd found my gentleman from this morning and that he wished to consult me. I omitted the matter of his true name and his announcement that someone had murdered him, both respecting his wish and wanting to know the full story before I assessed it.

"He will not speak to me if you are anywhere near, so I will meet you later," I finished.

Grenville was not happy, but he nodded. "Do take care. I will find a coffee house in the Piazza Navona and warm myself."

Brewster, predictably, refused to move.

"Mr. Grenville can do as he likes." Brewster's eyes held no capitulation. "But I don't stray a step until you come out of that lane with no harm to you. If you say he won't peep a word if I'm behind you, I'll keep out of sight. But I'll be here." He pointed a broad finger at the pavement beside the bulk of the Pantheon.

I had to concede. Grenville tipped his hat to us and continued along the lane until he turned west toward the piazza.

Brewster planted himself, back against the wall, bending his leg and resting the sole of his large boot behind him. He was hidden from the lane I made for, but anyone coming through his narrow way would have to get past him.

I expected Broadhurst to have fled while I spoke with my

friends, but he was still hugging the rubble-strewn niche when I returned, as though he'd be safe there forever.

"Would you prefer a more comfortable spot in which to tell your tale?" I asked him.

Broadhurst shuddered. "No, I would not. Never know who is about. I will be brief. My partner, Mr. Cockburn, was killed a year ago this January in London."

"I see." I did not entirely and waited for him to go on.

Broadhurst's cheeks reddened. "The killer meant to do me, and that's the truth. Mr. Cockburn had departed our office in Cheapside late one evening. It was dark, and he nipped along to Lombard Street, same as he did every night, heading for rooms he took on a street south of it. As far as I know, he was waylaid, nearly on his doorstep and stabbed through the back, enough times to kill him. They left him there." Broadhurst's throat worked. "I found him. Didn't half give me a turn."

"I am sorry." I imagined his horror when Broadhurst stumbled upon the man, his colleague and presumably his friend. "Mr. Grenville seems to think it was *you* who died. Are you telling me Mr. Cockburn was killed and buried in your place?"

"You have grasped it, Captain."

"What happened when you found him?" I persisted. "Did you not summon the Watch? Rush to find a magistrate?"

Broadhurst scrubbed a hand through his hair. "I scarce knew what I was about. I was terrified. I—I had to think fast. He and I looked a bit alike, and knew the murderer had mistaken him for me. I thought—why not have it be me who'd died? I found myself switching my coat for his—I had letters addressed to me in my pocket. I took Cockburn's pocket watch, his coin, all he had. I let myself into his house with his key and nabbed his passport papers and any money I could find, which wasn't much. Then I fled. I bought passage to the Continent that very night and sailed from Greenwich. The newspapers reported that Norris Broadhurst had been killed, likely by a thug who'd robbed him near Lombard Street. By that time, I was here. Safe, or so I thought."

I leaned heavily on my walking stick, unnerved by his blatant confession of so readily taking his partner's identity. A bit hard on poor Cockburn's family and friends, who believed he was still alive. "Why are you so certain that whoever this murderer was, was after you? It was Mr. Cockburn who was attacked and killed after all."

Broadhurst wet his lips. "As I say, he and I looked a bit alike, and from the back, one fellow from the City resembles another. And Cockburn, he was trying to put everything right. Our firm had got into a bit of ... difficulty. Honest mistakes were made, and the market never does what we think, but I was blamed. I knew I'd face the dock for it, but Cockburn was working diligently to pay back the money. Everyone made him out to be a hero—*I* was the villain of the piece. So it must have been me this killer wanted. I made sure it seemed he'd offed the correct man."

"What about your brother?" I asked. "Surely he would have known the dead man was not you."

Mr. Broadhurst shuffled uneasily from side to side. "He was away, in Canada. The magistrates decided they had enough cause to believe Cockburn was me."

I had the feeling he was leaving something out of his tale, but I decided not to press him at the moment. I'd pry it from him later, when he wasn't as nervous.

"You believed that ought to have been the end of it then," I finished for him. "Why have you begun to worry now?"

"Because I'm being followed." Broadhurst darted a nervous

glance behind me. "When I saw you this morning, I remembered meeting you at the Derby in Epsom year before last—Lord Dorland introduced us. He'd been speaking to me about investments."

I recalled the introduction now, a brief encounter. I'd been pulled away very soon to attend Lady Aline Carrington, who had convinced Grenville and me to escort her to the races. Broadhurst had begun his patter to convince me he was a trustworthy man for my investments, but as I had little money of my own, I'd paid him no heed and had gratefully used the excuse of assisting Lady Aline to escape him. I hadn't thought about Broadhurst again from that day to this morning.

"I'm not sure what you wish me to do, sir," I said stiffly. "If you fear retaliation, you ought to hire a man to guard you."

Broadhurst's eyes widened. "Thought of that, thought of that. I'm not certain I trust these Romans. Gut you and rob you as soon as look at you, I'd say. I cannot turn to an English servant, such as you have, because they gossip, don't they? I'd be found out."

I began losing patience with the man. "If you do not trust the inhabitants of this city, why do you live you here?"

"I am merely another tourist, aren't I?" Broadhurst waved a plump arm. "The British expatriates are mostly artists and writers or minor aristos, and I don't know them. They've never heard of Mr. Cockburn, let alone Mr. Broadhurst, of the City—"

"How can you be certain someone has found you out?" I interrupted.

Again his pale tongue slid along his lips. "Letters. Short missives left with my landlord. *You cannot hide. Repay what you owe.* That sort of thing."

"Perhaps I could have a look at these letters." I held out my hand. "Examining them might help identify the writer. His handwriting, the paper, quality of the ink."

Broadhurst shakily thrust a fist into his coat pocket and pulled out a folded paper. "I put most of them on the fire—I didn't want them anywhere near me. All but this one that I received when I returned to my rooms this morning. It clinched the matter of seeking you out."

I took the letter, opened it, and read. *You will pay for what you have done.*

That was all. The hand was rather neat, as though the writer wished to make certain his message was clear.

"If you receive any more, save them," I said, refolding it. "Shove them into a box if you can't stand to look at the things, but bring them to me."

Broadhurst's eyes filled with hope. "You will help me, then?"

"I will consider it." I tucked the letter into my pocket, where it hung like a weight. I continued in a stern tone, "Another tactic you might take is to give the money back. You told me that Mr. Cockburn was trying to make things right. Why not finish what he started? I imagine that a man who saw the money he lost returned to him would be more kindly disposed to you."

Mr. Broadhurst cleared his throat. "Not so easily done, you see."

I hadn't thought it would be, or he'd not have fled to the Continent at the first opportunity he found.

"You have spent all the money?" I could not find any kindness in me for his misdeeds. "You ought to have remained at home and faced the consequences, Mr. Broadhurst."

It had occurred to me that his story of finding Mr. Cockburn conveniently dead could well be a false one. Perhaps Broadhurst had realized that he faced debtors' prison, or worse, and had invented the scheme of switching identities with his partner. Blows from a knife in the dark, a flight to another country, and he was free.

"Perhaps I ought." Mr. Broadhurst fluttered his gloved hands. "But there's nothing to be done now."

I doubted that. He must have managed to squirrel away a large portion of the money he'd swindled before he'd escaped to the Continent. His clothes were whole and well-tailored, his hat a fine one, and he could pay for lodgings. He was not living in the gutter and suffering from want.

I grew annoyed with Mr. Broadhurst. His sins were coming home to roost, and he was asking me to help him avoid this fate. He struck me as one who would do anything to evade responsibility. Even murder? Possibly.

"I'd heard that you are rather good at hunting down those who harm others," Mr. Broadhurst went on. He spoke breathily, and I detected true shame in him. "If you can discover who is doing this, perhaps dissuade them from pursuing me ... The tame ruffian who follows you about would be just the thing." His face grew red. "I know it's an awful cheek, but I truly am frightened."

I firmed my mouth. "What I suggest, sir, is that you either move to another city or own up to your crimes and reimburse your victims, even if it ruins you. Become the hero, as you called Mr. Cockburn, rather than the villain."

"Would that it were so simple." Mr. Broadhurst stated this with feeling. "I vow, I would pay back all I owed if I could. And I did plan to move along. Rome is getting too frightening for me. But, please." His eyes held fear and some self-loathing, none of it feigned. "If you could see your way to discovering who stalks me like a gamekeeper and dissuade him, I would be ever so grateful."

"Are you certain you have no idea who is behind this?" Usually, a man wasn't threatened without cause or at least a knowledge of who wished violence against him.

Broadhurst's eyes flickered as though he'd thought of someone, but he shook his head. "It could be one of so many. That is the trouble. Please, Captain, if you do this for me, I could put some good your way."

I had no wish to take investment advice from a swindler, but as Broadhurst opened his mouth to bleat more pleas, I held up my hand. "I will look into the threats. For nothing else but my conscience in case someone does manage to murder you."

Broadhurst flinched but melted in gratitude at the same time.

"Thank you, sir. Thank you. You are an honest gentleman."

Truth to tell, I wanted nothing more to do with the man, finding him a bit odious. But also true, if I discovered tomorrow that someone had bashed him to death in the night, I'd not forgive myself for not preventing a murder. I could also discover, if possible, what had become of the cash he'd cheated out of his clients, and perhaps have it returned to them. Not all gentlemen could afford to lose their funds.

"Do not thank me yet," I said. "I will hunt for this letter-writer, but I will not promise to set my ruffian, as you call him, on him. Brewster is his own man, not my lackey."

Broadhurst had to concede this point, and stuck out his hand. I clasped it in a firm grip that caused him to wince then quickly withdraw.

"If you receive any other letters, bring them to the house next to the Palazzo Giustiniani and leave them with Mr.

Grenville's valet. I am departing this city tomorrow for a short time, and I have no intention of holding up my journey for your sake."

"Not at all, not at all." Broadhurst beamed at me. "Anything you can do is welcome, my dear fellow."

"I am hardly your dear fellow." I tipped my hat. "Good day, sir."

I turned away. Broadhurst did not follow me, and I heard nothing from him as I made my way back to the wider lane and the scowling Brewster.

———

I COULD NOT VERY WELL KEEP WHAT I DISCUSSED WITH Broadhurst from Brewster or Grenville. I would need their help, and I could trust them to keep the secret.

Brewster, to whom I'd told the tale as we walked, decided to remain outside the coffee house as I entered the dark, low-ceilinged room filled with pipe smoke and the heavy aroma of roasted coffee. Brewster's opinion was that I should find the letter-writer and lead him to Broadhurst and good riddance, but I pretended to ignore him.

I found Grenville in a corner table in the coffee house, reading an Italian-language newspaper, a small cup next to his elbow. I seated myself opposite him, and when he lowered the paper, I told him in a hushed voice all that Broadhurst had said.

"You amaze me, Lacey," Grenville said once I'd finished. "Not from your story—I am not surprised the man found a way to survive, likely with the funds intact, as you suspect. I am amazed that you agreed to help him."

I shrugged. "Not so much *him*, but this person who is

threatening him. If I can save that man from the noose, I will consider it a good deed. Why waste a life because of a pest like my new acquaintance?"

"Ah," Grenville said, his tension easing. "I take your meaning."

"I suppose we must interview every Englishman in Rome until we find the letter-writer," I said. "A tall order?"

Grenville folded his paper, creasing it before he laid it aside. "Not entirely. We may begin today. I am obligated to call on those of my acquaintance before I vanish from the city. They will feel slighted otherwise, and my reputation will be in tatters."

He spoke lightly, but I knew Grenville did not entirely jest. There was a code of conduct a gentleman had to follow in order not to be considered a boor, or even called out if his behavior was deemed too insulting. I'd always been grateful I was seen as a rough-shod army man and forgiven my lapses, but Grenville knew exactly how to tread the line.

We departed the coffee house, fetched Brewster, who'd made a friend of a lad who cleaned shoes at the side of the square, and made our way back to Grenville's. There I retired to my chamber so that I could be presentable when Grenville was ready to depart.

———

The English who'd exiled themselves to Rome, whether they'd departed Britain by choice or under scandalous circumstances, dwelled in abodes around the Piazza Navona or the Piazza di Spagna, near the lavish gardens of the Villa Borghese.

Grenville led me on foot early that afternoon, Brewster

trailing us, to a tall house that overlooked the Borghese gardens. Lord Matthew Roberts, our host there, was the brother of a marquis. He and his wife were middle aged, Lord Matthew's hair gray, his wife's a dark brown with only a few silver hairs. Lord Matthew had been an acquaintance of my mentor, Colonel Brandon, in their younger days, and professed to be delighted to see me.

"Splendid to meet you, sir." Lord Matthew pumped my arm, his grip solid. "Heard about you through Brandon's letters. Very proud he was, of his recruit."

I murmured something polite, wondering how detailed those letters had been. Colonel Brandon had been quite pleased about my rise through the ranks, he boosting me all the way, but our subsequent falling out had been tumultuous. However, Brandon was a private man, so perhaps he'd spared his friends the exact tale.

Lady Matthew—Millicent—welcomed us to her parlor, where other guests had congregated. The chamber with its high ceilings possessed the grandeur of a palace, though the gold leaf trim flaked around paintings that were dim from age. Many of these houses had been built a hundred and more years ago, when popes and cardinals had decided that Rome needed to show the splendor befitting their high authority.

Grenville settled in comfortably without betraying any awe at the ostentation of our surroundings. I kept myself from staring and accepted hock to drink.

The guests were unknown to me, though Grenville was acquainted with most. Colonel Ward, a retired military officer I did not recognize, greeted me warmly. He'd been artillery, laying down fire before the cavalry charged. Though he'd been in a different regiment from mine and our paths had not crossed, we'd shared the experience of the Peninsula War, which made him inclined to befriend me.

I did not have much time to reminisce with him, finding myself buttonholed by the ladies of the group—the colonel's wife; Lady Matthew; and one Mrs. Hetherington, who was perhaps ten years older than me and determined to keep a firm grip on her youth.

The three were not so much charmed by me as interested in my wife. Donata, the former Lady Breckenridge, was well known throughout aristocratic and genteel society, and speaking to her nobody husband—*why on earth did she marry that odd fellow?*—would give them fodder for conversation for days to come.

Mrs. Hetherington was somewhat of a bluestocking, or at least professed to be, all the while wearing plenty of diamonds and silk, her cheeks rouged. She was a friend to poets, she boasted, like the scandalous Mr. Shelley, who'd left his wife to run away with the Godwin girl, and poor Mr. Keats, whom she was trying to persuade to come to Rome for his health. As for Lord Byron, well, she could tell tales …

The three women, tossing questions at me one after another, managed to pry from me that Donata's son had journeyed with us instead of being shut into his school, that both my wife and I adored our new daughter, and that Donata continued to move in high society, though I was more content sitting at home.

Grenville was no help, deep in conversation with the gentlemen. Before the ladies could take me into the ring for another round, the butler entered and cleared his throat.

"Conte de Luca has arrived, my lord."

I rose in surprise as a rather stocky man of medium height and black hair entered and made a flourishing bow, a cape rippling over one shoulder. He rose but dropped his gloves, a wry smile creasing his face as he swiped them up from the floor and handed them and his cape to a patiently waiting footman.

This ungainly gentleman was the man I was to contact for Mr. Denis and from whom I was to obtain the costly artifact.

CHAPTER 4

*M*ateo." De Luca addressed Lord Matthew
Roberts with open arms, voice booming. "How
splendid to see you."

Lord Matthew, apparently used to the conte, consented to
his embrace and his noisy kisses on both cheeks.

"De Luca." Lord Matthew's greeting was more reserved but
no less warm. "How are you, my old friend?"

"As well as ever." De Luca spoke English with barely a trace
of accent. He next turned his attention to the ladies, beaming a
broad smile at them. "As beautiful a trio as I can ever hope to
find."

Lady Matthew flushed at his compliment, and Mrs.
Hetherington simpered as she gave him a curtsy.

Lord Matthew introduced us. "Mr. Grenville, Captain
Lacey. Conte Adolfo de Luca."

"An honor, sir." De Luca shook Grenville's hand hard, no
embraces for strangers. "I have heard of your collections in
London, so very tasteful and intelligent."

Satisfaction sparkled in Grenville's eyes. "One does one's best," he said with an attempt at modesty.

"No, no. It is a stupendous gathering of beautiful objects, I have been told. You have seen it, Captain Lacey?"

"Indeed." I let de Luca grip my hand, already liking the man's genial ways. "Mr. Grenville has some amazing things."

"I also have heard that you are under commission to purchase one of my, as you English say, bits and bobs." De Luca grinned at my surprise. "I keep my ears open. So many are interested in my treasures, but I simply gather what I like."

Sir Matthew chuckled. "A fine understatement."

De Luca opened his dark eyes wide. "No, it is true. I promise you. I might have a few interesting pieces, I suppose." He laughed, mouth open, a man amused by his own self-deprecation.

The ladies and gentlemen in the room smiled and nodded as though de Luca had made an excellent joke. I wasn't quite certain what to make of him, but I saw a gleam of mischief in his eyes, as though he acted the bumbling aristo to disguise keen shrewdness.

"You must come and see my house, Captain Lacey," de Luca continued. "Pick out what you like, and I won't be too hard on you about the price." His amusement told me he might indeed be a skilled bargainer, but I would face that when I came to it.

Grenville answered before I could. "We'd be honored, although we are in somewhat of a hurry. We depart Rome tomorrow. The ruins on the Bay of Napoli await us."

"Ah, you English. I resided for a time in Oxford, and I noticed that you rushed through your meals and coffee, though had time to linger for hours over your ale." De Luca's smile shone out again. "I cannot blame you. The food was terrible, the coffee sludge, but the ale was a marvel."

Again, all in the room laughed with him, and I could not help it as well. His humor was infectious.

"Never fear." De Luca's large hand landed on my shoulder. "You shall come when you return. I will put aside time for you, and you will put aside time to share a meal with me."

We could not disagree with such a generous offer. Both Grenville and I promised to attend.

Talk turned to art and antiquities as we drank more wine. Bonaparte had helped himself to many of the treasures of the Italian States as he'd created the Kingdom of Italy, with himself at its head. The artwork, in the five years after Bonaparte's fall, had drifted slowly back where it belonged, but by no means had all been restored.

"Plenty of works are still missing, or remain in Paris," Grenville said. "It will be a long while before what Bonaparte wrought is completely dismantled."

"What he wrought is idolized by some," Sir Matthew mused. "The new constitutions would have let Italians rule themselves—or so they believed, with Bonaparte as overall emperor, of course, and members of his family over the various states. But the point was, he rid them of Hapsburg rule." He waved his glass. "Now the Austrians have returned, their hold on the northern states tighter than ever, and they have control of Venice. A thousand-year-old republic, gone with the stroke of a pen."

Sir Matthew simplified the situation greatly, but it was true that Bonaparte, the wars, and the Congress of Vienna afterward had altered the map of Europe. No more Holy Roman Empire: the Hapsburg territories were now called the Austrian Empire, and France, while nominally a kingdom again, would never be the same. Only the Ottomans continued as they had been, though I'd no doubt Bonaparte's ambition would have turned to that realm if he'd prevailed in Europe.

Britain had escaped, but by the skin of its teeth. If Bonaparte hadn't had lost much of his army in Russia, he'd have focused his attention to annexing Britain at long last.

We debated the topic, which would give historians fodder for years to come. Grenville managed to slide in a mention of Broadhurst—beginning with swindlers in general and moving to specific ones—but from the blank stares of the company, I concluded they'd not heard of him.

The sun was slanting through western windows when Grenville rose and said we'd take our leave.

Grenville knew exactly when to end a call—he'd stay long enough to be cordial, but not long enough to become tiresome. It was a talent I lacked. When I found someone with whom I could be congenial, I wanted to linger and enjoy the conversation. Likewise, when the company was tedious, I'd find any excuse to rush away.

De Luca again clasped our hands in his tight grip before clapping us both on the shoulders. "Godspeed, gentlemen. Call on me when you return from your journeys, and we shall have a fine repast."

We agreed, I already looking forward to it, and took our leave, making our way down the stairs and to the street.

"Guv." Brewster emerged from a door a few feet down the lane, this one fronted by an iron grill that he clanged shut. "Best get indoors. There's those what are hunting for us."

"Hunting?" I asked in perplexity.

The sound of tramping feet made him grimace. "Too late, that's a fact."

A half dozen men I assumed were patrolmen rounded the corner from a wider street and blocked our way.

"You are Captain Lacey?" one inquired of me unsmilingly. "You and your servant will accompany us."

Brewster stepped in front of me, his bulk between me and the armed men. Their uniforms were a subdued blue, boots dusty from the streets.

"I beg your pardon?" Grenville gave the leader a haughty stare. "We are visitors here and will go nowhere with you. What is the trouble?" Grenville had not been included in the command, but he had no intention of stepping aside and letting me be arrested.

The commander shifted uneasily. "I have not the English to explain. The magistrate will tell you."

I agreed with Grenville and Brewster that I should go nowhere. Unlike in London, where the Watch kept a some-what ineffectual eye on the streets, cities on the Continent had more regular police who patrolled with more vigor.

I imagined the magistrate would not be happy that I, a foreign nobody, had resisted going tamely to him for whatever I was supposed to have done. On the other hand, I had no intention of letting myself be jailed until I understood the nature of my supposed crime.

The commander bore a scowl, not at all pleased with us. His soldiers—or constables, or whatever they were—watched with interest, as though curious about the outcome of the encounter.

A rumbling voice cut through our indecision. I recognized Conte de Luca's baritone, which was no longer amiable. He barked out questions in Italian, and the commander's expression grew still more irritable.

I heard the name *Trevisan*, and de Luca said "Ah," and bent a stare on me.

"What have you done to upset his worshipfulness, Conte Trevisan?" de Luca demanded.

I returned his gaze in puzzlement. "Nothing. I did visit him this morning, but I spoke little to him."

De Luca's brows went up. "I'm certain there is more to it than that. He is claiming you charged in and attacked him. His neighbors did see you entering his house." His gaze took me in. "They describe you well."

"Then they will have noted that I am lame." I tapped my left boot with my walking stick.

"I believe they noted you carried a stout weapon." De Luca indicated the stick. "And that you left in a hurry."

My ire rose. "Conte Trevisan was upright and in good health when last I saw him. If someone punched his nose for his arrogance, it was not me."

De Luca barked a laugh. "So many would like to bruise that appendage, and so many fear to. He is a powerful man. If you promise you did not pummel him, then I will vouch for you."

"I do promise," I said. "I did not like the conte, but I give you my word I never laid a hand on him."

Grenville broke in. "Captain Lacey returned to our rooms as I finished breakfast, and I saw no evidence that he had been in an altercation."

Brewster contributed nothing. His habitual wariness of any sort of police kept his mouth a thin line, his face hard in his silence.

I was grateful to them both for saying nothing of Proietti, and I wondered if Trevisan had accused him as well. Or possibly he'd chosen me on whom to take out his wrath so he would not upset Proietti's daughter by having her father arrested.

De Luca shrugged and settled his dark cape on his shoulders. "There you have it, sir. Captain Lacey had nothing to do with any assault on Conte Trevisan. Lacey is a friend of mine, and I will answer for him."

The commander scowled, but the bow he gave de Luca was deferential. "As you say, your lordship." He snapped a command at his troops, who backed away, their stances saying that while they'd let us pass without hindrance, they'd be watchful.

De Luca clapped his large hands together. "There, that's cleared up. Gentlemen, perhaps you will accompany me home, and we can chat about my collection this evening."

I did not know if Grenville had other outings planned but heading to de Luca's abode instead of our own might be wise.

I nodded before Grenville could speak. "Very kind of you. Of course, we will come, if it is no inconvenience?"

"Not at all. My man is used to me bringing home all sorts on a whim. He keeps my larder well stocked. Good day to you, commander." De Luca swung around, his cape fluttering. "This way, my friends. A bit of a walk, but safer than a coach or sedan chair. The bearers and drivers can be brutes."

The commander said nothing at all. No apologies, no snarls. He had lost the power in this encounter, and he conceded it with dignity. Grenville tipped his hat to the commander, and I gave him a nod. Brewster ignored him completely.

"'Tis why I don't like foreign parts," Brewster muttered as we tramped off after de Luca, who moved swiftly for so large a man. "When there's trouble, gents like that commander round up the first cove what's not from around his city and shove him into a dirty cell."

"Do not be too hard on the man," I said. "He's torn between answering to his superior officer and knowing that upsetting a prominent citizen will bring him grief. He loses either way. I have sympathy for him."

"Have as much sympathy as you like." Brewster tugged his hat tighter against the wind. "But don't let him arrest you and drag you God knows where because you feel sorry for him."

"No fear," I said adamantly.

Grenville had caught up to de Luca, but Brewster kept his steps slow to match mine. The two men were never out of sight as we followed them to the Piazza de Popolo, which sported yet another obelisk in a plaza being renovated. From there we skirted the gardens surrounding the Villa Borghese and continued past the Villa Giulia, where Pope Julius III had taken his ease in great splendor from his exhausting days at the Vatican.

Houses grew fewer and farther between, until we walked up a street and through a gate into a lovely courtyard.

The garden in this courtyard must have been laid out when men in the seventeenth century had made Rome a place of resplendence. Three fountains lay among well-trimmed garden beds, the largest one in the center of the broad walkway that led from gate to house.

As it was February, the flower beds were empty but the box hedges were dark green, and the fountains played, the late afternoon's weather too mild for freezing.

De Luca walked through this pleasant garden without pause, leading us to a columned portico. One of a pair of doors at the top of three shallow steps opened before he reached it, de Luca passing inside with a nod to the manservant who'd admitted us.

If this manservant was surprised to see his master return with guests, he made no show of it. The same height as de Luca, with dark hair and eyes, he made a brief bow to

Grenville and me as we entered. Without a word, he reached for hats, gloves, and greatcoats, which we all surrendered.

De Luca's house was narrow, tall, and echoing. Still in the city, it was hemmed in by houses on all sides, but within this space was a simple opulence. A travertine-stepped staircase rose to a gallery, both stair and gallery railing of ornate wrought iron. Tables of luxurious curves rested in niches along the walls, each holding vases of flowers or bronzes finer than any I'd ever beheld. Ancient or modern, I could not discern, but Grenville eyed them with appreciation.

Rooms opened from the main hall, and I glimpsed more quiet beauty. Though de Luca had claimed he only had a few interesting pieces, what I saw negated this declaration. Perhaps de Luca had decided to be self-effacing at the gathering to not appear conceited, just as a great painter might dismiss his own masterwork was *a mere daub*.

De Luca did not acknowledge these other chambers, but started up the stairs, gesturing for us to follow. Brewster, with a nod at me, left to find the servants' hall.

My leg was sore from our swift walk through the city, but I was too curious to slow and rest. We passed along the first gallery and up a second staircase, then up yet another staircase hidden behind a door in a side hall. From this we emerged onto what I supposed was the topmost floor.

Here, under a low ceiling lined with dormer windows, lay an astonishing hoard.

Grenville's mouth fell open, and I was aware of my jaw slackening. De Luca grinned as we beheld the shelves, tables, and cabinets holding a mass of statuary, urns, bronzes, bejeweled boxes, marble pillars, silver and gold plates and pitchers, ancient lamps made of both metal and stone, finely wrought gold bracelets and earrings, and what looked like bits of papyrus from Egypt.

The things were not all from the ancient world. Plenty hailed from more recent times, including ornate clocks made only a few years ago, very like ones I'd seen at Carlton House. Paintings and tapestries covered every inch of the walls between the windows, and marble and alabaster statuary peered from every niche and corner.

De Luca gazed about in satisfaction. "I collect what I like. No arrangement to it." He flicked his fingers at a gold monstrance—an ornate upright pillar with a round opening in the center, meant to display the host during the Eucharist. Next to it sat a clay tablet with square writing on it from the Persian empire. "I know I should have this all cataloged, but I enjoy discovering something new every time I enter the room."

"Where did it all come from?" I asked in bewilderment. This was a lifetime's collection.

De Luca shrugged his large shoulders. Without the cape, his suit was no different from Grenville's, dark and plain, though well-cut. His was more rumpled—a man unconcerned with how he appeared.

"Here and there. I bargain with my friends for their bits, and we sometimes trade. My father left a good deal, as did my grandfather. Both hoarded like rats." He waved a dismissive hand. "I scan through estates when wealthy men pass away, their heirs eager to sell precious objects to collect the money for them." He shook his head, despairing of the young.

"This is astonishing," Grenville said in wonder. Grenville's own room of treasures was neat and precise, everything in its place, but I saw the envy in his eyes.

"As I say, bits and bobs," de Luca said, offhand. "What is it that your acquaintance is looking for, Captain Lacey?"

Denis had written me, with his usual brevity, a description of the precise piece he wanted. I did not have the paper with me, as I hadn't anticipated meeting de Luca today, but I remembered it, having studied the short letter often enough.

A small Roman statue carved from alabaster. A seated Cupid, face propped on his hand, one wing broken.

I related this information to de Luca, and the man's thick brows drew together.

"I believe I do have such a thing." He turned in a slow circle as he scanned the many shelves and tables of haphazard items. "But I'll have to have a hunt for it." He strode to the top of the stairs and shouted down them. "Gian!"

Unrushed footsteps sounded, and presently the dark-haired manservant appeared, he betraying no surprise or resentment about the peremptory summons.

De Luca spoke to him in Italian, sweeping his hand to the jumble in the room. Gian nodded, as though understanding exactly which piece de Luca meant, and answered his master, his tone deferential, even fond.

Gian's puzzled gaze then rested on me. He asked me a question, and I shook my head apologetically.

"Forgive me," I told him. "My Italian is very bad."

"He is wondering at your friend's taste, Captain," de Luca said jovially. "As am I. If it is the statue we are thinking of, then your friend does not understand what he is asking for."

"No?" Denis had told me to agree to whatever price they asked, and I knew he did not want me to leave Rome before I acquired the statue. "Is it so very valuable?"

De Luca's laugh rang out, and Gian smiled with him. "The opposite," de Luca told me with delight. "It's not from Ancient Rome at all. There never was such a piece made in antiquity. The Cupid is a forgery."

CHAPTER 5

*B*oth Grenville and I blinked at him. De Luca continued to laugh at us, as though enjoying our dumbfounded expressions. Gian was less amused, but he also clearly believed us—and our buyer—simpletons.

I immediately thought that de Luca and Gian must be mistaken. Denis would not want an artwork that had been faked, unless he was interested in it for the artistry of the forger. He relished finding the most skilled of the criminal classes. But most likely, Gian and the conte did not know what they had.

"Did you realize the statue was a forgery when you acquired it?" I asked. "Or did someone tell you it was fake later?"

De Luca stopped laughing at last. "It belonged to my father. He told me it was not real. Chuckled when he said it. A family joke."

Then the forger was likely dead and gone. Yet, Denis was never wrong about artwork. He had more skill in distinguishing the valuable from the dross than even Grenville.

Perhaps Denis knew the piece was authentic and also knew de Luca believed it a forgery. Such conviction on de Luca's part might bring down the price.

"Nonetheless." I shot de Luca a faint smile. "My friend would like to have the statue. A whim, perhaps."

"Perhaps." De Luca scanned the room again as though trying to remember what was where. "Well, if we can turn it up, I'll sell him the thing. As long as you tell him without hesitation that it's false. I wouldn't want him taking me to court for cheating him."

"I will tell him." Denis researched his purchases well, but de Luca's conviction was true. I had to wonder.

"Take your journey to Napoli, and Gian and I will toss through my things until we find it," de Luca said jovially. "Now, we should have some wine. Real wine, not the weak stuff served in an Englishman's home. Surrounded by vineyards, and they bring out inferior vintages and ruin it with water and sugar." He shook his head, aggrieved. "Gian, bring the cups."

———

WE SPENT A PLEASANT EVENING IN THAT ROOM, SURROUNDED BY astonishing things, while the friendly Gian kept our glasses topped with thick red wine. I asked Gian to serve some to Brewster, waiting downstairs, and Gian snorted. He said something to de Luca, who told us with merriment that Brewster had already refused the wine, regarding it with distaste, and asking if there was any ale.

De Luca was a born raconteur. Grenville would touch an object, and de Luca would bound out with a tale of where it had come from, or what its original purpose had been. Many things he had from Ancient Rome were bawdy—lamps in the shape of a phallus; a small hermaphrodite lying nude on a sofa; a brazier stand in the form of three fauns with arms lifted, their penises prominently erect. De Luca found the things delightful, pleased that the Ancients were fond of bodily pleasures.

"I'm too old for all that now," de Luca said. "But in my youth, gentlemen, I was quite the one for the ladies." He conveyed a faraway wistfulness.

"You have been fortunate," Grenville said, his speech slightly slurred by the wine. "When Bonaparte charged through the peninsula, absconding with art right and left, it is a miracle all this escaped. Is that why you've hidden much of your collection up here in the attic?"

De Luca's brows rose, and he was off in merriment again. "It's here because it won't fit into the rest of the house. Again, we must blame my grandfather and then my father, and then me for steadily adding to it. But Emperor Bonaparte, he'd heard of my collection, and he came calling."

"Good heavens," I said in surprise. "How did you fend him off?" Bonaparte, like Denis, had not liked the answer *No*.

"I did not." De Luca took a noisy sip of wine. "I promised him the entire lot. I did ask that my things reside here until he had conquered the rest of the Continent and was happily ensconced in his palace in Paris. Then he could send agents around to collect it all. I even signed a document stating so."

"He agreed to that?" I asked in amazement.

De Luca's eyes twinkled. "I think, Captain, that he was put off by the chore of sorting through it. His chosen lackeys could do that later." De Luca spread his hands. "And then ..."

"He was defeated," I finished. "Rendering your document null and void."

"I made certain the promise applied only if he remained in power. Ah well. As your poet says, *The best-laid schemes o' mice an' men gang aft aglee.*" He delivered the line by Mr. Burns in fine Scots.

Conte de Luca had certainly proved to be an interesting man. I'd been reluctant to run Denis's errand, but I softened to the task because it let me meet de Luca, who I could count as a very intriguing acquaintance.

———

We finally made our excuses to de Luca—Grenville had other obligations that night as well as our early start—and we dragged ourselves away, the sky now dark. De Luca made us promise to visit the moment we returned from Napoli, and we agreed with enthusiasm. He again stated he and Gian would comb the rooms for the Cupid statue, and we departed.

We returned to Grenville's abode and dressed for the evening, then I followed Grenville to a soiree hosted by another Englishman. The ladies there were likewise disappointed my wife was not in attendance, and also made do with asking me questions about her.

Those I met this evening were similar to Lord Matthew Roberts and his circle—ladies and gentlemen related to aristocrats, or retired army and naval officers who had found nothing to do with themselves now that the long war was finished.

Mentions of Broadhurst were met with shrugs and indifference, except one brother of a baron asking, "Wasn't he the chap who vanished with everyone's money? No, that was his partner. This chap died, didn't he? Hard luck. Well, if he was a swindler, he got his comeuppance."

That was the extent of knowledge about Broadhurst. If the letter-writer was among these people he kept himself very quiet.

We departed after Grenville had decided we'd stayed the requisite amount of time. Brewster met us outside, he emitting a small belch.

"They have a chef here," he said. "Fellow from Sicily. He decided I should taste all the dishes he's cooking tonight. Apparently, those upstairs have no idea what's good and what's not. He's not happy, but the pay is too much to chuck." Brewster wiped his mouth with the backs of his fingers. "He's a dab hand, I must say. When one of the lackeys told him I worked for Mr. Grenville, he came over all eager and shoved food into me."

Brewster did not, in fact, work for Grenville, but neither of us admonished him for not correcting the chef. Likely the man hoped Brewster would convey his skill to Grenville, who might be looking for another cook someday.

"He spoke English?" Most of the servants I'd encountered so far had little English, and many spoke the dialect of their region, rarely using even the Italian that I recognized.

"Not as such. But we managed to get our meaning across. Mostly it was me eating. Even the ale he found me weren't bad."

High praise from Brewster. "You can stay if you like." I gestured to the door that led to the servants' area. "We'll call for you in the morning."

Brewster sent me a dark look. "Very amusing. Happen I also found out where that fellow, Proietti, has his lodgings. One of the maids in this house is acquainted with one of the maids in his. In case you wanted to visit him and explain how we were nearly arrested for storming into the house of that ice-cold bloke."

"He might have been threatened as well," I said, though the police captain had made no mention of Proietti. "I ought to see whether he is all right."

"Perhaps Trevisan blamed *you* so the father of his beloved wouldn't be dragged to prison," Grenville suggested.

"Saw that on the stage." Brewster's sniff was derogatory. "It's like we've landed in one of them operas."

"Rome is where they all began," Grenville tried to joke. "Though I doubt Conte Trevisan would do anything so dramatic. From what you said of him, he seemed a cold fish."

"We shall ask Proietti," I decided. "We will not have another chance to visit him until we return from Napoli, and I feel I should make certain he is well."

Grenville agreed, and we followed Brewster, who had not agreed but not argued, into the streets.

That Brewster had pried out the information of exactly where Proietti lived and knew how to reach the house did not surprise me. He'd had plenty of time to speak to locals today while Grenville and I took our time visiting expatriates. I remembered him gesticulating with the shoe boy in the square —no doubt he'd recruited helpers in this city already who'd told him exactly what was where.

We tramped down the hill and followed the river south toward the Piazza Navona, passing the mausoleum of Augustus along the way. Any other time, I'd want to linger at the crumbling building and have a look at it, but Brewster hurried us on. Darkness coated the city, and predators roved the night.

Where the river bent to the west, Brewster took us into a warren of streets, pitch dark and packed with houses. A taverna would open abruptly from a corner, the room inside filled with a glow of warmth and voices.

"Here we are, guv." Brewster stopped before a black-painted door that looked no different from the others in the lane through which he'd led us.

There was nothing to say who lived in this dark house, but cracks of light shone from an upstairs window behind the shutters of chipped green paint. Brewster, without compunction, pounded on the door.

After a moment, a bolt scraped back, and flickering candlelight revealed the suspicious countenance of a thin man, not Proietti. He stared at us without recognition and barked a question.

Grenville tipped his hat and spoke in Italian. As the name *Captain Lacey* slid from his tongue, the man became suddenly deferential.

"*Ah, si, si, si. Il capitano inglese. Mi segua, por favor.*" The manservant gestured us in, his candle waving wildly, and slammed the solid portal once we were inside.

The floor beneath our feet was hard stone, but the staircase that rose at the end of the entrance had polished wooden steps. The servant led us upward without waiting, and we had to hurry to keep within the glow of the candle.

The staircase was steep, and I ascended into darkness a few paces behind Grenville, Brewster's tread heavy behind me. For once, Brewster did not immediately find the servants' hall, he not trusting there would be no danger above.

The upper floor was as gloomy as below. The manservant's candlelight fell on chairs here and there and the occasional table with curved legs, all positioned on red-and-white checkered tile. The servant halted at a double door in the middle of this passageway, pushed it open, and waved us in with enthusiasm.

I stepped into a surprisingly pleasant room, which was well furnished and bright. Proietti rose with a start from a table near a large porcelain stove, its warmth penetrating the chill of the evening. The table held a jug of wine, a glass, and a half-empty plate of food.

The rest of the chamber was cozy, inviting. A sofa strewn with cushions with a long shawl draped over one arm spoke of a place where a lady could comfortably curl up and read. Books filled another shelf, and carpets warmed the tile floor. Paintings graced the walls, nothing brilliant, but colorful pictures of soft landscapes that one could enjoy gazing at.

"I beg your pardon, Proietti," I said quickly. "We did not mean to disturb you at your repast."

Proietti came toward me, hand outstretched. "No, my dear Captain, it is of no matter. But you must stay, partake." He waved at the man who'd admitted us and spoke rapidly in Italian.

"We should not presume." Grenville said, ever polite.

The servant instantly rushed away to obey Proietti, and Brewster, without a word, departed behind him.

"Of course, you should presume, sir." Proietti favored us with a bow. "You honor my house, though I am sorry to show it to you so sparse. My wife has left me on my own, you see. She has gone to her sister, most upset."

His daughter's flight had unsettled the entire household.

"My sympathies," I said. "I find your home most pleasant." I spoke the truth. I preferred this chamber to the overly cool houses of Grenville's friends and that of Trevisan, and even to the chaotic splendor of Conte de Luca's grand villa.

"You are kind. Please." Proietti gestured to comfortable

chairs drawn up to the table. He seized glasses from a side-board and sloshed blood-red wine from the jug into them.

Grenville and I exchanged a glance, and decided, without words, to join him. We seated ourselves at the table, which reposed near a green-shuttered window. This was where I'd seen the light from below.

Proietti returned to his chair, and we drank. The wine was glorious, a perfect vintage that tasted of air, earth, and a bite of spice. Grenville always stocked the best wines, and the one de Luca had served us had been fine, but this one, which Proietti kept casually in a jug, outdid them all.

Grenville, the connoisseur, raised his brows and studied the wine in approval. "Excellent, Signor. I thank you for sharing it with us."

Proietti sent him a quick look, then was mollified to find genuine admiration in Grenville's demeanor.

"Pardon my manners," I broke in. "This is my friend and traveling companion Lucius Grenville. I am here on the Continent as his guest. Grenville, Colonel Alessandro Proietti."

"Delighted to meet you." Grenville shook his hand across the table, knowing how to bend etiquette to the moment.

Proietti, likewise, had a comfortable informality about him. Gentlemen on the Continent, I'd found on my travels, could be even more sticklers about protocol than Englishmen. Conte Trevisan, for example, would likely insist on references from a host of those he trusted before he'd let me through his doorway—had I not charged through it on my own. Even Conte de Luca had issued his casual invitation because he knew Grenville's reputation and was well acquainted with Grenville's friends in Rome.

I lifted my glass once more to savor the wine and reminded myself why we were here.

Grenville broached the subject before I could. "You will think me terribly rude, good sir, but the captain nearly came to grief from your adventure this morning. The constables—or whatever you call them in Rome—wanted to arrest Captain Lacey for having a go at your Conte Trevisan. Naturally, as he is my guest, I am concerned."

CHAPTER 6

*P*roietti sprang to his feet and stared at Grenville, mouth agape. As we rose with him, he began a stream of anguished words in Italian, then switched to English. "I am devastated. Please forgive me, Captain, for ensnaring you in my troubles and bringing you grief. Why did they believe you had anything to do with it?"

Grenville answered before I could. "Conte Trevisan must have decided Lacey was a good scapegoat. Another friend of ours convinced the police that they had no grounds to detain him."

I noted that Grenville did not state Conte de Luca's name, perhaps not wishing to bring the man into it.

"Thank God for that." Proietti let out a breath of relief. "I again apologize to you profoundly, sir." His remorse was so profound that I regretted disturbing him.

I shrugged, trying to make light of it. "I'm certain he sent the police to me because I am a foreigner here. Easy to have an Englishman arrested and perhaps shipped back to London, as a warning to you, and others."

"Or perhaps because he thought Lacey might be a threat to him," Grenville suggested. "You, sir, Trevisan feels he can deal with, but Lacey and Brewster are another thing entirely."

"He could not know who you were, could he?" Proietti asked me in bewilderment. "Likely he believed you were one of my colleagues left over from the wars, and decided as you say, to punish you for my brashness."

"He must have discovered *some* information about Lacey," Grenville said. "As he had the police follow us to one of my friend's homes and lie in wait for us outside."

"Ah." Proietti sank to his chair, head in his hands. "Again, I am so very sorry."

My reassurances to him were interrupted by the arrival of the meal. The man who'd answered the door—he seemed to be the only servant in the house at this time—entered bearing a large, covered platter. Brewster followed with smaller dishes of steaming food, which he thunked to the table without ceremony.

The manservant gently laid the platter on the table and then fetched plates from the sideboard. Proietti lifted the cover to release an aroma of sautéed meat in a savory sauce. The plates Brewster had borne held potatoes and a mound of bright greens.

"May we forget our troubles and partake?" Proietti asked. "My cook is quite good."

Brewster cast a quick glance around the room, as though making certain we three were truly in no danger, and he followed the manservant back out again. I was surprised he'd let himself be recruited for servant duty but perhaps he'd wanted to assure himself I was safe here. Or else he'd felt compassion for the single servant having to lug everything upstairs by himself. An amalgam of both, I imagined.

Proietti himself served us meat from the platter before refilling his own plate. I bit into beef so tender it nearly fell from my fork, the juices holding a rich bite. Carrots and onions, also tender, rested in the sauce, which was excellent on the potatoes and greens. I hadn't eaten so well in a while, despite Grenville's expensive chef.

"My cook is an amazing woman," Proietti said as we praised the dishes. "Only do not try to enter the kitchen to tell her so. She is quick to raise a carving knife, and only my daughter can soften her."

His eyes filled with sudden tears, and he quickly bent over his meal.

I exchanged a glance with Grenville. "I know the subject causes pain," I said. "But can you tell us more about the situation? How can Conte Trevisan marry your daughter if he is already married himself?"

"Because he is a snake." Proietti's decisive words rang through the room. "As cold as one and as wily. His wife is from Venice. Daughter of a family who produced many Doges before the republic ended. They had a great amount of wealth and influence. Trevisan married that wealth and took his wife to Milan, but she bore him no sons. A daughter only, I believe, who is no longer living. His wife has retreated to Venice, from what I understand. I have no idea why Trevisan decided to come to Rome, but perhaps his wife's family is making the north too hot to hold him. He met my daughter, Gisela, and she claims he has fallen in love with her. Pah. I do not believe he knows the meaning of the word."

As Proietti savagely attacked his beefsteak, Grenville asked quietly, "Your daughter perhaps has been taken in by his wealth?"

Proietti shook his head. "Not Gisela. She has no use for it.

Trevisan can certainly be charming when he wishes. They attend church together, which is where he first met her. My only comfort is that he is continuing the sham of his virtue and has not laid a finger on her. I would have bodily brought her home at once if he had."

"Trevisan's mother truly lives in the house?" I asked.

"The contessa, yes. She adores her son, will do anything for him, but she is as iron-willed as he. *She* will let no scandal touch him, or Gisela, if my daughter is to marry him."

"And you believe he will marry her, once he is free?" I continued.

Proietti's sigh came from the depths of his soul. "I am by no means certain. And even if they do marry—what happens in a few years when the bloom is gone from my daughter's cheek? If she likewise does not bear sons? Will Trevisan tire of her and turn to yet another woman, one younger than she? Breaking Gisela's heart?"

If Trevisan was in the habit of putting aside wives who'd displeased him after he'd wrung everything he could from them, I understood Proietti's anxiousness.

"There is one advantage to marriage," Grenville said as he swirled his meat in its juices. "I am not familiar with all the laws of the Papal States or of Milan, but marriage settlements and legal issues can be made iron clad. You can ensure that if Trevisan ever tries to put your daughter aside, she will receive handsome compensation."

"Possibly." Proietti did not appear cheered by this. "But I do not believe Trevisan would agree to these things. His men of business are powerful. I've already had letters from them advising me not to interfere."

"He is powerful in Milan," I pointed out. "Can you insist

they marry here in Rome? Where your own men of business can draw up the contracts?"

"I will certainly try, if it comes to that." Proietti drained his cup and reached for the jug. "You might think it odd, gentlemen, that I do not wish my Gisela to marry a man so apparently prosperous and well-connected. She would be a contessa, live in a grand mansion, command the admiration of many. She will become a wonderful hostess no matter whom she marries—she has the gift of making anyone feel welcome and well-regarded." His eyes grew moist, gleaming in the candlelight. "But I do wish she'd never set eyes on the man."

"I comprehend," I said with feeling. "I would prefer my daughter to be happy instead of stuck in a loveless marriage, no matter how wealthy her husband."

"I have a daughter myself," Grenville put in. "Her choices have not been the best. I unfortunately was not there to prevent them."

Proietti refilled his cup and ours as well. "It is a perilous thing, having daughters. Especially when that daughter is your only child."

"Indeed." Grenville's answer was soft. His melancholy note made me wonder—would he and Marianne try for children? Marianne had a son, who was simple, poor lad, and Grenville had already declared he'd raise David as though he were his own. But they might want children of together.

"I have a second daughter," I said. "All of a year old. Already I have begun to fear for her future."

"It is a father's lot," Proietti agreed. He raised his glass. "To fathers of daughters, and the treacherous roads they travel."

We drank. The wine flowed after this, supper ended, and Grenville and I, despite our departure from Rome the next day, commiserated with Proietti to the small hours of the morning.

WHEN I ROSE FROM MY BED AT DAWN'S LIGHT, MY HEAD
pounded, and my tongue felt thick. I tried to quench my thirst
with the clear water my valet, Bartholomew, provided, but it
did little for me this morning.

Grenville, likewise, had red-rimmed eyes and pallid cheeks
as we attempted breakfast. Bartholomew and Gautier recom-
mended various remedies but nothing, I knew, would suffice
except time and rest.

Brewster, heartlessly, was fresh and lively, his booming
voice grating through my head.

"What happens when you drink too much of the grape
instead of the grain," he informed us. "Me old dad used to say
that. He weren't good for much else, but he were wise about
drink. No gin, and definitely no wine, and you'll not suffer
for it."

His cheerfulness made me growl. Grenville, whose motion
sickness could render him immobile, eyed the carriage he'd
hired to take us to Napoli with misgivings.

He had altered the interior so that one seat folded down
into a bed. This was the only way he could endure the rocking
of a coach, though I imagined we'd halt many a time while he
either rested or heaved the contents of his stomach out on the
side of the road.

Brewster helped load the bags into the carriage and took a
seat on the rear, to ensure no footpad nabbed our belongings.
Bartholomew and Gautier would follow in a smaller carriage
with more baggage for setting up the house in Napoli.

The carriage wound its way south through the city, heading
for the road that more or less followed the ancient Appian Way
to Campania and places south.

Mist filmed the streets, making the ruins we passed slide, ghostlike, around us. We creaked by a depression of weed-choked grasses that stretched a long way beside the road—the Circus Maximus. When we returned, I'd climb down into it and walk the path where charioteers had driven horses in a mad rush centuries before. Gladiators' games had been held here as well, as the Circus had existed long before the Flavian emperors built the grand amphitheatre in the heart of Rome.

The road took us along the ancient route, lined with tombs buried in weeds and mud. Several times I spied men in great-coats plying shovels through the earth. Historians and treasure hunters, searching for loot and knowledge.

As the road meandered south, the fog burned off and an azure sky appeared. An aqueduct, many of its ancient arches still standing, marched across a green field.

I was entranced by the juxtaposition of today and yesterday, but Grenville soon lay himself flat on his seat and closed his eyes. He was a man who loved travel but suffered much for it.

We moved slowly, ending up at a wayside inn for the night. The road was not easy, and several times I found it more convenient to walk ahead of the carriage until my knee grew too sore, and I had to climb back inside. I wished I'd had a horse—I could have covered the distance between Rome and Napoli much faster.

Grenville recovered enough at the inn to have a meal in the taproom with me. We drank a jug of wine that didn't match what Proietti had served us, yet was surprisingly tasty.

"Vineyards are everywhere in this part of the country." Grenville waved a vague hand at the dark window. "It is not surprising that vintners turn out delicious drink."

I'd observed plenty of bare vines marching down hills as we

went. "The volcanic soil, I have heard, is good for the plants." I spoke confidently, as though I were an expert grape grower.

"The north of Italy is best known for its wines," Grenville said, studying the red liquid in his ceramic cup. "But I must say, those of Campania and even farther south in Sicily are worth noting." As Grenville had long been a connoisseur, I bowed to his expertise.

I slept heavily that night, and in the morning, we resumed the journey.

The second day of our travels was as uneventful as the first, except that Rome was well behind us, and more vineyards climbed hills, the plants waiting for the first blush of spring. Another inn housed us that night, this one smoky and filled with travelers. We supped in the private rooms Grenville had hired, slept another night, and woke for the final day of our journey to Napoli.

We bumped through that city, which was a mix of splendid tall houses and industrial docks, until the chaise finally halted on a hill overlooking the bay.

I exited the carriage, unbending my stiff limbs, and gazed about in wonder. The homes of Napoli hugged the curve of the harbor, buildings climbing from the water to the hills. Our abode was among these villas at the top, with the brilliant blue water of the bay stretching under a cloudless sky. The squat, square Castel dell'Ovo stuck out into the water—I itched to explore it.

The house Grenville had hired lay on the south end of the city. From there it would be a short journey to the ruins, which we'd set off for the next day.

I eagerly faced that direction. The tall mountain of Vesuvius, which I'd read of since boyhood, rose before me, its distinctive double peaks misty on the horizon.

"Plenty of time to explore tomorrow." Grenville stepped down from the coach, drawing in a relieved breath that the journey had ended. "But it is beautiful, I agree."

"I could stay here forever," I declared.

"I'd advise you to speak with your wife before you entrench yourself. She'll miss her friends." Grenville's eyes twinkled, he knowing Donata well.

The house Grenville's agents had chosen was not overly large but opulent to my eyes. A gate led from the street to a small courtyard where a fountain delicately sprayed. Statuary graced the fountain's corners, greenery in urns and troughs lining the space. An elegant balcony with a stone balustrade ran around the courtyard on the second floor, with French windows leading into rooms above.

The courtyard was paved in travertine, that pale tile prevalent throughout the land. The walls cut the cold winter breeze and the stone absorbed the warmth of the sun, making it a pleasant place to linger.

A door at the far end of the courtyard led to the interior, where a staircase bent upward to the rooms above. A reception room to the right of the staircase had windows overlooking the bay. I stepped into the chamber and stood at the windows, unmovable for a time, admiring the glory before me.

Donata might agree that such a place was worth staying in. Though hers was a restless soul, loving the social whirl, I'd also observed her at her father's home in Oxfordshire, where she'd sit in the sunny garden and simply *be*.

"The Romans called it *Campania Felix*," I said to Grenville as he stood beside me. "Even they enjoyed its beauty."

"As a change from tramping over the world in their large boots and stealing the best bits for themselves." Grenville chuckled. "I agree, it is lovely. I knew my man would choose well for us." He yawned, rumpling his hair.

"I am happy for you to desert me while you recover," I told him. "I will take a walk."

"Have Brewster accompany you," Grenville said, his smile leaving him. "There are plenty who might believe a lone Englishman easy pickings."

"I tramp about plenty in London, which is as dangerous a city as any. But I will have a care."

Grenville sent me a look of misgiving, though he did not pursue the topic. Before he could make for the staircase and find his chamber, Bartholomew came charging through the courtyard and inside to the anteroom.

"Visitor for you, Captain. An Italian man." His creased face indicated that he did not approve of visitors pouncing on us immediately upon our arrival. "His bloke gave me his card."

Bartholomew thrust a pale rectangle at me. I took it in curiosity, then regarded it in astonishment.

"Conte Vittorio Trevisan," I read in a stunned voice.

CHAPTER 7

"Trevisan?" Grenville regarded me with equal amazement. "What the devil is he doing *here*? If he has sent men around to arrest you again, I shall have something to say about it."

That Trevisan had reached Napoli so quickly, or possibly even before us, did not baffle me. He could have used a swift carriage, or even ridden horseback, as I had contemplated, while we'd dawdled on the road and spent two nights en route.

The only way to solve the mystery of his presence was to ask the man. "Send him in," I told Bartholomew. "With your permission, Grenville."

"By all means," Grenville said crisply, his temper not improved by his motion sickness. "Let us quiz him."

Bartholomew quickly departed. Grenville planted himself by the window, so he was in place to turn, rather disdainfully, as Gautier, whom Bartholomew must have fetched, ushered the conte into the reception room.

"Conte Trevisan, sir," Gautier said, his tones haughty. "From Milan."

Trevisan entered, equally as arrogant. He halted just inside the door and made no move to advance into the small chamber. Gautier, his task complete, vanished like this morning's fog.

"Gentlemen." Trevisan gave us a polite bow, one far more deferential than what he'd bestowed on me when I'd first encountered him.

Grenville returned the bow. "Conte. Welcome. What brings you to my home?"

"The captain is the reason for my visit." Trevisan faced me and favored me with another bow. "I have come to apologize for the incident in Rome. I did not mean for the magistrate to send out his men to detain you and your man outside Mr. Grenville's friends' abode. The captain of the patrollers was imprudent and foolish. I vow to you, such a thing will not happen again."

I listened with growing incredulity, but his tone was sincere. Perhaps someone in his household had mistaken Trevisan's angry rantings for a call to have me arrested, as had King Henry with Thomas à Beckett. I suppose I could be thankful they hadn't tried to murder Brewster and me on the spot.

"You are good to look me up to tell me so," I said without inflection. "Quite a long journey for so simple an errand."

The conte's cheekbones stained red. "I have ... business ... in the area. I was told that you and your colleague had taken this house, and I decided to find you and offer my apologies. My servants, in their zeal, supposed you were a danger to me."

His explanation was smooth, but his manner held no guile.

"I see." I leaned on my walking stick. "Well, I am pleased you have decided to approach me. It was kind of you."

"Indeed," Grenville put in. "I would invite you to dine with us, but I fear I do not know how well the house is stocked, or what the cook can prepare."

"No, no." Trevisan raised an elegant hand. "I have no wish to disturb your household. I wanted only to explain to the captain what had happened as quickly as possible. You deserved an apology."

I nodded. "I do appreciate your trouble in coming here."

"Do you stay in Napoli long?" Trevisan asked, though I discerned the question was merely polite. I doubt he had any interest in us other than ensuring that I was not going to bring suit against him for wrongful accusations.

"A week perhaps," Grenville said. "We are keen to examine the ruins at Herculaneum and Pompeii."

"Of course. Many a foreigner comes here for that purpose. I know several gentlemen who catalog the work on Herculaneum. Scholars who know it and Pompeii well. I could ask that one of them show you the cities."

"A kind offer," Grenville said. "Actually, we would be delighted. Thank you, sir."

Trevisan bowed, exuding some relief. He must have expected more belligerence from us, and I conceded that he'd been brave to face us.

I again wondered why he had. His apology could have been made in a letter, or by proxy, or he could have asked us to call on him when we returned to Rome.

Whatever his reason, Grenville and I exchanged polite farewells with him. We were not overflowing with friendliness, but we returned his goodbyes without hostility.

Gautier reappeared to escort the conte from the room, the valet as icy as Trevisan. We waited without speaking until we heard the conte and Gautier traverse the courtyard, and the clang of the gate that told us Trevisan was again in the street.

Trevisan had said nothing of Proietti and the meeting he'd promised to set up with the man, and I had not wanted to ruin the cordiality of this visit, however stiff, by asking. But I would not forget about it.

"How very interesting." Grenville sat down heavily on a divan and crossed his dusty boots, his exhaustion evident.

"I agree." I took another chair, joining him in repose. "Whether Trevisan's tale of business in the area is true or not, I am amazed that he would call on us with contriteness."

"I am less amazed." Grenville's eyes glinted with good humor. "The explanation, my dear Lacey, is that he found out who you are."

My brows rose. "Who I am?" I was the son of a minor landed gentleman with a career in the army, now finished. "You mean the friend and guest of the famous Mr. Grenville? Or, that I am married to a woman from a powerful family?"

"That is part of what I mean." Grenville's smile was wise, but he would not explain beyond that.

———

WE TOOK A MEAL AFTER THIS AND I, AS TIRED AS GRENVILLE from the journey, retired early though I very much wanted to explore the city.

I woke later than I hoped in the morning to find Bartholomew preparing my shaving things. My chamber was large and airy, painted in light blues and creams. Sunshine poured through the windows—even in February, the temperatures were higher than what I'd find in London at this time.

"Did you rest, Bartholomew?" I heaved myself from the soft bed and reached for my dressing gown. "No need for you to wake at dawn."

"Plenty of sleep," my young valet said without hesitation. "Don't need much in any case. Are you off to look at buried cities today?"

Grenville and I had planned to use an inn near Pompeii as a base from which to explore both it and Herculaneum.

"Indeed, but I do not know exactly when Grenville wishes to depart. I go at his leisure. No matter what, I will have a walk, see the lay of the land."

"Mr. Brewster says we need to be careful." Bartholomew stropped my razor with a practiced hand. "Resentment of foreigners is high, the servants here say. When the Frenchies took over, they slapped harsh taxes on everyone in the penin-sula, expecting the natives to pay for being invaded. The Frenchies are gone, but everyone's still unhappy with foreigners."

Though Bartholomew spoke little Italian, he would have already found those he could communicate with and befriended them. He was an affable young man, as was his brother, Matthias.

"The British invaded Napoli not long ago," I reminded him. "Tying to suppress revolutionaries. Lord Nelson even handed the revolution's leaders over for execution. I imagine the English are not thought of warmly either."

"Then we all should be on the lookout," Bartholomew concluded.

I had to agree with him.

Bartholomew shaved me with his usual competence. Once dressed, I departed the house. I had not thought Brewster would be amenable to my early ramble, but he met me at the front door when I emerged, and we set off.

This morning the sweeping arc of the blue bay glimmered under soft sunshine. The same sunshine touched ships that pulled into the industrial port, masts like black sticks in the distance. Boats of local fishermen, already bringing in the morning catch, bobbed in the larger ships' wakes.

"Breathtaking, isn't it?" I asked Brewster. Climbing vines on the walls near the house moved in the breeze, and bells from church towers silvered the air.

"Aye, it's different from London," was Brewster's noncommittal answer.

Not many were moving on this street so early, the area quiet and serene. I set off higher up the hill, wanting to enjoy more of the grand view.

Brewster tramped behind me, his steps heavy on the stones. I halted in an open square at the top of the street, a small green for nearby residents. A few tall palm trees graced the tiny park, lending an exotic air to the scene.

"Napoli was a Greek colony, once upon a time," I informed Brewster. "They were rivals of the Etruscans, before the Romans came."

Brewster scanned the city below us. "Don't much look Greek in my mind."

"We've arrived several thousand years too late. But the very name of its inhabitants, the Neapolitans, remembers its Greek origins."

"Aye?" Brewster gave me a slow nod, as though pondering all I'd said. "Thank you for the lecture."

"I beg your pardon, Brewster," I said. "I'm excited to be here. Think of it—ancient Greeks and Romans paraded up and down these very streets, going about their daily life as we do in London."

"Romans wandered about there too," Brewster pointed out. "When it was Londinium."

Brewster might appear to be a ruffian, but knew his letters

well and read often, even long tomes about history and art. He'd told me he had to study up to know what pieces were worth nicking. His tone had held amusement when he'd related this to me, mocking me for my surprise at his book learning.

"We've erased the Romans from London," I said. "Save for the odd coins that turn up. Here, you can still see the plan of the old Roman city."

I pointed with my walking stick to the middle of the town and its grid of streets, where humanity packed itself these days.

Brewster stirred impatiently, finished with the history lesson, and I decided we should end our stroll and seek breakfast.

I took a side lane that led down a staircase toward Grenville's home. Greenery found holds in pockets of brick beneath peeling plaster, the plants already budding, even this early in the year.

As I stepped on one stair, it moved. Or rather, the entire staircase did. Brewster gave a shout, and I slipped, catching myself hard on my walking stick and the wall beside me.

"Devil take it."

Brewster's words were far more foul as he stumbled, and I realized that the hill itself was moving.

"Hold on," I shouted at him. "It's an earthquake."

"Bloody *hell*."

We both clung to the wall, the rough brick abrading my gloves. The stairs vibrated and rocked, and I closed my eyes, bracing myself against it.

The rolling seemed to go on and on, though in reality I supposed it lasted less than minute. Then, as abruptly as it had begun, the quake stopped, and the world stilled.

Shouts sounded, and dogs barked. Shutters in houses

around us clanged open, and people called out to each other, voices holding concern.

"'Struth." Brewster leaned against the bricks, dragging off his hat and wiping his face with a shaking hand. "Never felt anything like that."

"No?" I tried to make my voice light, but it was unsteady. "I experienced earthquakes often in both India and Portugal. Common here too, because of the mountain." I waved vaguely at Vesuvius, a volcano that was never quiet for long.

"I'll take England, me." Brewster sniffed and jammed his hat back on his head. "Dangerous enough already without the earth trying to shove you about."

"That was a minor tremor," I assured him.

I worried that the quake had been strong enough to reach my family in Grenville's villa, and longed to charge back to them. I reassured myself that they'd be safe in Grenville's large house north of Rome. Likely the villa was too far away for this rocking to have affected them.

Brewster and I continued down the steep steps, going carefully. I'd no sooner stepped off the last one, Brewster ahead of me, when the world moved again.

Such tremors often occurred in quick succession, and I prayed that this was not the prelude to a much larger earthquake.

I stepped sideways to catch my balance, and at the same moment, something pinged into the bricks where I'd been an instant before. Brewster shoved me roughly aside at the same time the tremor abruptly ceased.

Brewster started back up the stairs at a run, and I saw what had fallen to the pavement beside me. It was a knife, long and wicked looking, its handle wrapped in strips of worn leather.

When I lifted it, I found that it had the exact balance and weight for a precision throw.

Someone had aimed that knife at me, and only the fortuitous earthquake had prevented it from landing between my shoulder-blades and burrowing its way into my heart.

CHAPTER 8

*W*hat the devil are you standing here for?" Brewster bellowed as he came flying down the steps toward me. "Get yourself indoors, before he comes back and tries again."

"Who does?" I'd seen no one, and Brewster returned empty handed.

"Don't know. Never found him." Brewster scowled, angry at me for nearly getting killed and at himself for not preventing the attack.

"A local tough letting his anger at foreigners get the better of him," I suggested. I started off in the direction of Grenville's, but in spite of my words, I hurried my steps, my leisurely stroll spoiled.

Brewster strode beside me, though there wasn't much room in this lane, and his bulk hemmed me in. "Not likely. You've started interfering in things again, haven't you?"

I could not argue with him. Conte Trevisan had apologized last evening ...so that an attempt on my life today wouldn't be blamed on him? Or perhaps whoever was writing threatening letters to Mr. Broadhurst objected to my assistance. Then again, maybe I was correct that it was a disgruntled Neapolitan, tired of foreigners swarming into his city.

In any case, going indoors was the best thing I could do.

We reached the house and passed through the solid gate into the courtyard. Brewster pushed the gate closed behind us, earning him the wrath of the doorman, who I imagine wanted it open to allow air to circulate.

Brewster shot home the bolt, bringing the doorman's shout of protest. I left the two of them to argue and made my way into the house.

Upstairs, a private sitting room rested between our two large bedrooms, reachable via a double-door into the gallery. I entered the chamber to find Grenville seated at the round table by the open windows overlooking the courtyard, sipping coffee. The remains of his breakfast lay on a plate before him.

"Everyone all right?" I asked as I hobbled swiftly into the room.

Grenville set aside his cup and rose, his eyes alight with excitement. "We are indeed. We stumbled around a bit, and the crockery rattled, but no one was hurt. How was it on the street?"

"I didn't note any damage," I told him. "Lots of people gabbing about it, but nothing more." I produced the knife, and thunked it to the table. "Someone took the opportunity of the quake to chuck this at me."

"Good Lord." Grenville stared in horror from the weapon to me. He had once been stabbed and lain near to death, and the shadow of that had never left him. From the tightness around his mouth, he recalled the incident even now.

"They missed," I reassured him. "Thanks to the unsteady earth and Brewster. Brewster gave chase but found no one."

"Do you think Trevisan sent him?" Grenville's brows rose. "In spite of his smooth words to us last evening?"

"I thought of that, but I don't believe so. As you pointed out, he has learned that I have connections to powerful people who could make life difficult for him." I sat down at the table, giving Matthias a nod of thanks when he set a cup of coffee before me. "If Donata decided to sink her teeth into him, she wouldn't stop until he was whimpering for mercy."

Grenville's tension eased, though only slightly. "She is formidable, is your wife. A lovely and splendid lady."

"I think so." I agreed with both sentiments. Matthias reappeared with a plate piled with slabs of ham, toast, and pastries. The cooks in the houses we'd stayed in so far were used to English guests, and we were usually served a mixture of local and English cuisine.

I fell upon the food, hungry after my walk and unnerving adventure.

"I had a note from Trevisan this morning, in fact." Grenville returned to his place at the table. "He has arranged for us to meet a gentleman who excavates the ancient cities. We will find him waiting at a tavern near Herculaneum—he even sent a map so we'd not mistake it. Why should he do that and then try to kill you?"

"Why, indeed?"

"Well, no matter what, we will be on our guard," Grenville said decidedly.

I finished my coffee and did not object when Matthias instantly refilled my cup. "I haven't had a chance to look into Broadhurst's problem yet," I said. "None of your acquaintance in Rome seemed to know much about him."

"I noted that, but many in London did. Broadhurst was quite good at talking gentlemen, who should have had better sense, into handing him pots of cash. Do you remember the swindler who convinced many to invest in nonexistent canals?"

I did. A young gentleman swearing there would be canals through the Berkshire countryside where none had been planned had been very persuasive. He'd also been responsible for Grenville's stabbing injury, which was likely why he'd sprung quickly to Grenville's mind.

"Was Broadhurst doing the same sort of thing?" I asked.

"Broadhurst and Cockburn," Grenville corrected me. "Two very respectable men of business who'd given many of my friends excellent returns on the Exchange. Or so my friends thought. It turned out Broadhurst and Cockburn had simply moved the money around, paying dividends to some with others' money, while pocketing the lion's share. When they were found out—and of course couldn't pay the money back— quite a few who couldn't afford to lose the funds were ruined. Alvanley invested a bit, but he is wealthy enough to shrug when he sees thousands gone. Others are not so fortunate."

"And then Broadhurst was killed."

"Indeed. Waylaid by street ruffians as he walked home from his office, as the story went. But now we know better." Grenville frowned over his coffee.

"Was no one angry at Mr. Cockburn? Did no one try to take revenge on him as well?"

"Cockburn was able to convince everyone that he was as innocent a dupe as the investors," Grenville said. "True or not, he claimed he did only what Broadhurst told him to, and never had a good look at the books. He believed in the investments. When the swindle was revealed, he tried to pay the money back, but of course, there wasn't any. Broadhurst had either salted it away or lost it."

So Broadhurst had told me. "What type of investments?" I asked in curiosity.

"Very enticing stuff. Steam-powered ships, goods from India and the Far East—trade that has opened up now that Bonaparte is finished. There is much wealth to be had in new inventions and new horizons."

"He appealed to their sense of the novel and exciting," I concluded. "Pretending they'd be investing in the exhilarating future of England. So, not only did your acquaintances lose their money, they were made to look like fools."

"Precisely." Grenville nodded.

"Are any of these embarrassed gentlemen likely to strike down a man in the street outside his lodgings? Or follow him to the Continent and write him threatening letters?"

"Not many would. They prefer to grumble in their clubs. A few of my old school chums could be of the violent sort but might draw the line at waylaying a man in the back streets of London."

"Then it might truly have been an attempt at robbery," I mused. "I'd dismiss it if not for the letters and the fact that Broadhurst is truly frightened."

"Well, I will continue to ask about when we return to Rome." Grenville thumped his fingers to the table and rose. "Once you finish your breakfast, Lacey, we should make our way south and to our adventure. The past awaits."

I agreed that I had more entertaining things to do than ponder the threats received by a man whom people were rightly angry with or wonder who might have tossed a knife at me in a lonely street in Napoli.

I tried to put both problems out of mind while I finished my excellent meal and went to my room to ready myself for our journey.

———

For this leg we went on horseback, Grenville never suffering his motion sickness when riding. Brewster had made it clear long ago that he did not like to ride, but he was forced to this time in order to keep up with us. He guided his horse behind us, muttering to himself but keeping a sharp watch.

I remembered how, in Egypt, Grenville had never set out to see ancient ruins without bringing several servants and plenty of baggage. He'd erected a pavilion on the sands where we could cool ourselves and slake our thirst, with Matthias and Bartholomew tending to our every need.

Grenville journeyed alone today with only a few things in a saddlebag. Granted, this was a far different climate, cool to cold in this winter month, and there were plenty of villages and taverns along the way, even if many did not look salubrious. We had no need to carry our own provisions.

From our rented house to the site of Herculaneum was only about six miles, which we accomplished in an hour or so of leisurely riding. We found the man Conte Trevisan had promised to be our guide at the indicated tavern not far from the ruins. He was a gentleman of Grenville's height with dark hair and a slim, agile body.

"So pleased to make your acquaintance." He shook Grenville's hand and then mine with a ready smile after we'd introduced ourselves and Brewster. "I am Ettore Baldini. I hear you wish to see the ancient cities. I will try to show you the best of them." His English was only slightly accented, and he quivered with eagerness.

We thanked him, answering his questions that our ride had been without difficulty. Baldini insisted we rest and refresh ourselves inside the tavern, and we politely accepted. The wine he ordered for us was quite good, and we sat at a table and chatted.

Baldini seemed to be as anxious as ourselves to visit the site, and we departed the tavern after only a scant hour. We'd leave the horses and our belongings there, he said, and continue to the nearby site on foot.

We walked through a quiet village, the bay to our right, fishing boats gliding serenely through the harbor. Brewster, happy to be rid of the horses, strode along, arms swinging.

"Herculaneum was a city of great wealth," Baldini said as we went. His tall walking stick struck the pavement with rapidity. "Romans loved the place for its view of the sea."

Streets crammed with houses wove toward the bay, brick and plaster crumbling as it had on the homes I'd seen in Napoli and Rome. Many in this area dwelled in near poverty or worse, exhausted by the armies that had moved through their land and the constant changes in rulers.

Baldini said nothing of dirt and penury, leading us toward our destination with every enthusiasm. A true scholar, focused on nothing but his chosen study.

"Here it is." Baldini halted and spread his arms. "The ancient city of Herculaneum."

I gazed where he directed, but did not see much. A depression below us undulated with grass and weeds, the shape of the hill mostly square with one curve as it bent toward the bay.

"The city was directly on the sea in its time," Baldini said. "The shore is farther away than it used to be."

"But where is it?" I asked in some bewilderment.

"Below us." Baldini enjoyed our confusion. "Follow me, gentlemen. I will show you what most are not allowed to see."

Brewster had no intention of waiting for us to return from

our exploration. He walked behind me, the tramp of his boots heavy in the damp air.

Baldini took us along the edge of the hill and then plunged abruptly downward via a stair that had been cut into the earth. Grenville went ahead of me, and I navigated carefully with my walking stick, Brewster directly behind me.

"I don't like this, guv."

Brewster was not fond of enclosed spaces, but I knew that wasn't what he meant. Baldini, a man we knew nothing about, could be leading us into a trap.

Regardless, I was avid to see what lay below. An entire city, frozen in time, awaited us.

The bottom of the staircase gave way to a tunnel hewn through solid rock. Not rock, I realized, but the ash and mud that had buried the city in a mad rush. Sixty-five feet of the stuff had converged on the town, engulfing it in moments.

"Farmers discovered the walls about a hundred years ago." Baldini struck flint to steel and lit candles that lay in preparation on a bench below, enclosing them into lanterns. He handed a flickering lantern to each of us. "That is the official story. Truth to tell, I've found evidence of digging that must have happened long before that. Perhaps by villagers taking bits and pieces to shore up their own houses or to sell for extra coin. Why not?" Baldini shrugged, spangles of light moving on the walls as his lantern swung. "All these things down here that no one wanted?"

"It is fascinating." Grenville lifted his light and peered into the tunnel. "And gruesome at the same time. I remember having nightmares as a boy reading about the poor souls caught in the ash and heat."

"Indeed, I still feel the tragedy of it." Baldini put himself in front of us and headed down the dark tunnel. "Almost two thousand years between that day and this, and I am still heavy-hearted for those people. It must have been terrifying. My family descends from an Ancient Roman one, and I suppose I feel some affinity for them."

Grenville glanced at me, his face neutral. The likelihood a man could trace his family in an unbroken line to the deep past was improbable, but perhaps this was how Baldini explained his ardent interest in ancient times.

The more regular shapes of walls began to poke through the rounded tunnel, and my own interest was thoroughly caught. People had lived here, worked here, loved here, fought here, gone through the day-to-day minutiae of life. Not understanding the ways of volcanos—they'd not even had a word for it until after the eruption—they hadn't discerned the warning signs and hadn't known to flee.

Baldini halted in a doorway not far along, showing us the interior space of what had been a house. Our candlelight fell on walls that were as red as the day they were painted. A small bright blue, yellow, and red mosaic high on the wall depicted a woman, nude, her hips swathed in cloth, gazing imperiously at us. Though this image was made up of hundreds of tiny tiles, the shading of her skin was as well done as in any oil painting by a great master.

"Exquisite," I breathed.

"Venus, we think." Baldini swept his light over the walls on the far side of the room, where great chunks of plaster had been gouged out. "Who knows what she gazed at there? So much was taken over the past century, transported to palaces, hidden away from us all."

"Kings always nick the best bits for themselves," Brewster grunted as he scanned the room.

"They do indeed, Mr. Brewster," Baldini said in fervent agreement.

We walked on. Baldini took us through more doorways into rectangular rooms, a few with mosaics that had either been too difficult to chisel out, or else the treasure hunters hadn't thought them worth bothering about.

I found them beautiful. A craftsman all those years ago had hunched over his picture to get it just right before it was plastered into the wall for us to admire now.

No one else was in the tunnels. We were alone in our quest today, our footsteps the only ones in the muffled hush.

"Excavation ceased some years ago," Baldini explained when I asked him about the absence of others. "A few gentlemen—including Herr Winckelmann, who wrote so much about ancient art—protested about how Herculaneum was being looted instead of studied, and the treasure hunters went elsewhere. Easier pickings in Pompeii, in any case."

"Still, there must be much to find here." Grenville gestured with his walking stick at a wall painted to resemble pillars.

"Oh, yes. Much, much more. Alas, excavations are expensive, and those who fund them want to keep the best things for themselves. As Mr. Brewster observed, kings take treasures to gaze upon, and then Bonaparte robbed those kings to pile things in the Louvre." His tone held disgust.

"Much of what Bonaparte took has been restored," Grenville pointed out. "The horses of St. Mark's to Venice, for instance." We'd had a similar discussion with Grenville's friends, the topic a heated one in this part of the world.

"But so much has not." Baldini kept his words quiet, but I heard his outrage. "Many things are still sequestered away, and it will take years to find them all. What was robbed of us was not just wealth, but knowledge."

"I agree," Grenville said. "And I imagine the not-so-famous paintings and sculptures will be more difficult to reclaim."

"You would be correct, sir." Baldini took us around a corner into an even darker tunnel, ending the conversation. "Now, there is a mosaic in this room that is quite lovely."

———

IN SPITE OF BREWSTER'S MISGIVINGS, BALDINI DID NOT LURE US into a blind tunnel where men lay in wait to beat us, nor did he seal us into one of the many chambers he showed off so enthusiastically.

Some hours later, we emerged from the darkness, blinking at the bright sunshine. I gazed over the site as we left it, the hardened earth waiting to give up its treasures.

Part of the reason for my brief journey here with Grenville was to discover whether it would be safe to bring my family to see the ruins. I thought Peter would handle himself admirably, and Gabriella too was of a robust nature. My wife perhaps would not enjoy climbing over rocks and through tunnels, but she'd appreciate the artwork we'd seen.

We returned to the tavern in the village and retrieved our horses for the ride to Pompeii.

It was late afternoon when we reached the inn Grenville's man of business had arranged. We'd eat and sleep here tonight, starting out fresh in the morning.

The inn was full, with travelers from all over the world. More than a few were British, although Germans made up a good part of the crowd. Frenchmen had come as well, scholarly gentlemen who spoke quietly together in a corner.

The Englishmen hailed us, happy to greet fellow countrymen. Grenville standing them a round of local wine also helped to smooth the waters.

I ate and drank, but I was too restless to sit and gossip with the lot. Grenville, who enjoyed speaking with those who traveled to see art and antiquities, was deep into conversation with several gentlemen. I quietly excused myself for a stroll in the open air.

Much had happened today, the earthquake, the thrown knife, the descent into the chill darkness of the past. I would have much to write to my wife, Gabriella, and Peter.

As I tapped my way behind the tavern to enjoy the sight of stars shining on the sea, a man banged into me and sent me straight into the wall.

CHAPTER 9

I immediately threw my weight backward in an attempt to dislodge my attacker. He clung to me with strength, and I felt a punch in my ribs. I grunted, scrabbling to retain my balance.

Another smack, this one into the small of my back. A man who knew how to strike and do it well.

I swung around, attempting to grab him, but in this darkness, I could see nothing. While Rome at least had lights spilling from its densely packed houses, here there was no illumination at all, not even a moon in the night sky.

I struck out and was rewarded with a grunt. We wrestled with vehemence, I trying to grab hold of him, he trying to pummel me into submission.

My assailant seemed to be about a foot shorter than I was, and not as large, but he was strong and wiry. If I'd been less trained, I'd have quickly been beaten down.

I heard running footsteps and then the man was hauled from me and lifted to dangle between Brewster's large hands.

A knife was clenched in the man's fist, and I was relieved he hadn't had a chance to use it.

"Who the devil are you?" I demanded, my breath ragged.

No answer—it was reasonable to assume he did not speak English. I repeated the question in broken Italian, but the man only struggled valiantly with Brewster, who was having trouble keeping hold of him.

"Who sent you? Why are you after me?" Again both English and Italian received no response.

"Lacey?" Grenville's voice rang out, and he rounded the corner behind Brewster.

The man gave a desperate wrench and managed to break free of Brewster's grip. He tried to dash away but was stopped by Grenville, who bravely stepped in front of him.

A keening sound came from the man's throat, and then words, English ones I thought, but slurred and oddly formed. He ducked to the left, evading Grenville, then sprinted into the darkness. Brewster was after him like a shot but returned to us not long later in defeat.

"Sorry, guv." Brewster let out a heavy breath. "He vanished. Can't see him, can't hear him. He must know this place well."

"He was trying to speak English, I'm certain," I said. "Who on earth is he?"

"Who knows, guv? A gent what's gone mad living among all these dead places?"

"Not mad," Grenville said, strangely subdued. "Our fellow is deaf."

"Deaf?" I stared at him.

"How'd ye know that?" Brewster demanded. "Begging your pardon, Mr. Grenville."

"I will tell you." Grenville gestured with his gloved hand, his suit as pristine as it would be at a Mayfair gathering. "But I think we should head indoors. It is time we retired, and who knows if our swift fighter will return?"

We agreed that this was best, and the three of us reentered the inn, I deeply curious about what Grenville had to say. The other travelers tried to engage us again, but Grenville made our apologies, citing our early start, and we took stairs to the rooms he'd let for us above. Baldini, deep in a glass of wine with other Neapolitan gentlemen, waved us cheerily off.

We entered Grenville's large chamber, which had a settee, chairs, and a table for his breakfast in addition to a well-appointed bed. Even at a wayside inn, Grenville managed to procure the best accommodations.

Wine had been left for us and Grenville served it without ceremony, though Brewster declined.

"Happy for a good pint when I reach home," he said.

Grenville settled himself after he handed me a cup of wine, and I sank into one of the chairs, grateful for a modicum of comfort after our day of walking and riding, not to mention fighting in the darkness.

"I have told you, I believe, that my father sired several by-blows," Grenville began with a pained expression. "A few were brought to my nursery, and it was made out that they were my cousins, but of course we all knew the truth. Those were the siblings I knew about—who knows how many more my father had? He was a bit of a gadabout."

His flush told me that embarrassment about one's pater was not unique to me.

"One of the lads who came to live with us was deaf," Grenville continued. "He hadn't been born so but lost his hearing through a fever when he was very small. He had learned to speak, yet his words were never perfectly formed, very much like those of the chap who accosted us tonight."

I thought back on the encounter. "Was this half-brother of yours as wily a fighter?"

"No, indeed," Grenville chuckled. "I liked him a bit better than the other lads foisted upon me, and we still correspond regularly. James lives in France now, with a wife and son of his own. He took to written languages very well and is a translator for diplomats in Paris." Grenville's pride in his half-brother rang in his voice.

"Our assailant spoke English," I said. "I confess I could not make out what he was saying."

"It didn't help that he was quite agitated," Grenville answered. "Something to the effect of *You will not stop me.*"

"Stop him from what?" I rolled my wineglass between my hands. My ribs ached from my assailant's punches, and he'd known exactly where to hit me at the base of my spine. "I wonder if he was soldier. Or a pugilist." I glanced at Brewster.

"He didn't fight like a boxer," Brewster answered. "But, aye, he knew where to strike, and how. He twisted away from me easily enough."

"I suppose we will have to put our hands on him and shake some answers out of him." I grimaced. "I must sound heartless wanting to bully a deaf man."

Grenville barked a laugh. "James and I scrapped plenty. A fellow not being able to hear does not mean he is feeble of body or of wits. This chap could have killed you, had not Brewster and I intervened. Or at least he'd have left you greatly injured."

"Agreed." I hardened my resolve. "I suspect he is the same who threw the knife at me in Napoli. I wish I knew what I'd done to earn his anger."

"Mistaking you for another bloke?" Brewster suggested. "You do have a cousin what looks much like you."

Indeed, that resemblance had given me a great amount of trouble in the past. "Marcus is tucked into the Lacey estate making it run better than it ever has. Why should an Englishman follow us about, trying to kill me, believing I'm him?"

"You could write Marcus and ask him," Grenville said. "You've only known him a little over a year, and he's proved to be quite skilled at intrigue himself."

True, my cousin had begun our acquaintanceship by trying to assassinate me and did end up nearly killing Brewster. He could have tangled with other men in his past, angering them enough for them to seek revenge. I'd been mistaken for him and he for me before.

"I do not believe this is the case," I concluded. "It is well known that Mr. Lucius Grenville took a villa near Rome for part of the Season and is exploring ancient cities with his friend Captain Lacey. These facts were blasted in all the newspapers before we left home. Anyone would know that the man with Mr. Grenville is me."

"Then we are back to those *you* have offended." Grenville sent me a wry look. "A long list. But for now, I am weary." He set his wine cup on a table. "Tomorrow, we are for Pompeii. We will simply have to guard ourselves against our unknown attacker."

"The captain's attacker, you mean," Brewster said. "Didn't seem interested in knocking *you* down."

"True." Grenville rose, and I did with him, ready to retreat to my own chamber. "Guard him well, Mr. Brewster. I would say we should call off our exploration and return to the villa, but I know how quickly Lacey will refuse. Besides, we have come a long way, and I'm damned if I'll let a ruffian turn us away now."

"Not a ruffian," I said. "His coat was of a decent cloth, from what I felt when grappling with him. Though his knife was rather ordinary." I'd left it in Napoli, else I'd have used it to defend myself tonight.

"Sold in any shop in the Italian states," Grenville said. "I've seen many like it. You are correct that his clothes weren't a laboring man's, but nor were they tailor-made in Bond Street. Secondhand, I'd say. Didn't fit him precisely."

Even in the dark, in a fight, Grenville had an eye for a man's garb. He was a noted expert on couture.

"So, our decently dressed Englishman comes to Italy after me, realizes he needs a knife, and purchases one before he attacks?" I frowned as I finished. "It makes no sense."

"No, indeed. But it might in the morning."

Gautier entered at the precise moment, like an actor awaiting a cue. Without a word, he went straight to Grenville and took his frock coat as Grenville shrugged out of it.

We said our goodnights, and Brewster followed me out.

"If you are going to advise me to remain here or return to Rome, save your breath," I told him.

Brewster gave me the even stare he did so well. "Wouldn't dream of it, guv."

———

IN THE MORNING, WE PACKED WHAT WE NEEDED FOR THE DAY and set off for Pompeii.

Brewster hadn't slept much, preferring to stay wakeful in case our assailant returned. He'd seen nothing, and as far as he knew, the man had not approached the inn.

He looked surprisingly refreshed for his vigil and kept a sharp eye out as we walked. I confess I glanced behind and about me often, waiting for another knife to sail at me across the fields.

A mile or so from the inn, we came to the ancient city of Pompeii.

Vesuvius loomed above us, a serene and beautiful mountain that had caused so much destruction. We climbed a short hill and passed under the arch of a large gate into the ruins.

In spite of the cool weather, excavators were digging enthusiastically here and there around the walls. Unlike in Herculaneum, where we'd been the only visitors in that silent land, Pompeii was a hive of activity.

Men crouched on hands and knees, stretching out sticks for measuring, gesturing to assistants who'd make a note in a book. Workers dug with spades, watched over by gentlemen in dusty suits, boots to their knees. Other men worked smaller patches with hand trowels and garden forks.

I was reminded of the bustle of activity on the Nile, where gentlemen—and ladies—excavated zealously, albeit on a larger scale.

"Not much treasure left in Pompeii," Baldini said when I commented on the differences. "Many of the statues and bronzes earlier excavators found have been taken away, as in Herculaneum. But there is so much to learn—wall paintings, mosaics, and even notes scribbled on the walls tell us so much about how the Romans lived. Come, I will show you."

He led us onward, taking a narrow road that went straight between walls that rose into the blue sky.

Roman men and women had walked on this stone street, I marveled as we went. The houses were brick, or rubble where the brick facing had fallen away. Once upon a time these walls would have been lined with marble or travertine, or perhaps only plastered over and painted. From my readings, Romans

had used cheap materials to make the bulk of the walls—
crushed rock and volcanic dust mixed into concrete—and
then faced them with the more expensive bricks, stucco, or
marble.

As I gawped at the perfect arches, the columns that rose
startlingly from the ground, the capitals on those columns
preserved in fine detail, Baldini and Grenville, chatting
together, left me far behind.

Brewster made certain to wait for me. "Makes you think,"
he said as we emerged into an open area that my guidebook
had labeled as the forum. "All those centuries ago, but they
were as good at putting up artful buildings as any who came
after. Our Adams brothers and Mr. Nash can learn from them."

"They did, as a matter of fact," I remarked. "No coincidence
that all the buildings in London resemble Greek and Roman
temples."

"I know that." Brewster's glance was disparaging. "I mean if
our coves made their buildings more like the real thing and not
just *look* like them, they'd be sturdier. This place lasted thousands of years."

"Because it was buried in ash. Some of what these men are
unearthing are skeletons."

Brewster cast a suspicious glance at the mountain rising
over the ruins, as though it might blow apart any moment.
"Poor blokes."

"Indeed. It is difficult to walk in the place of tragedy."

"We do it every day, guv. London's full of ghosts."

"Which you do not believe in, Brewster, so do not grow
morbid on me."

"Aye, well. Any old city will have sad tales. And plenty of
things worth purloining. Not here, though. It's all gone."

"Perhaps." I gazed along the street and to the corner around which Baldini and Grenville had disappeared. "But there is so much more to uncover. Secrets of the past. It is tantalizing."

"I nearly lost you—and me—in a tomb in Egypt, scrabbling after secrets of the past. No more of that."

Brewster spoke firmly. He hadn't liked Herculaneum and its underground passageways, but at least here, most of what we walked on had already been uncovered. Pompeii hadn't been buried as deeply, and excavators had been scraping away the ash for many years.

Baldini and Grenville waited patiently for us to catch up before Baldini excitedly gestured to the small space we now stood in.

"This was a bathhouse, we believe." Baldini pointed to the square depressions in the ground, which did indeed resemble the pools of a Roman bath. "And a brothel." He chuckled. "The paintings revealed would shock your lady wives. It was meant for sailors putting into shore for a night or two."

"Bit far to come for that, wasn't it?" Brewster asked doubtfully.

"You can thank Vesuvius for your confusion," Baldini said, as though delighted one of us had voiced the question. "Its eruptions have changed the shoreline, moving it a few miles from Pompeii. Used to be this town, like Herculaneum, was very near the coast. Another seaside retreat."

"I can understand its attraction," I said. Even though it was a bit cool today the green and black mountain rose against a very blue sky as a backdrop. The town must have been a pleasant refuge from the stink and crowd of Rome.

"Yes, indeed, until that fateful day." Baldini grew somber. "The skeletons found are curled into the most pitiful positions."

I felt a qualm of sympathy. The inhabitants had been going

about their business—shopping, visiting, arguing, cooking, strolling—when their world had ended so abruptly.

"Before that, though, they lived happily," Baldini said. A fanciful statement, but I nodded. "The walls were vibrantly colored, floors done in beautiful mosaics, and they left us plenty of messages."

He led us into a narrow passageway, using his walking stick to point out scratches high on the walls. They were Latin letters, old and crooked, made by knives or whatever the writer had to hand.

"This fellow proclaims that Julia is the most beautiful girl on earth." The walking stick moved. "This one claims that the first fellow has no eyes. It is Lucia who is the most beautiful. And *this* one tells us that a man came to find a lovely woman and only ended up leaving his turds in the latrine by his lonely self."

I had to laugh. I'd read much Roman literature, from Cicero to Tacitus to Julius Caesar himself, and most were lofty tomes... the military ones often bloody. This annoyed young man who was disappointed in his shore leave was so human and real, he might have departed moments before we'd walked up.

Baldini showed us more writings, some of them rather bawdy, and we enjoyed the novelty.

We returned to the forum where most of the excavation work was being done and halted in an open area. Brick buildings surrounded us, arches to nothing, columns forlorn and lonely.

I *would* bring Gabriella and Peter here, I decided. I would have to find a more pleasant place for us to stay besides the nearby inn, which was fine for Grenville and me, but Grenville could likely find a house for us to let.

"Your knowledge of these sites is excellent," I said to Baldini. "You are good to show us about."

Baldini shrugged, trying to hide his pleased flush. "I have studied Herculaneum and Pompeii for many years. I have learned a bit about their pasts, and mine."

"You are a scholar, you mean," Grenville said. "I am surprised such a learned man as yourself has deigned to lead a band of ignorant tourists. But I am quite glad you did."

"The conte, he asked it as a favor." Baldini sounded surprised at Grenville's amazement. "Of course, I wished to please him."

I wondered if Trevisan funded his studies and Baldini had not wanted to refuse a patron's request.

"He seems a hard man, if I may observe," I said. "Though he was contrite he'd caused us trouble."

"A hard man to those who do not know him," Baldini returned. "He has the northern temperament, yet is erudite and knows much about ancient art. One of the foremost experts on it, I'd say. His knowledge of the Colosseum surpasses even mine, and I am an avid student. I will take you through that edifice if you have time when you return to Rome."

"You admire him." This puzzled me—I expected Baldini to be a reluctant toady, but he'd been warm and friendly to us and showed no animosity to Trevisan.

"I do indeed. A better gentleman, I have not met."

"His behavior would suggest otherwise," Grenville, as confounded as I, said.

Now Baldini turned a look of confusion to us. "Behavior? I confess he appears to not be the warmest of gentlemen, but I assure you—"

"They mean his nicking a bloke's daughter," Brewster interrupted, growing impatient with our hesitation. "Putting aside his own wife for a pretty girl to see him through old age."

Baldini's eyes widened in shock. "I beg your pardon, sir, but what are you saying? Conte Trevisan has not put aside his wife. He never would—he is devoted to her. If someone has told you he has left his contessa for a young woman, then that person is lying to you."

CHAPTER 10

I regarded Baldini with some perplexity. "I assure you, I saw this with my own eyes. I met the young lady's distressed father, and we burst into Trevisan's home to free her. Hence his attempt to have me arrested, and you guiding us as recompense."

Baldini's dismay was unfeigned. "The conte said nothing of this to me. He indicated that he owed you a debt, which he would pay by sending me to entertain you. I gladly accepted."

"'Tis the truth." Brewster rested a massive hand on a column. "We went 'round to see the girl's dad. He's that unhappy his daughter's head was turned by the conte's riches. This conte met her in a church, and wooed her, like."

"Met her in a church?" Baldini grew resolute. "No, I do not believe it. The conte, he is not one who fears God. He's more like Bonaparte's Frenchmen and their atheistic ways. He does not approve of the *power* of the church, in any case."

Baldini lowered his voice, as though cardinals might swoop from the pagan streets and arrest him for this dissent.

I spread one hand. "I can only tell you what I saw, and what Signor Proietti has said to me. Do you know of Proietti?"

Baldini's eyes held blank ignorance. "I have never heard of a Signor Proietti. The conte has spoken nothing of him."

Grenville broke in, his tones soothing. "How often do you travel to Rome? Or meet with Conte Trevisan?"

"I have not seen him in some time," Baldini had to admit. "He wrote to me and requested that I guide you—I did not see him in person. Only once since he has been in Rome have we met, and that was weeks ago. In the past, I have traveled to Milan, or he has met me in Napoli."

"And you say he is learned about art?" I asked.

"Oh, yes." Baldini's approval returned. "He has studied it throughout his life, not collecting much himself, but advising others. He excels at knowing what a piece is worth and its provenance. The pope himself consults with the conte."

Grenville's brows rose. "Though he dislikes the church?"

"The conte makes no pretense regarding his feelings toward the papacy. But his expertise is such that those in the Vatican overlook this to consult with him on worldly matters."

In light of this information, Trevisan might have gone to the church to assess artworks or meet with someone about them. He'd seen Gisela Proietti, and . . .

"Sometimes older men grow foolish," I said gently. "They forget their devotion in a mad moment."

"Not Conte Trevisan." Baldini gnawed his lower lip in consternation. "The afternoon grows late. Perhaps we ought to return to the inn?"

"Certainly," I said. "I apologize for upsetting you."

"I know you are mistaken, Captain," Baldini said decidedly. "I shall ask him to explain. It will be a misunderstanding or scurrilous gossip."

I did not argue. I knew from experience how difficult it was to discover that a man one had admired was not the paragon one had believed. Colonel Brandon had disillusioned me long before I'd found out about his affaire de coeur with another woman, betraying his wife and my dearest friend, Louisa. I'd felt an ass for believing in him.

Grenville likewise did not carry on the dispute. He agreed that we should retire and take a meal, returning in the morning to continue our exploration.

On the way back to the inn, Grenville, who was excellent at smoothing the waters, began a conversation with Baldini about the wall paintings and mosaics we'd seen today. This mollified our guide somewhat, and he chatted readily with Grenville about the motifs and styles of that period.

We dined at the inn, the landlord bringing us platter after platter of food, which included plenty of fish and shellfish, the sea being so readily to hand. We washed it down with good wine and excellent coffee.

I decided not to take my usual evening stroll, to Brewster's relief, though I longed to catch our knife-wielding friend and discover some answers.

If the fellow was deaf, I was not clear how I'd communicate with him, but Grenville presumably had experience with this sort of thing. Our attacker might be able to write his answers to my questions, even if Brewster had to threaten him with a dire fate if he did not.

As I took to my small chamber to pen letters to Gabriella and Peter of what I'd seen today, I pondered Baldini's certainty that Conte Trevisan would never abandon his wife for a young lady of Rome. Baldini simply must not know Trevisan as well as he thought, but I wondered. What would make a man change from his rigid ways?

Perhaps someone had threatened Trevisan's wife to coerce him to do something, and Trevisan had decided to pretend she meant nothing to him, thus taking the teeth from the threat.

No, I could not see Conte Trevisan being easily intimidated. He was a cool man, playing some game of his own. He'd realized his mistake in sending the law after me and had lent us Baldini to, as Donata might say, turn me up sweet.

I pondered more on the question of Trevisan's motives but drew no conclusions.

The night passed refreshingly without incident and we rode back to Pompeii after breakfast the next day.

Baldini had been restored to cheerfulness as he took us around more of the ruins. The site was so extensive I knew we'd need several days to see it all, and those was only the areas that had been revealed.

Today we viewed more of the forum and a basilica, with its heavy columns holding up a portico with an empty floor above that. Majestic, I thought, and yet somehow sad. It had been a mighty place, powerful, and now, it was a ruin, wind brushing it mournfully.

Baldini showed us a few temples that had been uncovered, their walls exposed, the space inside open to the sky. Each of these buildings would have held at least one large statue, Baldini explained, to the deity worshiped there. The priests took care of the statue, which they believed was visited by the essence of the god. Everything had to be pristine and the statue was often clothed in silks.

All gone now. Whatever had remained after the eruption had been carried off long ago.

We visited the theatre, a semicircle of stone benches that led down a hill to a natural bowl. Actors would have strutted on the stage, chanting their lines, while patricians and plebeians alike watched, imbibing nuts and other treats while they enjoyed the play.

I sat down on one of the seats to stretch my bad leg. The stone was warm, absorbing the sunshine, which felt good against the wintry breeze. Grenville and Baldini wandered away, Baldini pointing out inscriptions on the stones, while Brewster, as usual, stood stoically watchful.

Brewster was the first to see our man. "Oi!" he shouted.

He started off down the steps of the theatre, and then I too spied my attacker darting behind the stones of the ancient stage.

As Brewster raced along, the earth moved in another tremor. Brewster lost his footing and tumbled forward, his momentum carrying him down the hard stones. He rolled a few more times and came to a stop just below the last seats.

Grenville and Baldini were already hurrying to him, they too stumbling as the earth shook. I was on my feet, steadying myself with my walking stick as I picked my way down the steps.

Brewster lay unmoving. The assailant took to his heels, heading for the ruins of the outer walls.

I flung out my arm, pointing. "Grenville! Go after him. I'll see to Brewster."

Grenville looked, saw, and darted after the fleeing gentleman. Being athletic, he quickly closed the distance. I lost sight of them and continued to the weeds and stones below the seats.

The tremor had ceased by the time I reached Brewster. He lay on his back, cradling his arm, alternately groaning and cursing.

I bent to him, Baldini hovering worriedly. "Where are you hurt?" I asked.

Brewster, a retired pugilist, would know what injuries he'd sustained better than any surgeon. "Me arm." His lips thinned as he said the words. "Probably broke it. Bloody hell and all that's holy."

"Lie still," I advised.

"Well, I won't be prying meself up with this limb, will I? Did you get the beggar?"

"No," I had to tell him.

"Bleeding bastard." Brewster said a few more choice words about him. "Find him, guv, so I can tear him in half."

Brewster's face was wan with pain. He tried to hide his discomfort as we heaved him to his feet, but I saw his eyes tighten, and he swallowed a grunt.

"We must return him to the inn," Baldini said in distress. "I will send for a surgeon."

"Don't need some foreign quack poking at me," Brewster growled.

"At the very least, he can tie up your arm," I said. "Then Gautier can look after you when we return to Napoli."

"The Frenchie is a physician as well as a valet, is he?"

"No, but he seems to know how to mix remedies and concoctions to make one feel better."

Brewster grumbled, his temper in shreds. I understood that he was angry at himself as well as the unknown man. Instead of capturing and interrogating our assailant, Brewster had failed and had injured himself. He would be grim about this for a long while.

"We will take Signor Baldini's advice and return to the inn," I said. "Explore another day."

"Not without me, you'll not," Brewster snapped. "It's me job to keep you safe, and you'll not go wandering about until I'm well."

Which could be weeks if he was badly hurt.

"Ah, well." I said, trying to keep my tone jovial. "I planned to return to the villa and fetch my daughter and son, in any case. By the time we venture back here, you will be mended."

"Huh," was his only answer.

"Where is Mr. Grenville?" Baldini peered about worriedly.

I scanned the area behind the theatre and saw neither Grenville nor the man he'd pursued.

"I'll hunt for him." I set my walking stick on the uneven stones, ready to start my search.

"No you won't, guv. A grand idea, race to the very place your companion disappeared and see if you get thumped on the head with 'im. Help me fix meself a sling, and we'll all go after 'im."

"You ought to sit down," I began.

Brewster cut me off with a string of foul epithets. "Just help me."

He shrugged out of his coat and looped the arms of it around his neck, placing his bad arm in the cradle of fabric. Bits and bobs clinked from his pockets to the stones, and I fetched them without a word.

I slid his trinkets into my own pocket—coins, tiny stones, and minuscule tiles. The coins were not modern ones, and neither were the tiles.

Once I helped Brewster settle his arm, tying the coat tightly, Baldini declared he'd lead us, as he knew every lane and turn in the ruined city. Following him, we made our slow way to the open area of the stage.

Unlike on a modern stage, where actors remain on a raised platform, the ancient players stood in the semicircle in front of the benches. From the long, flat end of this semicircle rose a proscenium; the brick buildings would have had arches, pediments, and columns to be used both as a setting for the play and also a screen to cut off the view to backstage.

Any steps to the platform had long since crumbled away. Arches on either side of the seats, for the most prestigious visitors to enter and sit in style, led nowhere, blocked with rubble.

We had to scramble up onto the ledge of the proscenium, Brewster proving surprisingly agile even with his injury. From there, Baldini led us around the stage to the jumble of ruins beyond it.

Behind the theatre lay a flat, open area, choked with weeds now, but its shape so regular that I imagined this had once been a smooth and well-tended space. Columns marched around it, having once held up a roof of an arcade. What the area had been used for, I could not tell.

Grenville was nowhere in sight. My heart thumped with worry as we searched, and I paused to cup my hands around my mouth and shout for him.

No answer. We reached the city wall at the other end of the open area. To the left, volcanic rubble was piled high, this earth not yet excavated. Baldini, without pause, took us along the wall to our right, following it to a tumbledown temple where digging commenced.

The men working here regarded us in surprise and we hastened to them. Baldini spoke to them in rapid Italian, but they shook heads and appeared puzzled. They'd seen no one.

Baldini waved us on. I thought he'd take us to the forum, open ground a man could run over to make his surest way for the gates and out. Instead, he herded us back more or less the way we'd come, halting at a steep slope pressed between the flat space and the large theatre. The concave bowl of land and the regular stones ringing it spoke of another theatre, smaller than the other and much more ruined.

Baldini led us down the slope toward what must have been the stage. Instead of elegant stone screens, this stage sported a tall brick wall with only a few narrow openings in it. Baldini, agile, scrambled up the stage and through one of these gaps, Brewster and I more carefully coming behind.

Beyond this theatre lay a maze of walls, some cleared down to their bases, others buried in dirt and fallen stones. Baldini wove his way through these, perfectly at home.

"Keep him in sight, guv," Brewster said behind me.

I understood why. Baldini could easily vanish, leaving us stumbling through this labyrinth. We might exhaust ourselves trying to find the way out, rendering us vulnerable to attack. Baldini, after all, was loyal to Trevisan, a man we'd disparaged.

I followed Baldini's hat as it bobbed among the ruins. To his credit, he slowed and waited for us when he realized he'd left us behind.

"What was this place?" I asked, waving at the walls close around us.

"Some believe for gladiators," Baldini answered, barely out of breath. "They trained in the place with the pillars we went through and slept in these cells." He indicated an opening to a very small room. As famous as some gladiators had become, they'd in the end been slaves, living in cramped quarters with little hope of freedom.

Baldini started off again, and we moved as swiftly as we could through the warren formed by the rock-hard ash and mud. No Grenville.

"Where the devil has he got to?" I asked the air around me.

It did not answer. We returned to the flat area that Baldini had termed the training ground. Nowhere did we find a London dandy, slightly the worse for wear, engaged in battle with our assailant or out of breath and impatient for sight of us.

Exhausting the area around the theatre and gladiators' grounds, Baldini at last returned us to the forum, where we asked anyone we could find if they'd seen Grenville. All answered in the negative.

"Bloody hell." I planted my walking stick into the earth. "He could have chased the man anywhere in this city."

"Or outside it," Brewster added, sinking to sit on an upturned stone block. "There's the new town and then all the inns and roads between here and Naples."

"You are pessimistic," I said, my mouth tight. "I hope we round a corner and find him—maybe he will come striding back, our attacker in his grip."

"Let's hope the bloke got away from him," Brewster said. "And Mr. Grenville's simply resting from the chase. Don't matter whether that chap can hear or not—he's dangerous."

I agreed. Also dangerous was letting Brewster run about with his arm untreated.

"We will take Brewster back to the inn," I said, taking command. "His arm needs tending. We can return afterward and hunt for Grenville."

"Allow me to stay and search while you care for your man," Baldini offered. "I know Pompeii well, and you also could rest, sir."

Likely I was looking as peaked as Brewster. "A sound plan. Do you need to rest a bit before we go?" I asked Brewster.

Brewster heaved himself up from the block. "I think it's a bad plan, meself, but if I sit under this sun much longer, it will be the death of me. Send me pay packet to Em and take me out to sea and throw me in when I go. It's beautiful here. My ghost might quite enjoy it."

"Onward," I said sternly. "You'll not die of a broken arm, Brewster. Not in my employ."

"He's the Almighty now, is he?" Brewster remarked this to no one and marched toward the gate. He did not need to ask the way—Brewster was very good at speedily learning the lay of the land.

"Why do you think it a bad plan?" I asked once I'd said goodbye to Baldini, who assured me he'd said word the moment he found Grenville, and were through the gate and on our own. "Baldini can search more quickly than we can and he knows the grounds better."

"Because who knows who *he's* in league with. We'd never met the cove before yesterday, and he has strange ideas about this Trevisan gent. What's to say the man with the knife and this Baldini ain't thick as thieves? That Baldini weren't luring us someplace so his mate could have us? Our bad luck I had to fall on me arm."

"I believe Signor Baldini is genuinely bewildered at these events," I said. "He expected to take three slightly naive Englishmen through the ruins where he could show off his knowledge and boast of his connections to Ancient Romans. Now he's been pulled into our adventures and told that a gentleman he respected is duplicitous."

"So, you trust Mr. Baldini completely, do ye?"

"I never said so."

Brewster grunted something but said no more.

It was little over a mile to the inn and both of us were flagging when we reached it. I bade the landlord send for a surgeon and he sent a boy running off on the errand.

Not long later, a small man with eyes set rather too far apart in his narrow face, appeared. He shut himself with Brewster and me in Brewster's chamber, examining the broad arm Brewster presented him.

The man spoke no English, but he let us know through gestures and the rudimentary Italian I understood that the arm was not broken, only badly sprained. Brewster, with his knowledge of pugilists' injuries, concurred.

The surgeon expertly bound up the arm and left Brewster a concoction to drink for the pain. Brewster was reluctant to take the remedy, but I stood over him until he downed it. I knew he was in more agony than he wanted to let on.

The surgeon grinned at me and held his hand out for a fee. He nodded after I'd dropped several coins into his palm, then departed.

The drink soon had Brewster snoring. I made certain his arm was resting where it wouldn't be jostled, covered him with warm blankets, and left the room.

Outside, the boy who'd run for the surgeon waited for me.

"You are to come, Signor."

"Come where?" I asked in trepidation. Had Grenville been found? "Did Signor Baldini send word?"

The lad, who had more English than the adults in this tavern, shook his head. "You are to come," he said. "I lead you right."

He grabbed my sleeve and dragged me out of the inn, into the gathering night.

CHAPTER 11

*T*he lad would not tell me where he was taking me no matter how often I asked. I decided to save my breath, and also my strength, in case I needed it to fend off yet another attack.

We wound through the narrow streets of the village and out into open country. The moon had appeared tonight, glittering hard on the bay, its cold light contrasting to the warm glow of the boy's small lantern.

I had to walk quickly to keep up with the lad, who occasionally slowed to wait impatiently for me.

"This way," he'd urge.

He led me up a hill into which steps had been cut. At the top was a grove of trees, and among these trees a gate, which the boy easily wrenched open.

I had no idea where I was, though I could see lights far to the north of me, which I assumed was Napoli or other towns along the bay. The gate led to a gloomy path that I was reluctant to walk.

Again, the boy caught my sleeve and pulled me onward.

The lane was paved with brick and meandered through the trees, which cut out the moonlight. If the lad hadn't kept his hold on me, I'd have lost my way or tripped in the darkness, despite the tiny glow of his lantern.

We emerged from the grove, moonlight illuminating all once more, and I halted in surprise.

I stood before a villa. Its tall, pale walls were punctuated with windows at irregular intervals, shutters covering any light that might leech from behind them. Urns bore plants that twined their way around the doorway and up to a balcony on the next floor.

The lad seized an iron knocker and banged on the door, paint chips flying to land in the gravel at our feet.

The door was yanked open by a tall retainer, the glow of candlelight spilling out around him. The lad indicated me with both hands then held out one palm imperiously. He jiggled impatiently from foot to foot until the retainer had dropped a coin to him. The boy instantly closed his fingers over it, spun away, and disappeared back under the trees, leaving me to my fate.

The man who'd opened the door spoke to me in Italian mixed with a local dialect and gestured me to follow.

As I did not know my way back to the inn and would be hard-pressed to find it in the dark, I had little choice but to go inside. The retainer slammed the door behind me, sliding home the bolt.

The thick doorway directed me to, not a foyer, but a garden. Even in winter, much grew in this enclosure that kept out the winds, and the scent of greenery and blossoms engulfed me. A fountain pattered in the middle, moonlight rendering the water droplets diamonds in the air.

The retainer guided me at a slow pace around the outer

perimeter of this garden and opened another door. A flight of stairs awaited, and I bent my protesting knee to follow the man upward.

The stairs ended at a gallery much like the one in Grenville's house in Napoli. The retainer took me partway along this and opened a door. Beyond that was warmth, a sitting room, carpet, and soft furnishings.

The chamber also held Grenville.

He sprang up from a chair when I entered. "My dear chap. I tried to return, and they would not let me."

Grenville's face bore faint bruises, but it had been washed, and his hair, which had been mussed by the wind and dust when I'd last seen him, was combed and neat. His suit bore rents from today's ordeal, but it too had been brushed, as had his gleaming boots. From the look of him, the most exertion he'd done today might have been a stroll in the garden below.

I could only stare, my heart pounding in relief. Then irritation took its place.

"I see I worried for nothing." I pretended to joke, but I heard the annoyance in my voice. "Brewster has been tended and put to bed, thank you. I was about to return and search the ruins for you."

"Not a good idea, Captain Lacey." A hearty and very English voice assailed me. "Pompeii is treacherous after dark. Not only holes to fall into, but thieves to rob you."

The man I faced was tall and broad of torso and had a thick shock of blond hair going to gray. A military man, I surmised, from his bearing and the voice that was used to roaring commands.

"Lacey, this is Colonel Reynold Stanbridge," Grenville intervened. "He and his wife fished me out of a very bad place indeed. Stanbridge, Captain Gabriel Lacey."

Stanbridge laughed, the noise resounding through the room. He was an officer in the style of Colonel Brandon, very hearty with his friends, every inch the commander.

"He means that quite literally, Captain," Stanbridge boomed at me. "Now, come in, come in. Fetch the man some wine." This last was directed at a lackey, who bowed and moved to a sideboard to pour out.

"Do shut the door, Colonel," a woman's voice came from across the chamber. "I can't see the captain from here. You gentlemen are blocking my view."

Stanbridge laughed again and obliged. "Always keen to meet new neighbors, is my wife. Especially if they are fellow countrymen. And army men at that."

Once my eyes adjusted to the candlelight, I found myself in a comfortable sitting room, with carpet on the tiled floor and a fire crackling on a hearth. The furniture was of heavy carved wood, but plenty of cushions and rugs softened every surface.

The lady who rose from a chair near the fire was plump and middle aged, her gray hair covered by a lacy cap. She wore a fashionably cut gown of a dark color I couldn't make out in this light—brown or maroon possibly—enhanced with an embroidered jacket. Her face was round and pleasant, and she smiled amiably at me.

If Stanbridge was similar to Colonel Brandon, his wife was nothing like Louisa. Louisa Brandon was steely but delicate, while this lady exuded robustness.

"How do you do, Captain?" Mrs. Stanbridge extended a hand, and I bowed over it. "Mr. Grenville had fallen into a hole near one of the bathhouses. Possibly it was a well, or maybe another bath. The colonel found some rope, hooked him, and reeled him in." She chortled.

"They very kindly brought me home and leant me a valet

who helped me refresh myself." Grenville's tone was light, but I saw exasperation in his eyes. "Then they kept me prisoner, declaring I must take supper with them. Only great pleading allowed me to send word to you."

"Isn't he a one?" Mrs. Stanbridge crowed in delight. "As though tramping through the dark to a rough inn is preferable to a meal by our chef. He's a wonderful cook, Captain Lacey, as you will see."

"What about Baldini?" I asked Grenville. "The poor man is tramping all over Pompeii, searching for you."

"No longer," the colonel broke in. "I sent a chap to intercept the scholar and send him home. Baldini should know better—Pompeii is treacherous after dark."

"You know Signor Baldini?" I asked.

"Everyone who is interested in Pompeii knows the man. He's a foremost expert on the place, that and Herculaneum. The ruins in Rome too. He's loaned me some literature to help me understand them. A pleasant young man."

"I hear you gained the favor of his patron, Conte Trevisan." Mrs. Stanbridge gave my arm a coquettish tap. "Lucky Captain Lacey. He is quite wealthy and well connected. Anyone in his favor will do very nicely, thank you."

I could think of no reply, so I nodded politely. More who thought Trevisan a great man. It was curious. I wondered if Trevisan was as good a confidence trickster as Mr. Broadhurst had been.

There was nothing for it but that Grenville and I sat down to supper with Colonel and Mrs. Stanbridge.

The meal was quite good, the colonel's wife not exaggerating about their cook's talents. The chef sent up several meats, including sausage-stuffed veal, along with a flatbread coated with a sauce made from crushed tomatoes and a mild cheese melted over the top. I quite liked the flatbread, which I had seen vendors selling on the road from Napoli.

The conversation turned to our thoughts on Rome and the rest of the peninsula.

"There are those who like to say that things are back to the way they were," the colonel remarked philosophically. "A foreign king again rules Napoli, the Austrians are administering in the north, and the pope has regained his Papal States. But it is different. The average man got a taste of life in a republic when Bonaparte was here. Mark my words, they won't forget."

"Any reforms from the past twenty years have utterly vanished," Mrs. Stanbridge said. "I did not approve of Bonaparte marching all over the world to have his own way, but he did try to improve the lot of the ordinary man."

"*I* believe he simply didn't like anyone ruling but him," the colonel said. "Better to kick out the old kings and popes and put his own people in place—he could control *them*, couldn't he? The reforms were by the way."

"I suppose that's true, Colonel," his wife said cheerfully. "I couldn't help feeling sorry for poor Murat, though. A sad end to a brave man."

"Well, he did betray Bonaparte after Leipzig," Grenville pointed out. "Marshal Murat more wanted to be King of Napoli than anything else, in the end."

"An excellent cavalryman, though," I said. "I have experience of him," I finished feelingly.

"Most excellent," the colonel agreed. "Good thing for us on the Peninsula that he went to Russia, eh? One of the few who did return. Poor buggers."

We discussed that ill-fated campaign for a time. While Grenville was the only one at the table who hadn't been in the king's army—Mrs. Stanbridge had followed her husband throughout his career—he knew much regarding what had happened in 1812, which had eventually led to Napoleon's downfall, which in turn had brought about Murat's.

"And Napoli has a Bourbon king again," Mrs. Stanbridge said. "Though they share him with Sicily. Napoli and Sicily are known as 'the Two Sicilys,' and I do not believe the Neapolitans are happy with that."

"What made you come here?" Grenville asked her in curiosity. "It is lovely, of course."

Mrs. Stanbridge snorted a laugh. "England's climate—what did you think? Winter on the bay can bring cold winds and rain, but not for long. Most of the time the sun shines, and the bay is so blue. We grew used to warm weather on the campaigns, didn't we, Colonel? We debated returning to Spain but decided upon Napoli and its environs after a visit."

"Not Rome?" Grenville went on. "So many Englishmen find themselves there."

Mrs. Stanbridge waved this away. "I don't like to stay overly long in Rome. Too many Catholics."

Colonel Stanbridge brayed with laughter. "The pope does make his home there, my dear."

"You can smell the incense whenever you walk down the street," Mrs. Stanbridge said wearily. "We had business there a few days ago, and I nearly ran to reach the bay again. At least here the sea breezes carry all that incense away."

Finished disparaging an entire faith, Mrs. Stanbridge cheerfully called for the footman to take away plates and bring the pudding. This was a concoction of sponge cake soaked in some kind of liqueur with sweet cream between the layers.

At supper's end, the colonel and his wife declared it was far too late for us to walk back in the dark to our inn, and that we must spend the night. They had plenty of room, they insisted, and we'd each have a comfortable chamber.

We could not refuse. Prisoners indeed.

When Grenville and I retired, I learned another reason that the Stanbridges had made the Bay of Napoli their new home. Colonel Stanbridge had lost quite a bit of money in an investment that went sour, one headed by a Mr. Norris Broadhurst.

———

"BROADHURST SWINDLED THEM?" I HELD A WHISPERED conference with Grenville in his chamber. The rooms were indeed well-appointed and comfortable, and I could not be put out that we had been persuaded to stay.

"They had mentioned their loss before you arrived." Grenville pulled off his boots with the aid of a boot jack, then stood them upright. "Though not the particulars. Whatever bonuses the colonel received when he came home from campaigning, he invested in Broadhurst's schemes. When the bailiffs came for Stanbridges' things, they decided that it was time to retire to a southern clime. Stanbridge did not say it, but I imagine debtor's prison was a step away."

"They'd be pleased if Broadhurst suffered, then," I surmised.

We spoke softly, aware that any servant might overhear us and repeat the conversation to their masters.

"Possibly." Grenville unbuttoned his coat and slid it from his shoulders, hanging it carefully on a stand provided by the colonel's valet for the purpose. "The man swindled so many that I'm surprised an entire army wasn't after him. No mystery why he decided to play dead. Still, I suppose we should not let anyone actually murder the fellow."

I nodded. "If only to spare a would-be killer the noose. Trial for murder would only make things worse for a family that has already lost much because of Broadhurst."

"The desire for vengeance often overrides sense," Grenville said. "More to the point, are our hosts in league with the man attacking you? Or is he entirely separate from this business?"

"I suggest we lock our doors, in case," I said bleakly. "And leave at first light."

"Agreed." Grenville gave me a nod, and I said my good nights, retreating to my own chamber.

————

As wary as I was, I dropped to sleep quickly and slept hard. The tour of the ruins plus hunting for Grenville, coupled with the relief that he was well, unwound my limbs and made slumber impossible to resist. I had asked the Stanbridges before we finished supper to send word of our whereabouts to Brewster at the inn, though I doubted he'd wake before morning.

I'd taken the precaution of locking my door and window and added the barrier of a writing table in front of the door. It was a small table, but if nothing else, the clatter of it falling over would wake me if anyone tried to force their way in. As it was, the table remained undisturbed in in the morning. None had tried to intrude on either Grenville or me in the night.

The Stanbridges took breakfast with us—meat, bread, and cheeses of all kinds on offer—oblivious to the fact that they'd alarmed Grenville with the mention of Broadhurst the evening before.

"You mustn't rush away," Mrs. Stanbridge told me as we ate. "Signor Baldini will not have time for you today, I think—I hear he has had to head off on some errand for Conte

Trevisan. You must visit with us, and we can arrange a guide if you insist on returning to the ruins. Or remain here and enjoy the views with us."

"Indeed," her husband chimed in. "This house was built to resemble the Roman villas of old. We even have an ambulatory —a columned walkway overlooking the sea. Do say you'll stay."

I shook my head, trying to show regret. "My man was hurt, and I must make certain he is well."

"We can bring him here," Mrs. Stanbridge said at once.

I imagined Brewster's reaction to an enforced stay in a villa that might contain people who wanted to kill us.

"We are on a timetable," Grenville said, also making a show of reluctance. "We begin the return journey to Rome tomorrow, stopping at Napoli along the way, then back to our ladies. They will be adamant that we do not linger."

"What a pity." Mrs. Stanbridge brought her hands together. "Such a treat for us to meet fellow Englishmen, especially those who were on the Peninsula with us."

"Not the same regiment, of course, but that can't be helped." Stanbridge chuckled. "Now that you know where we are, you must return, Lacey, so we can reminisce until Mrs. Stanbridge and Mr. Grenville are at their wits' end. Come back to the bay and bring your ladies with you."

I had fully planned a second journey with Donata and family, but I only nodded noncommittally. The Stanbridges were very likely exactly what they seemed—a retired army couple lonely for company but making the best of their exile. Once I determined who was threatening Broadhurst, I could be more amenable to a visit.

After more protestations as well as thanks for their hospitality, Grenville and I at last took our leave.

We elected to walk back to our inn, as it was not far and

neither of us wanted to wait for Stanbridge to order a coach or horses for us. It was a pleasant morning, the rain and wind gone, blue sky welcoming.

"They are either very friendly, salt-of-the-earth people, or very clever villains," Grenville said. "I'd never suspect them of sending our attacker after you, but for the fact that the man knew exactly where to find us, and the Stanbridges were swindled by Broadhurst."

"The man chasing us might have nothing to do with Broadhurst," I said. "I have also offended Conte Trevisan, who many seem to think is a nonpareil. Perhaps our follower is bent on teaching me manners."

"Farfetched." Grenville adjusted his hat against the sun and scanned the fields on either side of this stretch of road. They were empty, fortunately, except for a trio of farmers digging on the far side. "This fellow is English, in any case. Why should he care about a Milanese conte?"

"There is another motive to consider—I have a commission to fulfill for Denis. Perhaps this man does not want me to get my hands on the forged statue. Is *he* the forger? And fears that Denis will discover his ruse?"

"Again, farfetched. We only have Conte de Luca's word that it is a fake. Perhaps de Luca simply does not wish to sell it to Denis."

I made a gesture of defeat. "I can think of no other reason this gentleman should throw knives at me or wrestle you into a hole in Pompeii."

"The hole was my own fault." Grenville reddened. "I had nearly caught up to the man when he turned to fight me. We exchanged a few blows, then I slipped and fell. He could have finished me off—I thought he would for a moment—but he fled. No matter how much I cried out, no one heard. I honestly

thought I'd be another body found in Pompeii by excavators."
He shivered.

"There are enough people crawling over the ruins that
you'd have been discovered eventually." I tried to sound reassuring. "By us, certainly, if the Stanbridges hadn't pulled you
out. Baldini was conducting a thorough search."

"Thank you, Lacey." Grenville adjusted his hat again. "Kind
of you to indulge me in my fears."

"Pleased to assist you, my friend," I said, keeping my tone
light. Grenville sent me a tight smile, and we spoke of it no
more.

We continued our walk, keeping sharp eyes out, and
reached the inn without incident.

Brewster was up and in the common room, his left arm in a
linen sling the surgeon had fashioned for him.

"Dining in the lap of luxury while I were laid low, were ye?"
Brewster shoveled a large helping of chopped mutton and a
round of thick bread into his mouth, an indication that his
sprain hadn't hindered his appetite.

"We hadn't much choice," I told him. "Safer to stay,
wasn't it?"

"That's as may be." Brewster mopped up the mutton's juices
with the last of his bread. "And they might have cut your
throats in the night."

"We thought of that." I told Brewster what we'd learned of
why the Stanbridges had moved to their villa, and he huffed,
wiping his mouth on his hand.

"Lucky you walked out whole, weren't it? An English bloke
keeps trying to bash at you, and nice helpful people who've
been swindled by the very man you've vowed to save offer you
a bed for the night? You have an angel looking after you, guv."

"Perhaps, when you are not available." I allowed myself

amusement at his exasperation. "Never mind. We are returning to Rome, as planned."

Adhering to our schedule mollified Brewster somewhat, and he readied himself to depart.

I wrote to Baldini thanking him for his assistance and reassuring him that Grenville was well, to be delivered to him whenever he returned from Trevisan's errand. I wondered what Trevisan was having him do, but I made no mention of my curiosity in the letter. I left the note with the landlord as we set off on horseback once more.

We kept the pace slow to accommodate Brewster, and later that afternoon we reached Napoli and Grenville's comfortable, rented house.

While I had enjoyed our scramble over Pompeii and Herculaneum, I was happy to dine in the dim coolness of the Neapolitan abode. Gautier entered the dining room as Grenville and I lingered over wine, the entire meal served competently by Matthias, who encouraged the tale of our adventures.

"A letter for you, sir." Gautier addressed me, not Grenville.

"Oh?" My brows went up. My first thought was that something had happened to any and all members of my family, but Gautier's expression was wooden, disapproving. Even the stiff Gautier had sympathy in him when he conveyed unwelcome news.

"From Rome, sir. From Lord Matthew Roberts. It arrived the morning after you left for the ruins."

Lord Matthew, Grenville's ex-patriate friend. More puzzling. "He wrote to *me*?"

"Yes, sir." Gautier seemed relieved I'd finally grasped the situation. He handed me a thick sheet of paper, folded and sealed.

Mystified, I broke the seal and opened the note. As I read the words, written in a slanting hand, my jaw went slack.

"What is it?" Grenville asked in alarm.

"The conte is dead." I said the words stiffly, my lips barely able to move.

"Trevisan?" Grenville stared in as much shock. "Good Lord."

"No." I shoved the letter at him. "Not Trevisan. Conte de Luca. He's been murdered."

CHAPTER 12

I *knew you were interested in one of his pieces, and you ought to know that he is dead,"* Grenville read. *"The police pronounced it murder. I am afraid access to his collection is now restricted."* Grenville dropped the paper to the table, his eyes filled with foreboding but also some disgust. "Roberts has always been a bit of a cold fish, no matter how he behaves outwardly. He's informing you not because we befriended Conte de Luca and would be sorry for his death, but because you might not be able to purchase the statue."

My heart was heavy as I accepted more wine that Matthias quickly poured. I had liked de Luca, with his friendly bonhomie, and I'd looked forward to introducing him to Donata.

"I will have to write to Denis," I said bleakly.

"Your pardon if I sound callous, but I imagine Mr. Denis already knows," Grenville said. "His agents are everywhere. He might even know who killed the man and has already taken steps to show his disapprobation."

Denis's disapprobation was dire indeed. "Was de Luca robbed?" I asked.

Lord Matthew's letter had not indicated this—I was wondering out loud. A killer would find plenty to steal at his home. I also wondered if his murder had anything to do with the statue Denis wanted.

"Speculating will only distress me," I said. "We must to Rome."

"We are going there anyway," Grenville reminded me. "Will you linger in Rome to find out what happened?"

I wanted to. I also thought of my wife, wandering the villa's garden, counting on my return.

"No," I said resolutely. "De Luca's death likely has nothing to do with Denis or the statue. Rome is a dangerous place, and de Luca's home had many valuable pieces of art in it." I thought of the monstrance, a marvel in gold. "A robbery gone wrong it must be."

"Very likely. Poor fellow."

"Yes."

I did not like to think on it. I had planned to approach de Luca about the statue again and enjoy his company. Now I would not have the chance, and I grew morose.

The rest of our evening was spent preparing for the journey. I wrote letters to my family, telling Donata of de Luca's abrupt death. To Gabriella, I gave a lighthearted version of Grenville's mishap and rescue by the Stanbridges, omitting any reference to his struggle with a would-be killer. To Peter, I sketched the outlines of what I'd seen in Pompeii and told him of Baldini's speculations that the flat area surrounded by columns had been the gladiators' training grounds.

In spite of how much I'd enjoyed this sojourn, we were a somber party that entered the carriage to return to Rome.

The journey was uneventful. No earthquakes, and no one attempting to waylay us. Our assailant was mercifully absent, but I wondered very much when he'd turn up again.

We reached Rome late in the evening of the third day and rumbled past the Circus Maximus on our way to the lane near the Piazza Navona. The house welcomed us, and Grenville took to bed right away, his motion sickness laying him low.

I wrote to Lord Matthew Roberts, thanking him for informing me of de Luca's death and asking if he had more details of the incident. I also wrote to Denis, explaining what had happened and inquiring if he wanted me to try to purchase the statue from de Luca's heirs.

Restless, I decided to walk to de Luca's house and see if anyone was in residence there. Brewster followed me, uncannily knowing the instant I shrugged on my coat to walk outside.

"Stands to reason someone murdered the bloke for his gear," Brewster said as we headed north toward the Villa Borghese. "He had plenty stashed in that house, didn't he? Wonder who gets it all."

"Someone in his family, I imagine. I hope they are grateful."

"Huh. If any is left. Thieves would have picked over the best bits, wouldn't they?"

"I have a feeling there is more to this than a simple robbery," I told Brewster.

"Always is, inn't there?"

We said nothing more as we moved down the lane to the gate that led into de Luca's mansion. I rang the bell, not expecting to be admitted but thought perhaps the footman who answered could at least tell me about de Luca's death.

I rang again, and after a few minutes with no answer,

decided my errand was futile. Perhaps the house was empty, waiting for the magistrates or bailiffs to admit the heirs.

As I turned away, a door banged behind the gate, and a man hurried out. I recognized Gian, de Luca's manservant. He waved at me and came forward.

In the dim light from the house, Gian looked haggard. His eyes were red-rimmed, his face blotchy.

"Please." He opened the gate. "Come in, Captain. Signor Brewster."

I'd never seen a man more sad or dejected. Gian was a servant and yet his grief was true. He must have been very fond of Conte de Luca.

"Can you tell us what happened?" I asked as we went through the garden to the main house.

"Please." Gian gestured us inside. The lower hall was dark, the only light coming from moonlight through high windows. Gian guided us to the chamber on the top floor we'd been admitted to before, where a lone candle flickered, creating shadows on the many objects in disarray.

Gian disappeared behind one set of shelves and returned, carefully bearing a statuette about a foot high. "This is what you were wanting?"

I accepted the heavy thing Gian gave me. It was a sculpted Cupid sitting cross-legged on the statue's base, which was carved to represent a bed of grass. One hand pressed against his cheek, while the other idly held his bow, as though the god contemplated who to shoot next. Instead of a chubby cherub, he had a more adult face, the god Eros rather than the child Cupid. His face was superbly sculpted, the expression of longing quite real. I felt certain he was thinking of his lover, Psyche.

One wing had been broken, and the alabaster that the crack revealed was milky pale.

"Beautiful." It was no wonder Denis wished to purchase it.

Gian shrugged. "Not from the ancient world, as the conte told you. But I give it to you."

I wasn't certain he meant "give" as in he wished no money for it. I also noted that Gian's English was quite good—he'd spoken only Italian on our previous visit, and I'd assumed he'd not understood English.

"I was instructed to pay whatever Conte de Luca asked," I told him.

Gian waved this away. "I do not want your friend to bring suit for selling him a fake. Please, take it."

"Are you certain? What about the conte's heirs? Will they object to items going missing before the estate is settled?"

Gian stared at me as though he didn't understand my words, then he drew himself up and pressed his hand to his chest. "I am the heir. He left all his things to me. No other."

Brewster, who'd been viewing the goods with his hands carefully behind his back, broke in. "His family might have something to say about that. Even with a bloke that has tuppence to leave, the family fights over it."

"He has no family. Only me. I am his son."

I blinked at Gian, and Brewster regarded him skeptically. "Not a legitimate one, eh?" Brewster asked with his typical bluntness.

Gian did not seem offended. "I will not become a conte and inherit his lands or this house, no. His cousin will have all that. But his things, his collection, are not part of his title. They all come to me. I have seen the will."

Giving him a powerful motivation to murder the man. But Gian's grief, I thought, was true.

"He was good to you," I said.

Gian's eyed filled. "He was. He could not make me his true son by law, but he raised me and trained me, taught me about art and its history, and how to value things. You are welcome to the piece. He planned to give it to you when we found it."

"Very kind of him." I regarded the statue again, Eros perfectly formed. "I will write to my friend and inquire if he will accept it as a gift."

Denis was very careful, I knew, making certain any artwork in his house could be verified as belonging to him if anyone came calling. He'd not be so clumsy as to be arrested over a stolen statue, even a forged one.

Gian opened his hands as though to say he was finished with the matter.

I set the statue down on a cluttered table. Brewster moved to examine it, but I faced Gian.

"How was he killed?" I asked.

An unashamed tear trickled down Gian's cheek. "I had gone out, visiting friends. We had dinner, eating and drinking and laughing. They were good friends, and I spent the night rather than walk home in the dark. When I returned in the morning, I found the conte in one of the sitting rooms downstairs, dead as a stone. His head had been knocked in. The marble vase that did it lay beside him, covered in his blood."

He broke off, his voice failing him. I went to him and dared lay a hand on his shoulder. "I beg your pardon. Most distressing for you."

"Distressing." Gian's eyes flashed. "I was sick. What is the word in English … devastated. He was my *father*. My friend. My protector …"

I tightened my grip on the man's shoulder, my sympathy flaring. "When did it happen?"

"Wednesday last." Gian deflated as I released him. "A week and a half ago. So few days, and yet it seems a lifetime."

That Wednesday night, Grenville and I had been on the road to Napoli, had been resting in an inn along the way when de Luca met his end. We'd arrived at Napoli on Thursday evening.

"Had someone broken in?" I asked gently. "Did you find the door open?"

Gian shook his head. "All was as I'd left it. The gate closed, as was the front door. They were no longer locked, but they had not been forced. I never noticed if any windows or other doors had been opened. I secured all before I went." He wiped his arm across his eyes.

"So, he might have had a visitor. Was he expecting anyone?"

"No. Not that he told me."

"Who else works in the house?"

"The cook," Gian answered readily. "He'd gone home—he does not live here."

"No one else? Just you and the conte?"

"He didn't like too many servants around his things. There is a woman who comes in once a week—Mirela. She sweeps and dusts. Complains that there is too much jumbled about." Gian's smile was shaky.

"Was there any sign that he'd had a visitor? Or do you know who else would have a key?"

Gian peered at me. "Why are you asking these things? I had to explain all to the magistrates, who are certain I have done this."

They were not entirely sure, I surmised, or Gian would already be imprisoned. The friends he'd dined with must have vouched for him. "I am curious, is all."

"Humor him," Brewster said disparagingly. "He'll ask behind your back if you don't tell him. It's his way."

Gian sent Brewster a puzzled frown but answered me, "I do not know who has keys—he might have given some to friends, but I know nothing of that. I saw no one, admitted no one before I went. If someone did come after I was gone … I do not know who."

"Was anything stolen?"

Gian studied the cluttered chamber before lifting his shoulders in a resigned shrug. "I do not know. I am going through all his things, but I have not missed anything so far."

"And the police? You said the magistrate suspects you."

"The *police*." The word was a growl. "Do you know what they say about the patrollers who protect Rome from the bandits in the hills? That they are no different from the bandits themselves. They take money to look the other way."

I recalled the men who'd surrounded me when the police commander had tried to detain me. They'd not looked civilized, it was true.

From what I'd heard of the justice system in the Papal States, the police could arrest and detain a man without trial for a long time. The idea was that the fear of being thrown into the cells for weeks would deter crime. Only the most heinous of cases came before a jury and judge. Trials were costly, Grenville had explained to me, and so avoided as much as possible.

"Would you mind if I looked over where he was found?" I asked. To Gian's skepticism, I added, "I might be able to discover what happened. To ease your mind. Or at least make certain the police don't arrest you."

"How would knowing ease me, sir?" Gian asked, but more

in sorrow than anger. "He gave me everything. Now he is gone."

He exuded misery, and I ceased asking my questions.

Gian, shoulders slumped, motioned us to follow him. He took us down the stairs to the main part of the house, leading us to a sitting room on the ground floor.

The room was no less cluttered, though things had been arranged more for display instead of a jumble of objects. Shelves held gold and silver items, porcelain, ivory, and boxes encrusted with semiprecious stones. Tapestries hung on the walls, their fine work and sheen attesting to their age and value.

I appreciated Gian's dilemma—unless he had a well-ordered catalog of all these things, how could he know if anything was missing?

"I found him there." Gian pointed with a sweep of his arm to the space before two chairs that had been set next to each other. De Luca's body was no longer there, but a small, dark patch stained the tile floor, where scrubbing had not removed all the blood.

"Was he facedown?"

Gian nodded, a scowl creasing his face. "Yes, the coward struck him from behind. The back of his neck was crushed." He flinched as he said the words.

"I am sorry," I said. "It was cruel. Perhaps I can help bring whoever it was to justice."

"How can you?" Gian's scowl deepened. "There will be no justice, even if you find the person. A man can be executed for stealing a bauble in Rome, but a murderer escapes more often than not."

I had heard such things spoken of at Lord Matthew's house, during the conversation before I'd met de Luca. The Stanbridges had said much the same thing. Crimes involving property seemed to be more important than the death of a person.

While Brewster studied the goods on the shelves and tables, I pictured the scene. De Luca had turned in surprise when whoever it was had broken into the room—or had he? Likewise, the chamber was neat, almost painfully tidy in spite of the many objects within it. A burglar would steal what he could lay hands on—there was plenty of choice—and flee. Even if he'd been startled by de Luca and struck him down, he'd have left with something, which Gian would have noticed gone.

Another explanation was that de Luca had admitted a visitor into the house, who'd had no intention of stealing anything, and invited him, or her, into this room. This would explain why the doors were unlocked but the locks not broken. The killer had calmly departed, closing the door and gate behind them, but not being able to lock them.

"Had de Luca fought?" I asked. "Were his hands bruised, or did he look as though he'd struggled? Anything knocked over, out of place?"

"No." Gian's anger mounted. "The terrible man must have waited until de Luca turned his back, then struck him down." He spat a word I did not know.

If de Luca hadn't fought, then he most certainly had known his attacker. He'd trusted whoever it was enough to lead them into a comfortable room and turn his back on them. He'd been a robust gentleman, and he'd have tried to deter the killer if he'd believed he was in danger.

That de Luca had been killed with an object from his beloved collection was an irony I did not like to contemplate.

"What did you do when you found him?" I asked Gian.

"I prayed for him." Gian's face was taut. "I prayed for his

immortal soul, and then I vowed I'd eviscerate whoever did this."

———

"I don't know how you're going to find out anything with this one, guv," Brewster said half an hour later as we walked from de Luca's house back toward ours.

The night had deepened, and with it came the bandits Gian had mentioned. I saw shadows flitter in the side lanes and was glad of Brewster near me. He scanned the streets as we walked, on the lookout for danger.

"I feel I owe it to de Luca," I said.

I carried the alabaster Cupid under my arm, the piece wrapped in a leather sack. Gian had insisted I take it with me.

"He were a jovial bloke," Brewster said. "Quick to make a friend of a cove. Probably was his downfall. He invited you and Mr. Grenville to his rooms readily enough. Who knows how many others he has? He liked to show off his loot, didn't he?"

Brewster had a point. De Luca had modestly laughed about his overflowing collection, yet at the same time, he'd been eager to reveal it to us. He'd obviously had trusted the wrong person at the wrong time.

"I believe it was someone de Luca knew already and who was familiar with his house," I said. "He waited until Gian's day out, obviously wanting de Luca to be alone."

"But how are you going to find out who this visitor was? Ye barely knew the conte. Ye don't know his acquaintances, his closest mates, or the ladies he might have thrown over. Could have been anyone."

"I have thought of that, Brewster," I said in irritation. "I suppose I will begin as always, by asking questions. De Luca did tell us that he'd promised all he had to Bonaparte. Maybe someone came to hold him to that promise."

"Frenchies, you mean?"

"Possibly, but not necessarily. Plenty of local men gave loyalty to the new emperor in exchange for power, or lands, or money—some sort of reward. Perhaps that person wants to give the collection to his new masters, hoping for a reward from them, or to persuade them to overlook his switch in allegiance to Bonaparte."

"Now you're grasping at straws," Brewster said. "The Corsican is gone, and everyone is trying to give back the things he stole, not take more."

"You are likely right." I let out a breath as we tramped up the narrow street that led to Grenville's house. "I truly don't know much about de Luca or his background. Grenville and I will simply have to quiz everyone we can about him."

"Just so you don't take too long over it." Brewster wiped his nose with the back of his hand and hunkered against the cold wind that sprang from the river behind us. "Or your lady wife will come and ask me why I didn't drag you home to her. I'll be buggered if I'll know how to answer her."

———

AT BREAKFAST THE NEXT MORNING, GRENVILLE WAS UNHAPPY that I'd gone out investigating the death of de Luca without him, but his remonstration was cut short when Gautier announced a visitor.

"Mr. Denis to see you, sir." Gautier intoned the name with much disdain as he held out a silver tray with a single card on it. "I have put him in the reception room downstairs."

CHAPTER 13

*J*ames Denis was indeed standing in the center of the downstairs reception room when Grenville and I entered, his gaze directed out the long windows to the narrow street. He wore a dark suit topped by a traveling cape, much like the one de Luca had sported, his hat and gloves in his hands. Gautier had not taken them, indicating the valet expected the meeting to be short.

"Good morning," Grenville said with his usual politeness, though I heard the strain in his voice. "An unexpected visit."

His civil greeting silenced my more perfunctory one. *What the devil are you doing here?*

"My travels had taken me to Florence," Denis said, as though I ought to have known he'd embarked on a Continental journey. "I heard of the death of Conte de Luca, which brought me here." He fixed me with a steely gaze. "Do you know what happened?"

"Not yet," I said tersely. "We only heard of it a few days ago ourselves. We were traveling to Napoli when he was killed."

"Yes, to explore the ruins of Pompeii." Denis's voice held

disapproval. I should have bent all my efforts to preventing de Luca's death, apparently.

Denis was about a dozen years younger than I was, his face smooth, his hair dark. His deep blue eyes held a soul far older than they ought.

I'd learned some of his history and understood that Denis had been forced to fight to survive from a very young age. He now controlled most of the underworld of London, and I was surprised he'd come to the Italian peninsula himself. He did not like to leave his demesne unattended.

"If you are worried about your statue, I have it." I indicated the ceiling. "It is upstairs in my chamber, well hidden. Though I have been told it is a fake, so I doubt anyone will steal it."

Denis met my gaze without a flicker. "Thank you for obtaining it for me. The price?"

"De Luca's man, Gian—who is his son, actually—gave me the damned thing. Neither he nor de Luca could understand why anyone would want it."

Denis did not seem to be interested in Gian's or even de Luca's opinions. "When you return to de Luca's home, offer this Gian the equivalent in *scudos* of one hundred guineas. That should be enough to satisfy him. Have him give you a receipt."

"When I return?" I asked in bafflement. "It is not likely anyone in that house will be receiving for a time."

Denis regarded me with his usual coolness. He was nearly as tall as I was, but I could tell he did not like looking up the slight distance at me. Hence why he usually received me in his study in Curzon Street, he seated and icy.

Today I saw a brief flare of emotion in his eyes. Anger.

"You will invent a reason. I need to discover what happened to Conte de Luca and why. I am fortunate you are here and excellent at such matters."

My perplexity continued. "You have much more effective means at obtaining answers. I have seen you and your men find out much, swiftly."

"I do not wish to inform the world of my interest. But you have a reputation for inquisitiveness. Use it. It is important."

"Is it?" Truth to tell, I was already greatly curious, as well as indignant, about de Luca's death. I rarely saw Denis this adamant, however, though anyone else would never realize he was anything more than indifferent. "Why?"

Denis's answer was quiet, ensuring no one outside the door would hear.

"De Luca was a connection between collectors and items. He could put anything into anyone's hands—he was a great source of objects and also information. His death could have serious consequences."

Both Grenville and I listened in some amazement. "He told me his father and grandfather had begun his collection," I said. "And he simply picked up what he liked."

"That might be true." Denis gave me the barest hint of a nod. "But de Luca had the gift for knowing what was valuable. He not only obtained objects, but information about people—who wanted what and who dealt in what. You need to lay your hands on that information, if he indeed kept it in written form."

"Good Lord," I said, my interest growing by the moment. "Did he have a dossier on you?"

"Possibly. But more likely he had one on anyone who ever worked for me. As you know, I have agents in many places. They are my eyes and ears. Exposing them is not what I wish."

I had encountered one of his agents in Egypt, much to my regret, and I knew he had men placed throughout the Continent and beyond to find things for him or commit deeds for him, or both.

"I believe I understand your worry," I said.

"You cannot grasp it fully, but I am pleased you have an inkling. I will provide you any resources you need, as long as you find out who killed de Luca, why, and if he had lists of his contacts and mine. I want to know if the person who killed him absconded with the information."

"I will have to write to my wife," I said dryly. She would not be pleased with me, and she, for one, never had fear of taking Denis to task.

"I have already done so," Denis said. "I imagine she will arrive soon."

While I had a momentary flash of pleasure that Donata would join me, it did not come without trepidation. Donata preferred me to remain whole and hale, not beaten down by murderers and ruffians as happened whenever I decided to investigate a crime. If she'd decided to come, it would be to keep an eye on me. She'd trust no one else with that duty.

My hesitation also stemmed from the fact that my last investigation involving Denis had nearly meant the death of Donata's son. She'd not quite forgiven either of us for that yet.

Denis had nothing more to tell us. He retained his cool demeanor when I asked how he found Florence.

"The city is a fine one. I suggest you add it to your travels. I am staying in Rome for now, so when you have information, bring it to the house next to the Palazzo Borghese. Good afternoon, gentlemen."

He glided out, opening the door himself. Gautier stood rigidly down the hall, watching Denis exit the house before he rather firmly shut the front door.

"Well." Grenville watched out the window as Denis

mounted a carriage and rolled away at an unhurried pace. "He has certainly set us a task."

"He must be worried." The carriage turned the corner, sunshine gleaming on its black top. "To cut short whatever business he had in Florence to race here and find out what happened to de Luca means he is indeed concerned."

"You are right," Grenville said. "Where do we begin?" He let out a breath. "If Denis is correct that Mrs. Lacey will soon join you—and I feel that my wife won't be far behind—I must have Gautier see to decent accommodations for them. This is rather a bachelor's house."

I noted the pride in Grenville's voice when he said *my wife*, but did not remark upon it.

"We'll begin by paying another visit to Gian," I decided. "If anyone knows where things were in that house, it is he."

Grenville agreed, and after he'd spoken to Gautier about readying rooms for the ladies, we made to depart for de Luca's home. Brewster joined us as we left the house, the dressing on his arm renewed.

"Your valet got to me," he told Grenville when Grenville remarked upon it. "Bloke thinks he's a surgeon."

"He knows about wrapping limbs," Grenville said. We trudged into a wind that blew from the north. "I've certainly given him practice, tumbling from horses and out of boats and off rocks I'd been adamant to climb."

"Aye, he did a fair job," Brewster admitted. "Cold fish, but competent."

"I will pass on your thanks," Grenville said as we walked on.

When we reached the lane that led to Conte de Luca's abode, we found a large crowd gathered at the gate. Some were simply watching, but others had joined in the shouting that sounded within the courtyard.

Brewster managed to shoulder his way through until we stood at the open gate. Inside the courtyard, Gian protested using much gesticulation with a group of uniformed men, who were attempting to carry things from the house. The more unruly of the watchers had taken Gian's side and were yelling and throwing hunks of mud at the police, or whoever they were.

"What the devil?" I demanded.

The crowd ignored me. When the commander of the troop swung about and made for me, I recognized the captain who'd previously tried to arrest me.

"You," he snarled. "You have caused enough trouble. Go home."

"Hardly." Grenville gaze at him with the imperiousness only he could conjure. "We are friends of the deceased gentleman, as you will recall. Why are you looting his house?"

"It is he who has looted others. I have orders to take everything away and discover where it all belongs." By his expression, the captain was not happy with his assigned task, but he would stoically try to do his job.

I would have hotly disputed his claim had not Denis's visit put de Luca's collection in a different light. Perhaps de Luca had conducted the same sort of business Denis did—to obtain things for people by fair means or foul.

I gestured at the pile with my walking stick. "These things now belong to Gian if he is correct about de Luca's will. Plus, I am certain the next conte will have something to say about you tramping through his house."

The captain gave me a curt nod. "I am aware of this, but the magistrate ordered me to empty the place of everything."

Brewster, who had had turned away as soon as the captain

approached, now quietly slipped into the house. Gian ceased his shouting and ducked in after him.

"I have no choice," the captain continued in a hard voice.

I could see that the captain would dearly love to abandon his task and march his men out. Bystanders were still pelting mud, a few darting in and trying to overbalance two officers who were carrying out a gilded settee.

None tried to actually attack the policemen or attempt to take what they were absconding with, which meant the rabble were not risking getting themselves arrested. They'd be a nuisance until the captain chased them off. That he hadn't also told me he disliked his assignment.

"Ah." Grenville had turned at the sound of carriage wheels and now he nodded at the coach that slowed at the end of the lane. "See who has turned up."

Two lackeys leapt from the coach and approached its door. One opened it while the other lowered steps and bent his back in a protracted bow.

The man who stepped out was tall and haughty, his coat a deep shade of blue. He removed his hat, revealing the graying hair of Conte Trevisan.

"It seems he travels as much as we do," Grenville murmured to me, then gave the man a nod when he strode to the gate. "Conte. We meet again."

Trevisan had no interest in us. He swept his freezing glare over the courtyard and the chaos there. I noted that no mud came his way.

He snapped his fingers. Another lackey appeared from the coach, this one dressed in a tailored suit, and joined Trevisan at the open gate.

The captain jerked around, peered at Trevisan and his man, and then took on a look of weary resignation, as though reflecting that this day could not possibly become worse.

As soon as the captain approached, the conte directed a stream of words at him that were full of fury. The captain listened with a scowl, attempting in vain to interject whenever Trevisan drew a breath.

Trevisan snapped his fingers again. The suited lackey produced a leather portmanteau, from which he withdrew a sheaf of papers. He thrust them at the captain, who cast his gaze over the top sheet.

With a growl, the captain turned and barked orders at his men. They looked around in surprise, and when the orders were repeated, they shrugged, set down whatever they were carrying, and began to file out of the courtyard. The men marched past the handcarts they'd already filled, abandoning them to disappear down the lane.

A small boy made to throw mud at one of the last soldiers, who turned and pointed at the lad. The boy dropped the mud and shrank back behind the rest of the crowd.

The abandoned furniture and carts sat forlornly in the courtyard, a few boxes overflowing with goods left on the seat of a finely upholstered chair.

Trevisan barked more orders, and his footmen, burly young men all, surged forward to move the goods back inside.

I signaled to Grenville then lifted a small box, hugging it in one arm, and lugged it to the house. Grenville picked up a graceful table and carried it, legs out, behind me.

Gian raked hands through sweaty hair but also ran out to hoist up an urn and a footstool. Brewster, in silence, passed us and returned with another small table held upright by his unhurt hand.

Between us and Trevisan's footmen the courtyard was

cleared in a few minutes. The bystanders, with nothing more entertaining to watch, faded away.

Conte Trevisan stalked through the downstairs hall as though assessing a palace he prepared to conquer. Grenville, at his most politic, met him at the bottom of the staircase.

"Conte." Grenville gave him a smooth bow. "I trust your journey from Napoli was comfortable?"

"It was not." Trevisan's words were clipped. "Why are you here?"

"We were acquaintances of Conte de Luca. We heard the tragic news and came to see if we could assist. Just in time, I gather. When we arrived, the police were busily emptying the place."

"They had no business. Everything must stay exactly where it is."

"I agree," Grenville said. "Were you friends with the conte?"

"No." Trevisan was as chilly as ever. "He was, as you say in English, a mountebank."

Grenville's brows rose, and I stepped closer to listen. "Do you mean to say he wasn't who he said he is?" Grenville asked.

"Oh, he is from an old family. The de Lucas have been in Rome for centuries. But how they obtained their wealth does not bear scrutiny. They take what they find and are in league with those who would gut all our lands."

Trevisan pinched his mouth shut as though he hadn't intended to say so much.

"That is quite an accusation," I remarked.

"But the truth." Trevisan bent his cold eye on me. "He was ever good at playing the *buon amico*, the good friend, the *mate*, as you might call it. To his own ends."

I was realizing this, which was too bad. Conte de Luca had been larger than life, and I'd wanted to become better acquainted with him. I reflected that I might dismiss Trevisan's claims as nothing more than his sour disposition had Denis not told us his convictions about de Luca this morning.

Trevisan's gaze turned steely. "You, Captain Lacey, must find out who has killed him. I need to know."

The second person today adamant that I solve de Luca's murder. "May I ask why?" I said, somewhat ill-temperedly. "I am here on holiday."

"I have heard of your reputation." Trevisan adjusted his gloves. "You find things out. We must know whether a ruffian thief killed him or if this is … political."

I did not like the thought that de Luca's demise involved the tangled politics of the Italian states. Unrest simmered below the surface up and down the peninsula, which I'd felt since our arrival. Too many changes at once on top of the collapse of the *Ancien Regime.*

I could scoff that of course a thief had done this for de Luca's great wealth, but I was no longer certain. A thief would have quickly helped himself to whatever goods he could carry before he'd realized that de Luca, alone in one room of this vast house, was even at home.

However, de Luca *had* been killed, and Denis's worry was real. I would need to stay close, in any case, if I were to find out if de Luca did have the dangerous information Denis claimed he did.

Grenville watched me closely as I debated with myself. Finally I squared my shoulders and sent Trevisan a nod.

"Very well," I said. "I will see what I can turn up."

CHAPTER 14

The corners of Trevisan's eyes tightened as though he was surprised I'd agreed. He'd been prepared to battle with me, and he no longer needed the arguments he'd been ready to grind out.

"You will tell me about anything you discover, and bring the culprit to me," he said.

"I beg your pardon," I answered with a coolness that matched his own. "I do not work for you, sir, nor am I a subject of this land. If I do find the killer, I will of course want him brought to justice. But you are not a magistrate, not here in the Papal States. You hail from Milan, which is in Lombardy, I believe."

"I do, and it is. But that does not matter. Until Conte de Luca's death is resolved not one thing must be removed from this house." Trevisan glared at me as though he knew all about me taking away the Cupid statue. I decided not to enlighten him about that.

I wondered at Trevisan's insistence—as I'd said, he was not a magistrate here, and he'd just told me he'd had no fondness for de Luca. Did he believe de Luca or his family had taken something that belonged to *him*?

"I will tell Gian," I said. "He will not want the things removed either."

Trevisan's lips pinched. "This person called Gian should not be the only man to look after things here. You should do it."

I was growing tired of Trevisan's imperious ways. No matter what good Baldini and the Stanbridges had said of him, to me he'd only been irritating and demanding.

"I will do what I can," I said. "That is all I can promise."

At last, Trevisan seemed to realize he could only intimidate us so much. He gave us a truncated bow. "Inform me of your findings." He turned and strode out, boot heels drumming on the stones of the floor.

Grenville blew out his breath once the gate had clanged behind him. "Did *he* ever meet Bonaparte, I wonder? And who was the victor in that exchange?"

I grunted a laugh. "He certainly expects obedience. I can scarcely believe he is the warm family man Baldini told us about."

"Very odd." Grenville glanced at the jumble of the downstairs. Gian was nowhere in sight, and Brewster had disappeared as well. "This will be a puzzle, Lacey. Anyone in Rome could have killed de Luca that night. The only people I'm certain are innocent are you, Brewster, and me. Baldini as well —he was waiting for us in Herculaneum, at Trevisan's command."

"But where was he the few days before?" I asked. "We traveled slowly. A man on horseback could ride all night and day after he killed de Luca, hiring fresh horses along the way, and be ready to show us about the following morning."

Grenville took a moment to consider this. "That man would be tired and agitated. Baldini was robust and pleased to see us."

"I agree, but until I know where he was, I cannot rule him out. Not that I can guess why he'd kill de Luca, or if he even knew of the man."

"The Stanbridges." Grenville fed the name to me, waiting to see what I'd conclude.

"Again, we met them several days after de Luca's death, and by Mrs. Stanbridge's statement, they'd recently been to Rome. But as with Baldini, I see no reason for them to commit murder."

"Gian claims to have been out with friends all night. That is easily confirmed, I suppose."

"Yes, we have only his word that he found de Luca and did not kill him upon his return. Though I hope it is not Gian. He seems to genuinely grieve."

"Trevisan himself?" Grenville suggested. "He certainly disliked de Luca. Loathing in every word he spoke of him."

"Possibly." My answer held caution. "Is your idea that Trevisan is adamant about us finding the killer to make certain we put the blame on someone else?"

Grenville leaned against the heavily carved newel post at the bottom of the staircase, the very picture of a dandy in the throes of ennui. "Trevisan was in Napoli when we were, but again, he could have traveled more quickly than we did, another thing we will have to inquire about."

"I wonder why he was in Napoli at all," I said. "I still find it puzzling he sought us out to apologize. He said he had business there but was close-mouthed about it."

"As I say, this will be difficult." Grenville straightened up and regarded the piles of objects left on the ground floor. "Where do we begin?"

"With the household." Servants always knew exactly what went on in a house. Donata's did, sometimes embarrassingly so. "Brewster can be a help there, and we can recruit Matthias and Bartholomew as well."

"They are itching for some excitement," Grenville acknowledged. "Cleaning our suits and keeping my house are growing too tame for them."

"I'll not begrudge them. I suppose we should start right away."

"I would say you were longing for excitement as well." Grenville's statement was too accurate, and I pretended not to hear it.

"I will tackle the kitchen," I said. "Brewster is down there already, I believe. Perhaps you could speak to Gian?"

"Pry more information out of him that is?" Grenville nodded. "Yes, best I do it."

"You'll be more tactful, you mean?" I asked, not offended.

"Exactly." Grenville grasped the newel post and launched himself up the stairs. "Tread lightly, Lacey. These are deeper waters than we know."

With that admonishment, he disappeared into the shadows, and I turned to seek the kitchen.

———

I FOUND THE DOOR TO THE BACK STAIRS AT THE REAR OF THE house, behind which tiled and narrow steps ran down into darkness.

At the bottom a more cheerful passageway, painted white and tiled in blue and yellow, led under high windows to a long, hot room with a fireplace and wooden table. Here a man with very black hair slapped dough onto the table's surface before rolling it out with what looked like a broom handle.

Brewster rose from a stool near the fire, a large tankard in his fist. "He speaks no English, guv."

"Enough to find you an ale."

"Aye, well. Some things are understandable."

The cook smoothed the dough into a wide circle. He set aside the stick and with his hands, rolled the thin dough into a long cylinder. Next, he took up a slender but frightening-looking knife and cut the cylinder into even slices. The pieces fell, unfolding into soft noodles.

"Are there other servants?" I asked. I saw no assistant to do the messy and tedious kitchen work, no footman, no maid.

"Not as such," Brewster answered. "This man makes all the meals, and Gian does the rest. Save for the woman who comes in and has a dust about."

So Gian had indicated. "I wonder why. The conte is—was— a wealthy man. Why only two people living with him? With one to do occasional cleaning?"

Brewster shrugged. "Fewer to nick things, most like. He trusted Gian and this cove." He gestured with his fingers to the cook, who glanced up.

I approached the cook, who quickly bent his head over his task. The noodles went onto a plate then he rolled out another round of dough.

"Have you worked here long?"

The man shook his head without looking up. "I have not the English."

I took a chance and addressed him in Spanish, speaking carefully. The man gazed at me in puzzlement a moment, then answered, very slowly, in Italian.

Five years. No, no assistant. The conte ate very little and almost never had guests for supper. Gian sometimes helped get the food in. No one else. It was an easy place.

"Did you see anyone the night he died?"

The cook scowled. He brought his knife down, point first, into the wood of the table. "No. I go home. I sleep. I did not kill him. Why should I? He paid well."

"Are you sure no one came before you departed?"

The man was finished with me. "No. You go now." He snatched up the knife and waved it at me, not really threatening, but in frustration.

"'Ere, enough of that," Brewster rumbled.

He spoke English, but the cook understood his gist. He said *perdonami*, laid down his knife, and went back to rolling his dough. He formed the cylinder once more and lifted the knife again but only to quickly slice off the noodles.

It looked like the beginning of a tasty meal. I'd love to sit and sample his cuisine, but the man was angry, not liking foreigners questioning him in his kitchen.

"Where will you go now?" I asked in painstaking Spanish.

"Go?" He glared at me. "I stay here. Cook for Gian. He is master now."

For how long? I wondered. De Luca might have left all his goods to Gian, but I imagined the conte's cousin would want Gian out of the house and might even contest the will.

The cook obviously did not wish to discuss the matter further. He would have to contend with the conte's cousin when he came calling, and I wished the best for him.

I thanked the man profusely. He finally nodded but turned his back and began rummaging in baskets for produce—bright carrots, white potatoes, and beautiful greens. De Luca had certainly had money to spend on provisions.

I drifted to the doorway, wondering if Brewster would join me, but he slurped his beer, seemingly content. If he could cajole more information from the cook, I would leave him to it.

I returned above stairs and climbed higher through the house. The police hadn't reached the rooms above the ground floor—these chambers held the same quiet splendor that I'd seen when de Luca had first admitted us.

On impulse, I stepped into one of the salons. A long settee reposed under a window draped in silk. A tall writing stand on slender, gilded legs rested opposite it, with a gold ink pot and pen holder arrayed on its top. Next to this desk, against the painted wall, was a cabinet holding artfully shaped glass and objects I recognized as ancient—a bronze drinking vessel, a clay lamp, and a set of jewelry, delicate and intricate gold. Nothing worth a fortune in their material alone, but the historic and artistic value must be high.

This was a showpiece of a room. Another slim chair sat next to the cabinet, placed so that a sitter could observe and admire what was on display. The half dozen sconces on the walls would light this room well in the evening.

And yet, the cook had told me the conte had few visitors. Who were all these arrangements for?

I doubted that what Denis searched for—a list holding all his agents throughout the Continent—would be here, but I could not be certain. I began a search, opening the drawers of the writing stand then the doors of the cabinet to see if anything had been hidden among or under the shelves.

I found nothing there but more valuable objects.

A door in this room led to the next one. The ceiling soared high in this chamber, which must have originally been a large drawing room, or even a ballroom. Arches framed the ceiling, forming a semi dome. Painted clouds floated above me, along with a scene of angels chasing away a lone and very evil-looking demon.

I'd seen such depictions in houses in England, which often managed to be overdone or insipid—very pink angels with too many draperies—but this was softly toned with real faces and true expressions. I'd seen such art before, and I highly suspected it had been done by Caravaggio or someone he'd trained.

I had a look through this room as well, but I found nothing that resembled documents or notes.

The rest of the rooms on this floor were similarly grand and also yielded no more information. I wondered if an inventory existed for de Luca's collection, and if Trevisan and Denis were correct that de Luca and his family had stolen most of these things, or at least obtained them illicitly.

De Luca had been so open about his treasures, declaring they'd been in the family for decades and that even Bonaparte had not been able to grab them. De Luca had been a canny man if he'd convinced the headstrong emperor to trust him.

I mounted the next flight of stairs and up the side staircase in search of Grenville and Gian. They proved to be in the collection room, Gian holding a bronze statuette, a primitive carving of an upright man.

"Etruscan," he was saying to Grenville. "Very ancient. My father had several Etruscan pieces. Scholars came to study them," he finished proudly.

"Do many scholars visit here?" I asked in curiosity.

Gian swung to me, startled, as though he hadn't heard me approach. "Not often. But they travel from England and France from time to time. The conte had antiquities and books as well."

"Can you tell me about the conte's family?" I asked. "Besides yourself, I mean."

Gian's teeth flashed in a smile, and I saw a younger version of de Luca in him. "I do not mind that I am not his lawful son. The conte raised me from a boy, as soon as he discovered my existence. My mother had died, and my grandmother had the care of me, but she wanted nothing to do with me. The conte paid her handsomely and took me away, and my grandmother did not regret seeing me go. She's dead now too. I grew up here, taking care of the conte while he took care of me. It was just the two of us."

Very kindhearted of de Luca, I thought, but perhaps he'd been delighted to find he'd had a son. Love did not need legal ties to be real. "He never married?"

"No, no. He loved the ladies but did not wish to marry. As far as I know, I was his only offspring. He had no brothers or sisters. Only the cousin, Gregorio, who will be the conte now. They did not get on." Gian's shoulders slumped. "He will come to take possession of the house soon, I imagine."

"Perhaps he'll keep you on," I said. "I'm certain no one knows this house as you do."

"I will not work for Gregorio." Gian's answer held anger. "I assisted my father because he was my family. I know the cousin is my family too, by blood, but I do not think he will regard me so."

"I beg your pardon," I said. "I wish I could help."

Gian gave me a bow. "You are kind. But nothing can help." His eyes filled again, and he swiped his hand across them.

"We'll leave you alone now, my dear fellow." Grenville gently lifted the bronze from Gian's fingers and replaced it on a nearby shelf. "You have my condolences on your loss."

"Thank you." Gian sniffled.

"Of course," Grenville said quietly. He signaled to me that we should go, and I began to follow him out.

At the door, I turned back. "One more thing, Gian, and then I will disturb you no more. Did you or the conte keep an inventory of his collection? Or lists of people he purchased things from or purchased things for?"

Gian went rigid, and his tears dried. "Why do you wish to know that?"

I shrugged, as though I did not care one way or another. "Thought it might help you sort things out."

Gian wiped his eyes again. "I do not know. I will hunt."

I noticed that when Gian wanted to be evasive, his grasp of English waned. He'd spoken quite eloquently about the conte's fondness for him, but as soon as he grew worried, his sentences became short and blunt.

I gave Gian a nod. "Good day to you, sir. If you have need of assistance, send word to us at Grenville's lodgings."

"Thank you."

Again, the words were stilted. Grenville and I at last took our leave, saying nothing as we descended the stairs through the silent house and exited via the jumbled foyer and the now empty courtyard, and emerged onto the street.

Brewster appeared through a side door as though he'd been watching for us, and fell into step as we turned south through the lanes.

"Do you think Gian killed him, then?" Brewster asked me.

"He could have," I admitted. "He could have returned home much sooner than he claims. De Luca wouldn't have had reason to fear him. I am certain he'd readily turn away from Gian without worry. Did the cook tell you anything more?"

"Naw. Just repeated that he went home and saw no one."

"The woman who cleans might know something as well," I said.

"If you ask her, be careful," Brewster said. "These people don't like the police. The only reason the cook opened up as much as he did is because I'm *not* police, and I don't like them either."

"I don't blame them," I said. If the police were wont to lock someone in a jail without hope of trial, I'd avoid them myself. "It would be helpful to have an interpreter if I need to question them further."

"Luckily, you did make an Italian friend," Grenville said.

I'd been thinking of Proietti before Grenville's answer. I did not know whether he would assist me if Trevisan was involved, but I could ask.

We fell silent the rest of the way home. The day had turned blustery, with wind drawing in clouds. I smelled rain in the air.

When we entered Grenville's hired house, we found it buzzing with activity. Bartholomew and Matthias hurried up the stairs, their arms full of linens, while Gautier tried to make himself understood—loudly—to the Italian servants who did the everyday cleaning.

Gautier abruptly became his cool self as soon as he spied Grenville. "Her ladyship has sent word she will be arriving, sir. We expect her upon the hour."

I tried without success to hide my gladness. Though I had been thoroughly enjoying my sightseeing, I missed Donata and looked forward to her arrival with the eagerness of a young swain.

Gautier made no mention of Gabriella or Marianne, so assumed they'd stay behind. Grenville did not ask him, also pretending nonchalance, though I knew he longed to see his wife as well.

Grenville and I retreated to his upstairs chamber, Grenville pouring brandy, while we went over the events of the day.

I was restless, however, and when I heard a carriage halt at our door, I was out of the room so quickly I forgot to set down my glass. Grenville's laughter followed me down the stairs.

Donata, the former Lady Breckenridge, glided into the house, servants swarming around her like drones to a queen.

A wife generally curtsied to her husband, but I had dispensed with that formality on the first day of our married life. I slammed my glass to the nearest table, went straight to her, took her hands, and kissed her lips.

"Gabriel," Donata said calmly, but her eyes sparkled with pleasure at my greeting. "I hear you have inserted yourself into other people's troubles yet again."

CHAPTER 15

*D*onata had read my letters I'd sent to the villa, and she forestalled me launching into the entire tale again.

"Let us walk. I am cramped from sitting in the carriage."

The wind had let up, though a gentle rain pattered down. We took our leave of Grenville who waved us away good-naturedly. Donata had brought him a missive from Marianne, and we left him seeking a quiet place to read it.

Brewster started to accompany us, but Donata forestalled him, telling him she wanted one walk alone with her husband.

Donata wore stout boots against the wet, a long redingote, and a wide-brimmed bonnet. She kept her hand on my arm, and I held an umbrella over us both.

Did I puff with pride that I walked with a most beautiful woman at my side? I am afraid that I did.

"Gabriella, Peter, and Anne are well?" The first question popped from my mouth as we strolled toward the Piazza Navona.

"All are in excellent, roaring good health, especially Anne.

She toddles everywhere, and her voice could bring down the rafters. I thought it best they remain at the villa."

"I had thought you might. Most sensible."

Donata's laugh was like silver in the rain. "No, you are annoyed that I left them behind, but Grenville's small house on a dirty street is hardly a place for children. Marianne was happy to see me depart—Grenville's servants defer to me because of my rank, but she is in truth the lady of the house. She needs time to be just that, without my interference."

"You'd never deliberately interfere," I assured her.

"Rubbish. I'm the most interfering woman I know. I like things to be a certain way. The only reason you do not notice this at home is because you pay no attention. You have no idea how to run a household, in any case."

"True, though you perhaps could sound more compassionate when you say so," I said, my tone light. "Poor Captain Lacey never had the chance to be master of his estate."

"You could have been, but you gave it away to your cousin Marcus."

Donata was still not happy that I'd stepped aside without a fight so my cousin, who by rights was the true heir to the Norfolk house and lands, could come into his birthright. The proofs were still going through the courts, which took time— Marcus had certainly already paid many fees to solicitors—but I granted he was a much better steward of the estate than I had ever been. It had even started to produce now that the weather was more salubrious than it had been a few years ago when we'd hardly had a summer at all.

"I prefer to live in Town with you," I explained.

Donata sent me an assessing glance and did not reply. She knew I did not consider myself a farmer, and that the memories of my home in Norfolk were not happy ones. The memories I built now were much better.

The rain ceased as we entered the Piazza Navona, and I shook out and folded up the umbrella. Others were strolling the long square, mostly tourists from other lands, with a few Romans hurrying about their business.

Clouds broke, and sunshine eked through. I'd already learned that the weather in Rome was changeable, with the winds blowing up the river from the coast to meet colder air rolling down from the mountains.

A man whose hair was a riot of dark curls stood in the middle of the piazza, playing a violin. The sweetness of the melody called to us, and we wandered that way.

The man continued to play, his eyes closed, his entire being absorbed in the music. I recognized a piece from Hayden, something from a symphony, I supposed, but pared down to its basic theme. The tune was heart-wrenching, but not in a sad way. I saw more than one handkerchief emerge from his listeners as the tune continued.

The last note of the melody sang as he drew the bow out in one long glide, the sound fading into the still air.

His listeners burst into applause, as did I, and money clinked into the hat he'd laid upside down before him. I tossed in a few coins myself.

The man grinned at Donata and sent her a cheeky wink, before he went into a rousing, lively piece. His arm moved rapidly, elbow wrenching up and down as his fingers danced over the strings.

Donata listened in delight. She was a patron of musicians in London, bringing forth new talents in her musicales all Season. Members of the *haut ton* finagled for invitations to these musicales, mostly in vain. Donata was very particular that only those who could do the musician some good attended.

The piece continued, the man twirling in place as he played the whirlwind notes. He lifted on tiptoes as the pitch rose, until he slammed home the final chord and made a bow at the same time.

More applause, cheers, and coins raining into his hat.

Donata and I waited in delight, ready for more. The man abruptly spun to us, reaching forward to brush a gentle finger over Donata's chin.

Before I could make my objections, he'd flitted away, laughing at me. Donata's flush and starry eyes told me she was not offended.

The man lifted his bow again. "For the lady," he said in heavily accented English. Then he began to play another sweet melody that tore at our emotions.

The music stormed at us then withdrew, then stormed again, then wound down to a lovely series of notes. The man finished with the highest note fading, his eyes closed, his face twisted with emotion.

He lowered his bow as we applauded, and wiped his eyes.

Donata had a card out of her reticule and shoved it at me. "Give him this. Sir, you must look me up in London. I will introduce you to people."

I handed the man the card. He took it with a bow of thanks and tucked it into his pocket, but whether he understood Donata's invitation, I could not tell.

As he lifted the violin again, a sudden tramping of feet sounded at the south end of the piazza, beyond Boromini's Sant'Agnese church. The tourists peered curiously, but any Italian who'd been lingering to listen to the violinist suddenly faded away.

The violinist likewise vanished. One moment, he was beginning a new piece, the next, he'd swept up his hat, coins, and violin case, and had disappeared into the lane I'd run down the day I'd spotted Mr. Broadhurst.

A group of patrollers marched in, gazing about as though hoping to catch anyone doing anything at all. The foreigners eyed them warily, then continued their walks.

Donata and I strolled on as well. "I'd like to show you something," I told her.

She peered over her shoulder at the patrollers. "I believe they wish to speak to you, Gabriel."

I turned to find the now-familiar captain of the squad, who looked as harassed as ever, accosting me. "Captain Lacey."

"Sir." I gave him a bow.

He glanced at Donata and forced himself into a respectful stance. "I have arrested de Luca's servants. One of them must have killed him." The captain was tight-lipped, as though irritated he'd had to follow these orders. "The one called Gian implored me to tell you. I was heading for your home but saw you here."

"Damnation," I exclaimed. "Quite right Gian should protest. I don't believe he or the cook did anything of the sort."

The captain lifted his shoulders in a shrug. "I was told to arrest the murderer, and there are no better suspects. If you can prove otherwise ..." He spread his hands, leaving it up to me.

"I will." I bent him a glare. "Where did you take them?"

"To jail. You may not visit them. If you bring me another murderer, I will let them go."

"Bloody hell." I felt sudden irritation at de Luca for getting himself killed and causing others so many troubles. "I will find the correct culprit, Captain. You have my word."

"Good." The captain touched his hat. "Good day, Signor."

"Shall we walk on?" I asked Donata, my tone chilled, not bothering with a polite farewell.

Donata had said nothing at all, but she sent the captain her iciest look, one that told the receiver she wouldn't soil her shoes stepping on him. From the captain's flush, he understood.

I ushered Donata away, making for the lane that led to the church with the Raphael fresco. People melted out of our path, clearly wondering what we'd done to merit the attention of the police.

We proceeded as sedately as we could through the streets to the church, and I guided Donata inside it, as though nothing important had deterred us from our sightseeing.

A service was being conducted, a Friday mass of some kind. We hovered in the entrance while near the altar of the rather small church, a priest in flowing robes and the men who surrounded him sang a Latin hymn in melodious baritones.

The Raphael fresco was in a side chapel near the front door, so I could quietly point it out to Donata without moving farther into the church. She loved art and paintings as much as she loved music. She admired the fresco, which depicted sibyls and angels, her hand squeezing mine in her enjoyment. If not for our unfortunate encounter with the police captain, this might be an enchanting moment.

The hymn wound down, the priest moved up the steps to his pulpit, and Donata and I quietly exited.

"I need to visit a friend," I said as we wended our way back to the piazza. "I will return you to Grenville's first, where you can rest. I'm certain Gautier will treat you like a queen, though Grenville calls it living rough."

Donata's brows rose, she ignoring my attempt at humor. "I

have no need to retreat indoors. I shall visit this friend with you."

I shook my head. "Rome is not the most salubrious city, as grand as it is."

"Nonsense. It is vibrant and robust." Donata rubbed my arm with her gloved hand. "So many eras in history, and yet the people here live firmly in the present. Or is this friend a young woman you do not wish me to know about?"

Now it was my turn to be surprised. Her tone was offhand, indicating she did not speak in earnest, but there was a watchfulness in her eyes that bothered me. Her first husband had been unfaithful to her from the day of their wedding until the morning he was killed.

"Not at all. It is Signor Proietti. I wrote you of him."

Her expression cleared. "Yes, whose daughter has been lured away. Have you news of her for him?"

"No, unfortunately. I am going to ask Proietti a favor. Though perhaps I should let him be."

"Do not treat the poor man as though he is an invalid. Perhaps this favor will help him take his mind off things until you can bring his daughter home to him."

I huffed a skeptical laugh. "Do you believe I can? Trevisan is an odd man, and a very determined one."

"I know you well, Gabriel. You will leave no stone unturned."

If she knew me well, she'd know I'd never dream of going to another woman. "I suppose you are right," I conceded. "And I suppose I am still smarting over what danger my last investigations put our son into."

Peter, a vigorous lad, had quickly recovered from his ordeal and spoke about it as a good adventure. His mother, however, who'd been faced with the real possibility of losing her child, had been inconsolable for a long time and very, very angry.

"I believe I have told you that the incident was not your fault." Her words were crisp. "I hold Mr. Denis and Mr. Creasy entirely to blame. Using a young boy in their war against each other, and a boy who is a viscount at that ... Mr. Creasy was a bloody fool." Rage filled her voice, in the cold way of Donata's anger.

We walked a few steps in silence before I said, "I did not have the chance to tell you that Denis is here in Rome."

Donata's falter would have been indiscernible to any but me. "Is he? He wrote to me from Florence."

"He came because he is incensed at de Luca's murder and fears de Luca had information that might expose his agents."

"Hmm. Well, if this information only exposed Mr. Denis, I would say wash your hands of it. But some of these agents might be working for him under duress and do not need more trouble."

"Precisely my thoughts."

"I imagined they were. You always strive to help others."

"Because I never know when to leave off," I said with some bitterness.

Donata squeezed my arm. "That was not an admonishment. It is a reason I admire you so much."

I glanced at her, wondering if she jested once more, but she'd turned her head to continue our walk, and her bonnet hid her face from me.

We went north through the piazza, Donata pausing to take in the grand fountains along the way. The violinist was firmly gone, and I hoped he'd reached a safe place to continue his playing.

Bells rang out from church towers around us, marking the

hour as we exited the square. I kept a sharp eye out as we traversed the narrow lanes to Proietti's abode, though most of the passers-by had no interest in us, and I saw no sign of our attacker from Naples and Pompeii. I hoped the man had stayed at the bay and had not ventured to Rome.

I found the door with chipped paint in the narrow lane and knocked upon it. After a few moments, the retainer who'd answered before flung it open, no reticence this time.

"*Capitano, entra, entra.*" He was agitated and harried. When the man caught sight of Donata behind me, his eyes widened, and he executed a low bow. "*Signora, perdonami.*"

"It is no bother," Donata said in English. "Admit us, please."

The servant might not understand the words, but he recognized the command. He opened the door wide, stepping back from it so we'd have plenty of room to enter.

He continued his apologies as he closed the door and led us to the stairs. Voices raised in argument poured down the staircase as we ascended it behind the retainer, and he turned a sorrowful face to us.

"*Sua figlia,*" he said. "*È tornata.*"

"*Figlia?*" I asked in surprise. "His daughter?"

"*Si, si, capitano.*"

The man did not sound happy. I heard the high-pitched but lovely voice of the young lady I'd met at Trevisan's home. Answering her was Proietti, in a blazing fury.

"Perhaps we should not interfere," I said.

Donata apparently did not agree with me. She released my arm and marched up the stairs, the retainer trotting to keep ahead of her. It was obvious from which chamber the argument emerged. Donata went straight to it, and the servant quickly opened the door of a small sitting room.

Proietti was in full voice. He stood several feet from his

daughter, arms raised to make a point. Gisela faced him, head up, mouth set in a stubborn line, not cowed one whit by her raging father.

"Good afternoon," Donata said into the noise.

She did not shout, but her words cut through Proietti's rampage and Gisela's impassioned ripostes.

Proietti whirled, arms still high. An expression of amazement crossed his face, and his arms came down.

"*Signora? Chi sei?*" I stepped into the room behind Donata, and Proietti became even more nonplussed. "Captain Lacey?"

"Proietti," I said hastily. "May I present my wife, Mrs. Lacey."

Proietti's face went crimson. Gisela stared with as much embarrassment and bewilderment. Father and daughter looked very alike at this moment.

"Perhaps, my dear, you will explain to me why you are bellowing enough to shake the walls," Donata said to Gisela. "You may translate, Signor Proietti. My husband has written to me all about you, and I am interested in your dilemma."

Gisela, today dressed in ivory cotton, sleeves gathered at her wrists with a fall of ribbons, unlocked her frozen stance and gave Donata a practiced and deferential curtsy.

"Please, madame." Gisela drew a large armchair from the shadows, positioning it near the warm stove. She then gave an order to the retainer, delivering it in dulcet tones, very unlike the infuriated ones I'd heard on the way up the stairs.

The manservant rushed away and quickly returned with a tray bearing cups and a decanter of wine. Gisela carried a footstool to Donata, solicitous of her comfort.

"You have very pretty manners, my dear." Donata smoothed her skirt and accepted the cup of wine from the manservant. "Which is likely why you are in this predicament now. A harridan would hardly have caught this conte's eye, from what I hear of him."

Proietti and I stood away from the ladies, watching the little tableau, making no move to intervene. The manservant brought me a wine cup, and I took it gratefully but did not drink.

"Thank you, madame," Gisela said quietly. I could see that Gisela wanted to argue, but also that she'd been raised to be deferential to her elders, in spite of what I'd just heard between her and her father. Her parents had not taken the spirit out of her, but neither had she become harsh and spoiled.

"I can understand why Conte Trevisan is taken with you," Donata continued. "And more than that, why his mother did not kick up a fuss when he brought you home."

"Contessa Trevisan is a great lady," Gisela assured her. "She is good to me."

I'd found the contessa as cool and arrogant as her son. She'd be unforgiving of any misstep.

"You are fortunate that she is being kind," Donata said. "At least for now."

Gisela flushed. "For now?"

"It is never flattering to believe that a gentleman has any intentions toward one but the most honorable and most welcome ones," Donata said calmly. "But from what I understand, those close to the conte say he is very fond of his wife and is not likely to leave her. That could mean he is simply relieving his appetites, as many gentlemen do, though I do not believe that is the case here."

Gisela's eyes widened. "No, madame. Never."

The shock and outrage in Gisela's voice told me that Proietti had been correct when he'd said that Trevisan had not made any illicit advances toward his daughter.

"Then my dear, we must consider," Donata went on. "If Conte Trevisan is not interested in the baser side of things, and he dotes on his wife, what is his purpose in bringing you into his house? He cannot be both a devoted husband and a philanderer who is ready to throw her over for a pretty young thing. He must be one or the other. Please look past your excitement that such a man chose you, and let us ponder why exactly he did so."

CHAPTER 16

Gisela gazed at Donata in stunned silence, and I saw her growing dismay. She might be headstrong and proud, but she was no fool.

"What do you mean?" Her question was quiet. No protests that of course Trevisan loved her, that she wouldn't hear a word against him.

Donata opened her hand. "He is far from home, he is not liked in this city, and yet he obtains a house here and settles in. He is very upset at the death of Conte de Luca and has requested that my husband look into it, though we do not know quite why."

Proietti shot me a glance, and I gave him a minute shrug.

"I know little of the Conte de Luca," Gisela said. "I am aware that he was a wealthy and prominent man, but I have never made his acquaintance."

"It makes me wonder why Conte Trevisan is so interested in him and his demise," Donata said. "As well as why he is in Rome at all."

I had been pondering these very questions. "Perhaps," I

broke in, keeping my voice gentle. "Letting the people of Rome believe he is interested in a second marriage will distract them from speculating on the true reasons for his visit." I knew what I said was cruel, but I also might be correct. Better she knew now.

From Gisela's stricken look, she hadn't thought such a thing was possible, but I was pleased that she did not dismiss the idea out of hand.

"I would better like it if he pursued my daughter for great love of her." Proietti's voice was thick. "But I know much of the world."

Gisela faced her father squarely. "Conte Trevisan is an honorable man. Much admired."

That might be true, but sometimes honorable men were forced to make difficult choices. There was a reason Trevisan was adamant about every bit of de Luca's home remaining intact, and I wondered if he'd caused Gian and the cook to be arrested so they'd be unable to take anything out of the house. What the devil was the man looking for?

"I am not questioning Trevisan's honor," I said truthfully. "I have met many who speak highly of him."

Proietti turned a scowl on me at this declaration but did not argue.

"He sounds a paragon," Donata said. "But no man is, so we may dismiss that notion."

"His mother told me he is in Rome to complete business transactions," Gisela said, her mouth firm. "That he has taken a house here because he does not know how long this business will take, which is also why his mother has journeyed with him."

"He has not stated the nature of that business," Proietti said sourly. "And my daughter refuses to ask him."

"I will not be rude, Papa." Anger returned to Gisela's eyes. "Both he and the contessa are unhappy. Conte Trevisan is a kind man and takes care of me well."

Donata's mirthful laughter wafted into the somber mood of the room. "So has said every young woman since the beginning of time." She set down her wine cup and folded her gloved hands. "There are two sorts of gentlemen a lady can find herself obligated to, my dear. A *bad* man will take and take all you have to give and then throw your devotion in your face whenever he likes. He will demand from you whatever he wishes until you are weary and despairing, and he will call it *duty* and *obedience*. A good man will ask nothing of you and accept only what you are willing to give of yourself."

"Then Conte Trevisan cannot be a bad man," Gisela said stoutly. "He has demanded nothing of me."

"Yet, he is putting aside his wife for you, or so some claim," Donata replied. "Perhaps she did not give him enough even when he said he did not require it. Some gentlemen make their demands very subtly, but they exist, and they are vexed when you do not discern them."

Gisela stared at her, lips parted. I imagined her thinking over all that had happened since she'd met the conte and putting those events in another light. Her next statement surprised me.

"His wife is very ill," she said softly. "He is saddened by it."

Sad. Yes, Trevisan did seem deeply sad, behind his chilly demeanor and high-handed ways. Perhaps he could not face the inevitable loss of his wife and had sought Gisela as consolation.

"I will take as a point in his favor that Trevisan did not object to you coming home to visit your father," Donata said. "He did not try to stop you, did he?"

"Not at all." Gisela's answer was swift and strong. "He believes Papa is wrong to try to dissuade me, but he understands I cannot be cut off from my family."

Either that or Trevisan did not fear Proietti's powers of persuasion. Gisela had made up her mind to be with Conte Trevisan, and Trevisan must have noted her strong will.

Gisela deflated once more. "His mother took a bit more convincing."

I predicted a battle of wills between wife and mother-in-law if Trevisan actually did marry Gisela.

"I would be interested in visiting Trevisan's mother," Donata said. "I might have mutual acquaintance with her, if they are from Milan."

Gisela started, then looked pleased. "I will inquire, madame. I am certain she will be happy for the interest of a great lady."

"You are quite charming, Signorina Proietti. It is no surprise that both the conte and his mother enjoy you living in their house. You must be a breath of fresh air."

This seemed to bewilder Gisela. "I try to be polite. My mother raised me to be."

Her eyes moistened with sudden tears. Her mother was notably absent.

"Your mother succeeded admirably. Please do convey my good wishes to the contessa and have her send word whether she will allow me to call on her."

"I will, madame."

There seemed to be no question that Gisela would return to Trevisan's house. If her father had hoped he'd argue her into remaining here, he now saw those hopes dashed. His shoulders drooped, a man defeated.

"A moment, Signorina," I said to Gisela. "Your father tells me you met Conte Trevisan in a church. Which church?"

Gisela turned to me in puzzlement. "Sant'Agnese en Agone," she answered. "In the Piazza Navona."

The very church where I'd spied Mr. Broadhurst the first morning I'd walked in Rome. Interesting.

"Do you attend there often?" I asked.

"Saint Agnes is my patron saint," Gisela explained with patience. "That church has a relic of her, and I pray to her there. Conte Trevisan saw me one morning and asked one of the priests, who knows my family, to introduce me to him and his mother."

What could be more respectable than an introduction made by a family's clergyman? Trevisan had chosen his opportunity well.

Donata's skirts rustled as she moved her feet from footstool to floor and rose. "You have a lovely home here, Signorina Proietti. Will you show me more of it? The captain came here, in fact, to ask your father's advice, and we ladies rather usurped his purpose. Shall we wander while they speak?"

I doubted Gisela had any desire to take Donata over the house, but as I'd observed, she was a lady of fine manners. She immediately agreed and offered Donata her arm.

Donata took it and they sailed out, Donata not bothering to look my way as she went.

"Please accept my apologies for interrupting you," I said to Proietti as soon as the manservant had closed the door from the other side. "You must have been very glad when your daughter turned up."

Proietti heaved a sigh and headed for the wine jug. "I was indeed. I'd despaired of ever seeing her again. You instructed Trevisan to set a meeting with me to discuss things, but I have yet to hear of it."

"So I gathered. He followed me to Napoli, claiming he had business in *that* city as well."

"He possibly did." Proietti trickled wine into a glass for himself. I had yet to taste mine. "He does business in many cities. Sometimes even his own." Proietti did not disguise the scorn in his voice. He set down the jug and drank deeply then faced me. "Your wife said you wished my advice."

"Your help, rather." I outlined what had happened at de Luca's house and how Trevisan, then the police captain had admonished me to discover what had occurred. "My knowledge of your language is poor, and it would help to have a local man assisting me. That is, if you do not object. I have no right to claim your time."

Proietti swept his arm about the room, wine spattering from his cup. "My wife has left Rome, my daughter insists on living with that conceited northerner, and I sit here and fret. I have more time than I want. Of course, I will assist you, Captain. That is, if you do not believe *I* murdered de Luca myself."

I sent him a look of astonishment. "Why would you say that?"

"My daughter spoke the truth when she said she knew nothing of de Luca, but I was acquainted with him." Proietti let out a sigh. "Times were hard when Bonaparte came. The wealthy were able to invest in lands he seized from the church, but if a man did not have the money to purchase them ..."

He opened one hand. "Rich men gained, and those of us who did not have as much lost investments and other income. I decided to sell de Luca a few heirlooms—a silver service that had been in my wife's family for generations as well as an Etruscan antique I'd purchased in my youth. He was eager to buy them from me, and he gave me a fair price, I must say. I was able to recover my income somewhat once the restoration began, and I no longer had to worry about being destitute. However, when I went to de Luca to purchase our things back, he refused to sell them."

"Did he?" The statement was at odds with the seemingly jovial man I'd met. "Perhaps he'd sold them to someone else in the meantime?"

"He had not. I saw both the service and the antiquity displayed nicely in one of his reception rooms. He simply did not want to part with them."

I recalled Gian proudly showing Grenville an Etruscan statue, and wondered if it was the same Proietti had sold him.

"Did he give a reason?" I asked.

Proietti's open hand closed to a fist. "De Luca said he liked them and did not wish to give them up. Once he had his fingers on something, he told me, he was loathe to release it. I explained to him how precious the silver set was to my wife, but he only laughed and said ladies had their whims."

I was coming to realize that my first impressions of de Luca might have been very wrong. "Perhaps he was trying to keep them for your own good?" I suggested.

"Reasoning that my family needed the money more than they needed the trinkets?" Proietti shrugged. "He might have had such a thing in his mind, but I more believe he liked them and did not want to part with them. He was an odd man."

That description I could agree with. De Luca's house of treasures that very few saw, with only two people to help him run it, and his jumbled private room closed off to all but the privileged few, indicated such. That he let in the woman to dust at all was surprising.

"This would be your motive for murdering him?" I asked.

"I was very angry." Proietti turned to the window and

peered at the patch of gray sky over the buildings across the lane. "I shouted at him. I'm certain his man and the cook in the cellar heard me. I vowed to have my belongings back no matter what it took. When de Luca laughed at me, I wanted to throttle him."

"When did this happen?"

"The first time I asked him for my things was a few years after the restoration began. I could afford the pieces by that time. I tried again a few weeks ago, right after Trevisan goaded Gisela into leaving us. I thought if I could not recover our daughter for my wife, I could at least recover her coffee service."

Proietti covered his face with his hands, and I saw his shoulders shake once. My heart went out to him, and I stood in sympathetic silence while he calmed himself.

"Forgive me." Proietti wiped his eyes with the heel of his hand and took a long sip of wine.

"If you give me your word you did not return to de Luca last week and cosh him, then I will welcome your help clearing up this mystery. Perhaps Gian will sell you your things back—he seems a reasonable man. And Trevisan is definitely up to something. I will do everything in my power to find out what, and convince your daughter he is not worth her regard."

Proietti stared at me throughout this speech, then he shook his head. "You are an interesting man, Captain Lacey. I am happy that I stumbled into you wandering lost in my city. You have no doubts that all this will come right, do you?"

"I have been in desperate situations before and prevailed, and I do not only mean in the war. If you will act as my interpreter, we will discover what has happened, recover your things and your daughter, and my wife and I can return to the luxury of Grenville's villa. To which I am certain he will extend an invitation to you and your family."

I watched Proietti move from despair to disbelief to amusement with my declarations, which is what I'd intended. For myself, I had no idea how I would prove what had happened to de Luca and find the information Denis wanted, but I'd meant to cheer up Proietti, and this I think I did. I gave him a glimmer of hope, at least.

As we descended the stairs in search of Donata and Gisela, I realized that Proietti had not, in fact, given me his word that he hadn't killed Conte de Luca. But we found the ladies quickly and I had no opportunity to ask him again.

———

It was dark by the time Donata and I departed, the February evening falling early. Gisela had decided to spend the night at home, looking after her poor papa, she told us, with the air of a long-married woman tending a father in his dotage. I hoped the evening would pass for them without rancor.

I took Donata's arm and headed through the narrow warrens, seeking the larger streets and the way to Grenville's.

The attack came when we walked through a particularly dark patch. A man with a cudgel charged out at me, his roar of rage drowning out Donata's scream.

CHAPTER 17

I fought hard, recognizing the fellow who'd attacked us in Napoli and Pompeii. He'd been joined by several hardened men, who were wading in to beat me senseless.

Donata was shouting at them, clearly promising them dire outcomes if they did not leave me be at once. No fleeing in terror or standing in the lane wringing her hands. I'd prefer it if she *would* flee, but she'd snatched up the walking stick that had fallen from my struck fist, and I heard it thud on a back or two.

These were honed fighters, and any moment one would turn on her. I did not believe they'd be gentle because she was a woman.

I punched and grappled, trying to keep to my feet. My back was to a brick wall, slick with rain, and the rough stones dug through my coat.

I knew how to fight, but so did the toughs, who were dark-haired Romans, contrasting the pale Englishman. I might have been able to best the man if we'd fought one on one, in spite of his cudgel, which is no doubt why he'd recruited help.

They'd beat me to a pulp. I shouted at Donata to run, but she ignored me, damn the woman.

I heard the pounding of large boots, and then Brewster was there, his sling gone, yanking a ruffian from me and hurling him to the pavement. Brewster's face was set in a scowl, rage radiating from him as he tore the second tough from me and smashed his good fist into his nose.

As he drew back for another punch, I shouted, "Leave him. Get *him*."

I pointed to the Englishman who'd decided to flee. Brewster released the man he'd pummeled, leapt over his body as he fell to the cobbles, and raced after my assailant.

The ruffians dragged themselves to their feet, decided I wasn't worth the trouble, and hobbled off into the darkness as rapidly as they could. I pushed away from the wall, catching my breath and trying to brush off my ruined coat.

"Donata," I said to my wife as she came shakily forward to hand me my walking stick. "What the bloody hell did you think you were doing?"

For a moment, she glared at me as though ready to admonish me in return, then her face crumpled. "Damnation, Gabriel, I thought they'd kill you."

She came at me, my usually cool and composed wife, and I caught her and pulled her close. We stood there in the tiny lane, swaying a bit as we held each other, I breathing her scent and thanking God she was whole and unhurt.

I heard Brewster stomping toward us, and a second set of scrambling footsteps interspersed with his. Donata and I drew apart as Brewster hauled the knife-wielding man around the corner to us. Brewster had twisted the attacker's arm behind his back and held him up by the collar, half strangling him.

"You," I said, gazing into the man's apprehensive but determined face. "You are going to tell me who you are, and what you are about."

Our attacker made a few desperate noises and tried to shove a hand into his coat pocket. Brewster twisted the arm tighter, and the man let out a gasp of pain.

Donata darted forward and dipped into his pocket herself, retrieving a small card with handwriting on it.

"Please understand that I am deaf," she read. "Good heavens."

"So Grenville told us. Brewster, please escort this gentleman to our lodgings. I have many things to ask him."

"Should toss him in the river instead." Brewster jerked on the man's collar, enough to make him grunt.

"No. Don't let him go, but keep him alive, please."

Brewster muttered something, but he pulled the man away with him. Brewster strode rapidly, the captive's boots dragging as he struggled to keep to his feet.

"The poor man is deaf?" Donata asked. She was still shaking.

I took the card from her, studied it, and dropped it into my pocket before winding her arm through mine.

"The poor man is excellent with a knife, and he pushed Grenville into a hole and left him there. I will shackle him if necessary." I knew I should give the attacker over to the police, but I did very much want to know why he was pursuing me.

I'd never seen him before in my life.

———

Brewster and his prisoner reached home before we did, and when we entered Grenville's house, Grenville was in the ground floor reception room, studying the wreck of our assailant. The man still hung in Brewster's grip, Brewster on the point of fracturing the man's arm in vengeance.

"Ah, Lacey," Grenville said as though we'd entered a soiree at his Mayfair home. "I see you've brought a visitor. I was just scolding him for knocking me into that well in Pompeii."

The man was much subdued, the wildness in his eyes replaced by pain. Brewster knew how to restrain a captive.

"Can he understand you?" I asked.

"As my half-brother does, by reading lips," Grenville said. "And, like my half-brother, pretends he cannot when he wishes to plead ignorance. But he understands me perfectly. Hand signals help—my brother and I worked out our own form of it, though of course this fellow can't know what we contrived."

The man's dismay as Grenville spoke told me he did indeed understand every word.

I faced him. "Who are you?" I asked carefully.

"It isn't necessary to twist your mouth with every syllable," Grenville said in amusement.

"Very well." I calmed myself and spoke normally. "The question remains. Who are you?"

The answer was unintelligible to me, though I was pleased I received any answer at all.

Grenville's brows had shot skyward. "Say that again, my good man. Is that truly your name?"

The man nodded and repeated the words.

"Good Lord." Grenville turned to me, stunned. "His name is Joseph Cockburn."

"Cockburn?" I stared at the man. "A relation of Leonard Cockburn, who was killed in London?"

This time I understood his answer, hurled with fury. "He was my brother."

"Ah." Now I understood the reason for his rage, a frustration born of grief. "I am so sorry, my dear chap. But why have you decided to take revenge on Mr. Grenville and me? We know nothing about your brother."

Cockburn hesitated, but it was clear he didn't believe me.

"We might be much better served if we sat down," Donata said. She'd handed her wet wraps to Bartholomew, who'd hurried in at our entrance, and now settled herself on the most comfortable chair in the room. "Do let him go, Mr. Brewster. Bartholomew, bring us all a pot of coffee. Something rich to cut the chill."

Bartholomew, who always instantly obeyed Donata, hurried away.

Brewster was more uncertain. "I turn him loose, who knows what he'll do?"

I did not trust him any more than did Brewster, but I wanted to hear the man's story.

"If you give me your word you will sit and speak to us, Brewster will release you," I said to Cockburn.

Cockburn hesitated. He glanced at Donata, who gave him a cool nod, a great lady promising him sanctuary.

"I give you my word," Cockburn said. I was beginning to catch on to the cadences of his voice.

I gestured to Brewster, and he, with great reluctance, eased his grip. Cockburn untwisted his arm, rubbing it, both relief and anger on his face. Brewster would not let him stray a step, however, until he'd searched the man and relieved him of several more knives.

Cockburn wore breeches and boots rather than trousers, the better for tramping about. As Grenville had observed before, his coat didn't fit him exactly, which spoke of second-hand gear, but the cloth was serviceable, whole, and sturdy. Not a wealthy gentleman, but not one in penury either.

Grenville, still the congenial host, waved Cockburn to a chair. Cockburn brushed off the back of his breeches before he sat. He did not plop into the chair or lower himself gingerly but took the seat as though comfortable chairs were usual for him.

Grenville waited until I'd also sat down, and Brewster had retreated to the doorway, where he planted himself like a pillar. Grenville pulled a delicate-legged chair around to face Cockburn and lounged on it, crossing his ankles. Any moment, his reclined pose said, he'd call for a brandy and box of snuff.

"Now then. Let us proceed in a civilized manner." Grenville fixed Cockburn with a stern gaze. "We were very sorry to learn of your brother's demise in so horrible a fashion. We also know that the world believes the dead man to be his partner, Mr. Broadhurst. You know differently, obviously. But why are you throwing yourself at the captain and myself? We had nothing to do with it."

"I saw *him*, didn't I?" Cockburn shot an angry glance at me. "With the coward Broadhurst, thick as thieves."

"You wrote the letters," I said. "Threatening him." The handwriting on the card had been the same as on the letter Broadhurst had given me.

Cockburn nodded without repentance.

"Mr. Broadhurst sought me out because he feared for his life," I explained. "Your letters worried him, and he asked me to discover who was writing them. Before I had the chance to investigate, you began throwing knives at me and chasing me through ruins."

Cockburn had proved his resilience though, evading Brewster and besting Grenville, who was an excellent fighter. Broadhurst was right to be worried.

"I assure you, I had nothing to do with your brother's death," I continued. "Broadhurst approached me because he knew of my reputation for handing criminals over to the Runners. That is all. Why do you believe *he* killed Mr. Cockburn? He found the man after the deed was done."

"So he says." The words were filled with wrath. "I know he killed my brother. Stole his name and escaped to Rome. Broadhurst knew he'd be held responsible for all the swindling. So he killed my brother and ran."

It was plausible and something I had considered. Broadhurst had been fortunate that ruffians had murdered Cockburn at that very moment and to be the first to find the man was very convenient.

"He also beat my brother's face with a brick to hide his identity," Cockburn announced. The blood-marred brick was found beside him."

All three of us gazed at him in horror. I thought of Broadhurst with his fleshy hands, his nervousness when he told me his story.

"He omitted that detail," I said. "I'd have walked away from him if he hadn't."

"Likely he knew that," Grenville said, his expression as grim as mine.

"How do we prove Broadhurst's guilt?" I asked Cockburn. "The killing happened in London, and your brother is buried there as Norris Broadhurst."

"Catch him," Cockburn said readily. "Pummel him until he confesses and give him to a magistrate. He'll never break free from a prison here."

"Or, the papal authorities will simply ship him back to

England," Grenville said. "Where of course he will be investigated, and at least punished for disfiguring your brother, stealing his identity, and fleeing the country."

"For murder," Cockburn insisted. "He should pay."

"What is your plan?" I asked him abruptly. "To kill him yourself? Then *you* will hang. Is that what your brother would want?"

Cockburn stared at me, lips parted, then to my distress, the man began to weep. He buried his face in his hands, wet noises coming from his mouth, shoulders heaving.

"Steady," Grenville said. He rose and moved to a table that held a decanter. Matthias at that moment swept in with a tray of coffee and cups, which he deposited next to the brandy. Grenville bypassed the coffee and brought a glass of brandy to Cockburn, shoving it under the man's nose. "Drink that."

Donata had moved to the edge of her seat, pity in her eyes. "He and his brother must have been very close."

Cockburn raised his head, grasped the goblet, and poured the brandy into his mouth. He swallowed, coughing, then dug a handkerchief from his pocket and wiped his eyes and face.

"Forgive me," he said.

Grenville settled in once more, and Matthias handed cups of coffee all around. "Not at all, my dear chap," Grenville said in sympathy. "Tell us about your brother."

"He looked after me when we were lads." Cockburn drew a ragged breath and composed himself before he continued. "I was born deaf. No one understood what was wrong with me— Leonard was the first to conclude I could not hear. He taught me to speak and to read lips. He taught me to fight, to keep the other lads off me."

"He certainly did *that* very well," Grenville said feelingly. Brewster, at the doorway, grunted assent.

"I always had to defend myself," Cockburn went on. "Leonard became a clerk at a stockbroker's and he gave me a job, assisting him. I'm good with anything written down."

His story continued. He worked with his brother until his brother joined forces with Mr. Broadhurst about five years ago. Our Mr. Cockburn had not liked Broadhurst, who was jovial but sly-eyed at the same time, so he'd left to work for another stockbroker. He'd tried to warn his brother, but Leonard Cockburn, too trusting, had taken no heed.

Broadhurst finally lured Leonard into a scheme to make millions. Broadhurst had assured him that everyone would make money.

But then it began to go wrong. People demanded their money returned, and Broadhurst couldn't do it. He'd dragged Leonard Cockburn down with him, and they were on the verge of debtors' prison, or worse. In any case, they were both ruined.

Leonard had walked home from the office on the evening of his death. He'd been preparing to meet with finance men from the government the next morning to sort out the mess and find the money to repay their investors. Our Mr. Cockburn had wanted to join him but had been waylaid with last minute paperwork at his stockbroking job. Our Mr. Cockburn had hurried through the darkness to the lodgings he'd shared with his brother, and found Leonard on their doorstep, dead, his face caved in.

When the City watchmen came, they'd examined the coat and belongings on Leonard's body and declared the dead man was Broadhurst.

"I tried to tell them, no, he was my brother, but they couldn't understand me," Cockburn went on. "They took me for a madman. First, they believed *I'd* killed him and then decided I was imbecilic. The magistrates concluded my brother had murdered Broadhurst and escaped, but I knew the truth. But no one would *listen*."

A person had to attend carefully to Cockburn to understand him, and I imagined the harried watch and magistrate had brushed him aside, thinking him incapable of coherent speech. It must have been dreadful for him, seeing his brother labeled a criminal and buried under another man's name.

"I even wrote to the magistrate," Cockburn continued. "But he said I needed more evidence to prove his identity. Everything pointed to the man being Broadhurst, in the magistrate's eyes."

I wondered which magistrate—my friend Sir Montague Harris would have been more careful. But Lombard Street was in the City, which was a separate jurisdiction.

"No wonder you were maddened," I said to Cockburn. "I cannot blame you for wanting to find Broadhurst and make him pay. But I understand the magistrate's caution—it would be helpful if we had proof that Broadhurst committed this crime."

Cockburn shook his head. "I have tried to discover any, but I have been unable to. But I know he did it," he finished resolutely.

I believed him. If Broadhurst had indeed smashed Leonard Cockburn's face to confuse identification, it was not difficult to assume he'd done the initial murder himself. Or, if he had not actually wielded the knife, hired someone to commit it for him.

I agreed with Cockburn that the best way to find the truth was to locate Broadhurst and wring his tale from him. But if I sent Broadhurst back to England, I would need some evidence of his misdeeds. Sir Montague Harris, to whom I would write of this, could arrest him, but no judge and jury would convict him on my word alone.

An independent witness would be best—if I interrogated Broadhurst, he might say anything to make me call off Brewster, and we'd not discover the truth in this manner.

I had a few ideas on that score, however.

"Where are you staying in Rome?" I asked Mr. Cockburn.

"In rooms near the Colosseum."

There were a number of boarding houses near the ruins of the grand amphitheatre. The area was a bit marshy, I'd been told, the air insalubrious. Cockburn wasn't a pauper as I'd observed, but still it would have cost him a fair bit to pursue Broadhurst across the Continent and into Rome. He'd not have much to spend on luxurious accommodations.

"I will help you, Mr. Cockburn," I said. "I did not like Mr. Broadhurst, and I too would not be surprised if he in fact killed your brother himself, or at least had a firm hand in his death. If he did, I assure you, I will make certain he pays."

I spoke grimly, and Mr. Cockburn brightened. "You will beat him down?" He glanced at Brewster who stood like a sentinel near the door.

"I will deliver him to authorities in England," I returned. "You must cease trying to exact revenge yourself."

Mr. Cockburn shook his head. "What choice do I have? Everyone believes me a madman."

"Write your story and your suspicions again, clearly and concisely. I will send your letter to another magistrate in London—he is at the Whitechapel House—whom I know will give it the attention it deserves. Even if the crime was committed in the City, he commands enough respect to have the matter investigated once again."

Cockburn did not appear convinced, but he nodded. "I will try."

"Good. Now, Mr. Brewster will escort you home—no more coming at me with knives if I am going to help you. Though the throw you did in Napoli was quite skilled."

Cockburn reddened. "I thought you in league with my brother's killer. You have my most profound apologies."

"Hmm." I remembered my fright as I hugged the wall, and the knowledge that I'd barely escaped with my life. "I will let you make it up to me somehow. Good day, Mr. Cockburn."

Brewster, without returning Cockburn's weapons, led the man from the room. I heard him growling at Cockburn as they left the house, the door slamming behind them. A cool draft scented with rain flowed into the reception room and then faded.

Donata rose, signaling for Matthias to leave the tray and asked him to fetch her a shawl. Matthias disappeared at once.

"Well," Grenville said. "What do we make of all that?"

"That Mr. Cockburn is a desperate man," Donata answered. "I confess I have sympathy for him, despite the fact that he very thoroughly attacked us. I hope he ceases his violent ways and allows Gabriel to deliver Mr. Broadhurst to London."

I tried not to flinch at her conviction that such a thing would be simple.

I took up my walking stick as Matthias returned with a long ivory embroidered shawl that Donata accepted from him gratefully. I helped her drape it around her shoulders, longing to close my hands on the soft garment and draw her into my arms. But Grenville and Matthias hovered, and I had errands to run.

"I'm off to visit Mr. Denis," I said as I stepped back from her.

CHAPTER 18

Donata turned from me and drew the shawl closer. "Please do not bring him home with you," she said crisply. "I have no wish to set eyes on the man."

Her chill tones touched me, but my visit to Denis was of a practical nature. He had eyes and ears both here and in London that could be very useful.

"Take Bartholomew with you," Grenville advised. "Since Mr. Brewster is engaged conveying Mr. Cockburn safely home. I will keep Donata company, if she will allow it."

"Of course," Donata said, her tone a trifle warmer. "Though in a more comfortable sitting room, I think. I want to hear your version of all these events."

"Delighted to oblige." Grenville extended his arm, and Donata took it.

I followed them out, asking Matthias to fetch his brother. Grenville and Donata ascended the stairs, the two much alike in their manner, background, and place in the world. As I watched them, I realized how outside their sphere I was, and wondered anew at my good fortune of finding the esteem of both.

I pressed these thoughts aside to focus on the task at hand. Not long later, Bartholomew and I strode through a finely falling rain north toward the Palazzo Borghese, near the river. Brewster would not be happy that I did not wait for him, but he could catch us up.

"How are you faring, Bartholomew?" I asked as we went. "I haven't given you much to do on this sojourn."

Bartholomew regarded me in surprise. The tall, fair-haired young man trod evenly as though he never noticed the rain.

"Mr. Gautier keeps us plenty busy, Captain. He can't abide idleness. There is a reason Frenchies fought the war so long— doing little drives them spare."

"So that is the reason for Bonaparte's ambition," I said in amusement. "Can you escape Gautier's strictures to assist me?"

"I'm your man, sir," Bartholomew answered quickly. "I work for you now, so he can't stop me."

"Well, do not upset him—Grenville does not need discord among his staff. What I'd like is for you to chat with maids and other servants. In particular, the woman who did the dusting for Conte de Luca. I realize you don't speak Italian, so it might be a tall order."

Bartholomew shrugged his large shoulders. "I've learned much already. Matthias, though, he's very good at picking up other lingos. I'll take him with me."

I wasn't certain how both young men would escape Gautier's watchful eye, but I'd leave them to find a way.

"Thank you. I'll discover where Conte de Luca's maid lives."

"No bother. I'll ask in the houses around his. The other servants will know. Probably they can tell me a fair bit as well."

Bartholomew and his brother indeed had a gift for making

others talk to them. They were handsome, personable, and of sunny dispositions, and most people ended up speaking with them readily.

We walked on through dark rain that began to beat down harder until we arrived at the house that, as Denis had told us, lay next to the Palazzo Borghese.

The palazzo itself was massive, lining one side of a square and running along an entire street beyond that. There was more than one house on the opposite side of the square, but I decided Denis must have taken the one that was large and square but with a plain facade. His house in London was equally understated.

Bartholomew and I approached the front door, and I tapped on it with the wide brass knocker.

The door opened after a long interval to reveal a large man with a scar where his left eye should be. He glared down at me, though Bartholomew, straightening his frame, was the same height as this specimen.

"*Si?*" The one word held disdain.

"Mr. Denis, please." I removed a card from my pocket and held it out. Easier than trying to explain who I was.

The man glanced at the card but didn't reach for it. "*Non è qui.*"

I knew that meant *He's not here,* but I did not budge. "I have important business with him. Perhaps I can wait for his return."

The man regarded me with his one eye. Whoever had taken his other must have been formidable indeed.

After a moment, he snarled and slammed the door. I exchanged a nonplussed glance with Bartholomew. Before I could ask his opinion on what we should do, the door was yanked open again, this time by a London man.

"Captain." He looked as much a ruffian as the other, but I recognized him as one of Denis's bodyguards. "Better come in."

"I'll nip to the kitchen," Bartholomew said. "All right?" he asked the bodyguard.

The man let out a laugh. "Suit yourself, mate. But Luigi, he'll eat you alive."

"Never fear." Bartholomew gave him a confident grin and sought the entrance to the staff area with an unerring sense of where it would be.

Denis's man shut the door against the rain and led me deep into the house's interior.

The squareness of the abode was more evident inside. The ground floor hall was an open space between four stone walls, with a staircase leading to a gallery above us. That too formed a perfect square, with rooms opening from it. The large columns of stone that held up the gallery were topped by capitals of flowing elegance, and a frieze of carved maidens chased vines of flowers around the upper eaves. The grandeur was understated but graceful.

The bodyguard took me up the stairs and around to a room that sat in the right front corner of the house. He knocked on the door and admitted me when we heard Denis say, "Come."

I half expected to enter a study with Denis seated behind a blank-topped desk, as happened whenever I visited him in London. Instead, I found a cozy library lined with bookcases, a thick carpet covering the floor, a fire on a hearth, and Denis rising from a chair, setting aside a book. The only other time I'd seen him look this human was the day I'd caught him eating a meal.

"Lacey." His greeting was neutral, as though he was not surprised I'd turned up on his doorstep. A large man lounged near the window, as one always did in his London house. Denis was never left alone.

"My apologies for springing myself upon you," I said.

Denis gave a nod to the man who'd admitted us who then ducked out, closing the door. Denis gestured to a chair near the fire.

"Sit and rest your leg. I know the damp pains it."

Denis was rarely this solicitous, but I decided not to argue. I sank to the chair as though I'd come for a friendly visit.

He too resumed his seat, reaching to the side table to straighten the book, which was a treatise on ancient pottery. He said nothing more, only waited for me to state the intention of my visit.

"I would like to ask a favor," I said as though the request did not discomfit me.

"I assumed so." Denis steepled his fingers, waiting for me to continue.

"I need to know what happened on a night in London about a year ago, in the City. Lombard Street, or a lane just off it." I spoke quickly, my idea seeming farfetched now.

Denis did not change expression. "A tall order."

"But necessary. I thought perhaps if you had people reporting to you unusual things that occurred around London, I could find out the truth of how a man named Cockburn—who was misidentified as Broadhurst—met his death. If he was killed by Broadhurst or someone hired to carry out the deed, or if he was simply struck down by a passing ruffian."

"Ah. You refer to Mr. Broadhurst, the swindler. He cheated powerful men."

"And not-so-powerful ones. Left them destitute."

"All stockbroking men are swindlers of some sort," Denis said philosophically. "They manipulate the markets, and when those markets fail, they climb out of the mess in innocence, with their fees intact. A reason I do not invest my money in the City."

"Very cynical," I said.

"But true. So the man killed was not Broadhurst at all." His eyes flickered, his only indication of surprise. "I assume you know that for a fact or you would not state it to me. I read of the man's death in the newspapers at the time but thought no more of it. What is your interest in the matter?"

"I wish to assist the dead Mr. Cockburn's brother, a man I pity." I briefly told him about meeting first Broadhurst and then Joseph Cockburn. "Cockburn believes Broadhurst himself was the murderer, and this is entirely possible. I need to find evidence so that Broadhurst can be tried and the Cockburn family cleared of stain."

Denis tapped his fingertips together. "As I said, a tall order, but I believe it can be done."

"True evidence," I stressed. "Not a convenient witness who likely witnessed nothing. The magistrate must believe it, as must a judge and jury."

"Your confidence in the justice system is somewhat amusing, Captain," Denis said. "But you are correct that my men are everywhere in the metropolis and they tell me about any untoward events. They possibly did not consider the death of Broadhurst of any interest to me, but I will ask about it."

"Thank you." I was slightly surprised he agreed so readily, but Denis never revealed his motives for anything he did. "As we are talking of favors, I tried to offer Gian the money for the statue you requested, but he thought me foolish. I insisted but did not have the chance to pay him before he was arrested. Might I assume you still want the piece?"

"I do. Do not bring it to me until you pay him. And before

you ask why, that is my business. Have you discovered anything of note about de Luca and his death?" Denis could switch topics with breathtaking rapidity.

"Not yet." I told him how I'd searched through several rooms in the house but found no hiding places for the list Denis sought.

"He would not have hidden it somewhere so obvious," Denis said. "Or it could be he had no such tangible list at all."

I hid my exasperation. "Why do you think he might have had one?"

Denis gave a minute shrug. "He was ambitious. De Luca liked to be the person everyone came to for items they wanted. A record would help him keep his sources organized, and also give him a hold over any of those people if he needed one."

More cynicism, but Denis had seen much in his life.

"Even Napoleon came to him," I remarked.

"Just so. That must have been an interesting meeting—both men liked to manipulate a situation for their own gain. De Luca might have won."

"He claimed to."

"Possibly." Denis made another shrug. "Or possibly he told you what you wished to hear. He might have kept the list I want in his own head or stored it in another location entirely."

"Then how the devil do you expect me to find it?" I asked in irritation.

"You looking at all is helpful. You might unnerve a confederate to try to destroy the list, and then my men will stop him. If everything was committed to de Luca's memory, then we have nothing to worry about."

Somehow, I did not think the solution would be that easy. "How many others would think there might be a list?" I asked. "Would they try to find it?"

"I do not know, but we can assume more than a few. De Luca was acquainted with every legitimate buyer and seller of antiquities, but also every thief, every receiver, and every under-the-table dealer."

"This list would be of great interest then."

"Indeed." Denis's answer was short and emphatic.

I pondered. Trevisan had been very concerned about the method of de Luca's demise and had strongly insisted his goods remained in his house.

Was Trevisan a dealer himself? Legitimate or otherwise? Such a thing might explain why he'd moved himself and his mother to Rome for a time. He might have brought antiquities from Milan or Venice to sell to others here. Possibly de Luca was his go-between, or possibly a buyer, and perhaps Trevisan did not want his goods going missing or anyone to know about his true dealings with de Luca.

I heaved a sigh. "Then I will continue to search. Is there any chance you could arrange for me to see Gian? He would know de Luca's hiding places better than any other."

Denis's brows twitched. I wasn't certain he'd have influence on the police of Rome or its justice system, but he had magistrates in his thrall in England, so why not Rome as well?

"I do not know, but I will see."

"Also, Mr. Broadhurst is in Rome. At least he was here. Can some of your men keep an eye on him?"

"Where does he lodge?"

I shook my head. "I don't know, exactly."

Denis's gaze bore a tinge of exasperation, but he nodded again. "I will find him."

I wondered how long he'd put up with my requests before he decided his debt to me was paid. It was a very odd feeling, I thought as his bodyguard returned with brandy for me to sip, to be the one who held Denis's strings. It was usually the other way about.

———

I DEPARTED AFTER THE GLASS OF BRANDY, MEETING Bartholomew as he emerged from the servants' hall. Bartholomew's cheerfulness was undimmed, but he looked a bit wan in the foyer's lamplight.

"Luigi is the cove who first answered the door." Bartholomew shuddered. "They were right that he's a hard man. Picks his teeth with a knife. Even Mr. Denis's blokes give him a wide berth."

"I wonder whether Denis sought him out or if he came with the place," I mused. When I'd remarked on the beauty of the house, Denis had only given me one of his barely discernible shrugs and said he had an agent who found abodes for him to rent when he traveled.

"Couldn't say, sir," Bartholomew said. "No one would talk about him, not with him there, glaring."

Luigi was nowhere in sight, fortunately, and we left the house without hindrance. Outside, a large shadow detached itself from the dark and stepped in front of us.

"Couldn't wait ten minutes before ye ran off, guv?" Brewster raged at me. "If ye get yourself killed when I'm elsewhere, it won't be my fault. This is a dangerous city after dark, by all accounts. Ye stick by me side, and that's all."

"Which is why I brought Bartholomew," I told him. "I knew I'd be perfectly safe in a house leased by James Denis."

"Aye, but that don't mean you're safe *from* 'im," Brewster declared. "Or his toughs. They'll end you quick the minute His Nibs snaps his fingers."

I experienced a qualm, knowing Brewster had the right of it. Denis and I were in a state of truce but that could end at any moment. "You used to be one of those toughs," I remarked.

"That's how I know what they'd do. But now I work for you, and it's my job to keep you whole. Next time you pay a visit to His Nibs, you make sure I'm with ye."

"I apologize, Brewster. You are correct. Bartholomew's presence helps keep the thieves of Rome at bay, but I should not drop my guard with Mr. Denis."

"Too right, you shouldn't." Brewster said nothing more but tramped beside me into the narrow street off the square, his boots ringing on the stones.

When we reached home, Brewster went off to bed, still annoyed with me, though he did tell me he'd tucked Cockburn safely into his lodgings near the Colosseum.

Donata, who was used to staying up all hours of the night, was writing letters in the sitting room upstairs. Grenville was having a late repast in the downstairs dining room, Matthias told me, but I was not hungry and mounted the stairs in search of my wife.

Donata's maid had released her hair from its elaborate style, and it hung down her back in thick dark waves. She'd told me that when she'd been a debutante, she'd had it cut off to her neck as was the fashion. It had made her head marvelously light, but she'd decided to let it grow it back again.

I was glad she had. I came behind her and brushed back a lock of that luxurious hair, kissing the top of her head.

"Gabriel." Her pen did not cease, but she sounded pleased to see me. "I want to know what you dashed off to command Mr. Denis to do, but later. I must finish these letters. I have fallen behind on my correspondence."

She could sit up writing all night. I kissed the side of her neck then left her to it.

Bartholomew, transforming himself from bodyguard to valet, caught my clothes as they came off in my chamber, shaking them out, sorting those that were to go into the laundry and hanging up others.

As he opened the elaborately carved wooden clothes press, my eye fell on the leather bag that contained the statue Denis had sent me to obtain from de Luca. On impulse, I took it out an examined it.

It was a heavy piece, a foot wide by a foot long and a foot and a half high. Eros, with his broken wing, sat dejectedly—a metaphor for how love can go wrong?

The stone was alabaster, presumably solid. In the middle of the base, where Eros's legs folded on top of the mound of grass, was another crack. The creamy gold of the alabaster was darker, as though someone had broken open the entire piece at one time.

Perhaps, I thought with a gleam of excitement, to hide a list of men who provided de Luca with his goods, including the information that Denis sought. I lifted the statue above my head, ready to dash it to the ground and find out.

CHAPTER 19

"Sir?" Bartholomew blinked at me, my coat dangling from his big hand. "What are you doing?"

I stilled, gazed at the statue above my head, then lowered my arms, cradling the thing carefully in my hands. "Nothing. My brain is addled, and I am weary."

Bartholomew let out a breath of relief and turned away to brush the coat. "Were you thinking the conte was killed with something like that?"

The statue had plenty of heft and was a solid weight, but I shook my head. "We know the murder weapon—a marble urn left beside him. This statue is innocent."

After this cheerful observation, I tucked the Cupid away, finished undressing, pulled on my nightshirt, and went to bed. Bartholomew puttered about for a time, then doused the lights and departed.

I fell asleep to dreams of being chased through the ruins of Pompeii with a man wielding a knife and the alabaster Cupid. Denis stood by and admonished my assailant not to break the statue, as he hadn't yet paid for it.

I jumped awake to a touch and a warm body sliding into bed beside me. My dreams dissolved, forgotten, and I turned to embrace my wife and demonstrate to her how much I'd missed her in the past weeks.

———

IN THE MORNING, GRENVILLE, WHO ROSE AS EARLY AS I DID when he was interested in a problem, breakfasted with me, then we both returned to de Luca's house, Brewster tramping along behind us.

We reached the abode to find two members of the captain's police troops guarding the door. I apparently had leave to enter, on the captain's orders. They tried to detain Grenville and especially Brewster, and I had to argue that I could not do what the captain wished without them. After a debate between the two, they reluctantly stood aside to admit all three of us.

I'd left my wife sleeping soundly, as she usually did in the mornings, but my disposition was more buoyant than it had been all week. Brewster and Grenville grasped why and shot me irritated glances when I grew too ebullient.

The three of us divided up the search, and we each went through a series of rooms, leaving no stone—or precious object—unturned.

The chambers I took on the first floor revealed wonders—small, exquisite miniature paintings, bronzes both ancient and modern, urns from ancient Athens, paintings by Canaletto and one that appeared to be by Raphael, to my amazement. I studied the last, not certain I was correct. I'd have to ask the opinion of Grenville, who carried an art catalog in his head.

I found no ledgers or lists, not even one inventorying the

collection. I finished that room, propped the possible Raphael against the wall, and went in search of Grenville.

He was in a chamber above mine, trying to make a desk reveal all its secrets. He liked desks with hidden compartments, and as I watched from the doorway, he busily opened drawers, pushed knobs, and finally lay down on his back to examine the desk's underside. His body disappeared under the piece of furniture until only his boots showed.

"Anything?"

Grenville must have heard me coming because he didn't jump. "No." He sounded morose. "Plenty of crannies in this one, but nothing in them. It's a beautiful piece." He slithered out but remained seated on the floor and patted the polished mahogany beside him. "Perhaps Gian will sell it to me."

"If Gian sells the lot, he'll be vastly wealthy." I leaned against the doorframe. "Though I suppose his government will take a part of the proceeds."

"No idea how inheritance laws work here." Grenville hoisted himself to his feet and brushed off his trousers. "I know that duties on my estate will be hard for my heirs, but I have plenty of gewgaws they can sell, as long as they go to people who will treasure the things."

I thrust aside the thought that I ought to sort things out for my heirs and asked Grenville to follow me downstairs.

When I showed Grenville the painting I'd set aside, his eyes widened, then he stepped back and studied it, chin on his fist.

"If that is genuine, and I am fairly certain it is, it should not be *here*," Grenville said after a time. "The last person who owned it was the Austrian emperor. It hung in Schönbrunn." He named the emperor's summer palace near Vienna.

"Bonaparte himself moved in there for a time after he gave the Austrians a drubbing, didn't he?" I asked. "He sent the things he stole back to France, I thought. But he stopped in Rome to visit de Luca at some point."

"And stashed the Raphael here?" Grenville regarded me with skepticism. "Are you supposing Bonaparte carried it about under his arm and decided this was a good place to hide it?"

"Perhaps not so literally ..." I trailed off, gazing at the variety of treasures that littered walls, tables, shelves. "And the painting might be a copy."

"If so, it's a damned good copy," Grenville said. "I'd have to take it to an expert. But it is odd. I've found one or two other things that, if they are genuine, are supposed to be in cathedrals in Lombardy and Florence, or in the Vatican."

"I imagine a thorough inventory of this place will turn up many oddities."

I felt a tingling on the back of my neck, as I sometimes did when I was close to the truth about something but couldn't quite grasp it.

"Why isn't there and inventory already?" Grenville asked. "De Luca was cavalier, but he wasn't dull-witted. Surely, he'd have kept a note of all these things, even if only to prove what belonged to him if he was burgled."

"Perhaps Brewster has turned up something," I said.

We left the room, I giving the Raphael one more glance. I'd never been to Schönbrunn Palace, but I knew it was vast. I wondered if the genuine painting was still there or, if it truly had been stolen, if anyone had noted its absence.

Brewster's searching methods were more rapid than ours. He'd shifted everything in a ground floor sitting room from one side to the other, examining each piece as he went. His movements were practiced yet careful—he'd never mar something valuable.

"Nothing yet, guv," Brewster said as we entered, anticipating my question. "He's got cheap trash mixed in with things worth thousands. Strange chap, weren't he?"

"Strange is a good word for all this," Grenville said. "I believe that instead of looking for an inventory, we ought to be making our own."

"Already started, guv." Brewster set down a beautiful porcelain vase and strode to a table on the other side of the room.

A sheaf of papers rested there with words scratched on the topmost one in Brewster's blocky handwriting. A pen lay on the paper, blotches of ink falling from its nib. His list was precise and divided into categories—furnishings, paintings, sculpture, objets d'art, hangings, musical instruments.

"Neatly done," I said.

Brewster shrugged. "I remember them ledgers when we did the Carlton House job. Denis's bloke knows how to catalog. Thought I'd do the same."

Clever of him. He'd found the paper in the writing table, and Grenville and I hunted up more pens and pots of ink. We took the writing things with us and returned to our respective rooms to catalog our findings.

We worked for the rest of the day, taking particular care with the attic room and de Luca's bedroom, as the most likely place he'd hide confidential information, but turned up nothing. We found no inventories of de Luca's things or lists of his agents—no papers or letters of any kind, in fact, except innocuous ones, such as a few bills for foodstuffs.

Odd, I thought as we decided to leave off our search that afternoon. Aristocratic gentlemen usually had quite a number of papers. Donata's father had an office stuffed with them—the earl liked to keep abreast of what happened on his large estate.

That we found not even casual correspondence with friends was bizarre.

Tired and discouraged, the three of us helped ourselves to wine in the kitchen then departed. Today the changeable weather gave us sunshine and a few high clouds, with plenty of people, both locals and tourists, walking about under the strains of church bells.

When we reached home, Grenville carried the inventories we'd begun to his desk to lock them away, Brewster sought the kitchens in search of dinner, and I went to the upstairs sitting room Donata had commanded. As she had been last night, she was busily writing letters.

"Good afternoon, Gabriel." Donata glanced at me fondly when I kissed her cheek. She reached for a thick paper tucked into a cubbyhole. "I have received an invitation from Contessa Trevisan to a musicale at her home tonight. Shall we attend?"

She asked, but I already knew her answer. Whenever Donata did not wish to appear at a gathering she simply never mentioned it to me.

"Trevisan's mother is hosting it?" I studied the letter with its gracefully exact handwriting. "Will anyone come? I note a distinct prejudice between southerners and northerners here." We had a similar rivalry in England.

"They will." Donata took the invitation from me and set it on top of a stack of letters. "The ladies of Rome will wish to be favored by such a highborn woman, and if nothing else, they'll go out of curiosity to witness any scandal firsthand. It was kind of her to include me."

"Gisela's doing, no doubt," I said. "Also, I believe Trevisan and his mother are curious about us."

"I agree. Let us remain composed no matter what happens

this night. Remember that Conte Trevisan tried to have you arrested and he likely can do so again."

"I have that thought firmly in my head," I assured her. "But you wished entry to the house, and now you have it."

Donata took up her pen. She gently touched my cheek with it, then turned to business. "Excellent. I will send her a reply that we are happy to attend."

————

DONATA WAS CORRECT WHEN SHE'D SPECULATED THAT THE society ladies of Rome would not turn down an invitation from Contessa Trevisan. When Donata and I arrived, along with Grenville, who had likewise had an invitation, the street in front of Trevisan's leased home was choked with carriages, ordinary citizens having to hug the walls as the coaches slid past.

Inside, the house was lit with what must be a thousand candles, sconces glowing on the walls, candelabras and candlesticks filling every niche. I guided Donata up the stairs, the travertine smooth beneath our feet, the lights reviving the faded glory of the place.

The musicale was held in a larger room than the one in which I'd first met Trevisan and his mother—this one spanned the front of the house, with high ceilings painted in Baroque splendor. The room was filled with ladies and gentlemen dressed in the finest frocks and well-tailored suits. Shades of blue, green, and violet adorned the matrons, with younger ladies in yellow, ivory, and cream.

All wore the first stare of fashion—neither war nor the unrest it stirred nor the growing poverty outside this bubble stopped them from showing off the latest Parisian modes.

Donata, in silver and gold, black feathers in her hair, was admired by all.

Conte Trevisan greeted the guests as they entered the long room, Signorina Proietti at his side. What the creme of society thought about him courting the very young daughter of a war hero they kept to themselves while they exchanged bows and curtsies. As soon as the guests moved out of earshot of their host, however, heads came together, and whispers began.

The contessa roamed the room, moving slowly with the aid of a tall walking stick, halting to greet clumps of guests. She kept her expression carefully neutral, a great lady who'd never betray what she felt to those who tramped through her house.

Her eyes did brighten when she spied me with Donata on my arm, and she stumped over to us.

"Lady Donata." The contessa gave her a regal nod, no curt-sying. She addressed my wife as an earl's daughter, Lady Donata Pembroke, rather than the widow of a viscount, Lady Breckenridge, or even as plain Mrs. Lacey, the wife of a former army captain.

"Contessa." Donata made a graceful curtsy and took the contessa's outstretched hand. "How kind of you to allow us into your home. It is lovely."

The contessa's slight curl of her lip dismissed the glittering room. No doubt her son's palazzo in Milan was much more lavish. "I am pleased you chose to honor us," she said in her flawless English. "Captain," she greeted me, an afterthought, then she closed bony gloved fingers around Donata's arm. "You will sit with me, my dear."

"Of course."

I was not to be included in this invitation, I saw. I bowed with as much politeness as I could and withdrew.

Donata glided away serenely with the contessa, who led her

through the crowd to a divan that reposed by itself near the pianoforte. The place of honor.

The contessa sank to the divan. Donata made certain the woman was comfortable before she sat down next to her, the contessa reaching for her arm again.

Gisela detached herself from Trevisan, after first gaining his approval to leave his side, and moved to the divan. She curtsied before Donata, then began gently arranging pillows for the contessa, signaling to a passing footman to bring them small glasses of dark red wine.

The contessa accepted all this attention as her due, but I stilled when her gaze fell on Gisela as Gisela turned to the footman. The contessa's face held not contempt for the chit who'd caught the eye of her son, but a deep fondness combined with profound sadness.

I sipped wine to hide the fact that I was staring, but her expression struck me sharply. The longing in her eyes ceased as soon as Gisela turned back to her, and the contessa became a haughty, demanding aristocrat once more.

Donata caught my gaze and gave me a minute shake of her head. Whether she'd observed the contessa's manner, I could not say, but I understood. I turned away and left the contessa to her.

Grenville drifted through the crowd on his own, waylaid by almost everyone he passed. His fame reached well beyond London, he the dandy who'd taken over the world's attention since Brummell had fled a few years past.

No one paid much heed to me, so I wandered toward the tall stove to keep warm. A man lurked in the shadows there, and I found, to my surprise, that the lurker was Proietti.

"Trevisan did not bar the door when he saw you approach?" I asked, keeping my voice light.

Proietti's morose gaze flicked to his daughter. "I was sent an invitation—I know Gisela insisted on it. Trevisan greeted me quite civilly, if coldly, but his mother froze me out."

"What do they object to about you? They can't blame you for demanding the return of your daughter. Any father would."

"In the world of Conte Trevisan, none would dare. I ought to be honored that my daughter has been so chosen by them." Proietti exuded unhappiness. "Do I give up? Let Trevisan have her? He'll take her back to Milan, and we'll see her no more." His eyes filled.

"She might be well cared for," I pointed out. "His mother looks upon her fondly, and Trevisan seems concerned for her well-being."

"That might be true." Proietti's dark eyes held pain. "If it were your daughter, would you be, as you English say, sanguine to let her marry the conte and depart your life forever?"

"No." My answer was immediate. "My daughter was taken from me when she was a child. During that time, I had no idea whether she was living or not. I found her again a few years ago—she is about the age of Gisela. Now she spends most of her time in France and wants to marry a Frenchman. Ever do I fear I will lose her again." That emptiness I'd experienced when I'd realized my first wife had gone with my daughter had never quite left me.

Proietti regarded me in vast sympathy. "I am so sorry, Captain. It is no surprise then, that you turned from your path to help me that day."

"I was happy to." I set my glass onto the nearest table with a decided click. "Do not give way. Trevisan cannot marry your daughter while he is still married to another, and you will be quite justified in preventing her leaving with him. But I am trying to decide why Trevisan is so interested in Conte de Luca. Who knows? I might be able to pin de Luca's murder on him, and we will be rid of him."

I meant to make Proietti laugh, but he shook his head. "He did not, damn him. I saw Trevisan that night. He and Gisela and his mother." Proietti's scowl darkened his face. "In a church, listening to a concert. Blast the man."

CHAPTER 20

*I*n a church. Of course. An impeccable alibi for a highly respectable aristocrat.

"You saw him?" I asked. "Is it your church as well? The Sant'Agnese in Piazza Navona?"

Proietti flushed. "They were at the Basilica Sant'Andrea della Fratte, near the Piazza de Spagna. There was a concert that evening, choirs, and a few noted opera singers. All divine music, nothing entertaining, like Rossini," he finished in disparagement.

"Ah, you went to attend the concert yourself."

"Do not try to give me excuses, Captain. I was following them, as you well know, watching what Trevisan was up to. He sat like a stone, while glorious music in a beautiful basilica flowed over him. Dear Gisela was touched by it. As was I."

"And the contessa? Was she moved by this splendor?"

"I do not know. She left Trevisan to sit with friends. As Trevisan is a foreigner in this city, he had seats away from the pews of the nobles, but the contessa managed to finagle her way into one of the enclosed pews, where she and her high-born friends can lounge in luxury."

I imagined the contessa had been welcomed by some aristocratic lady who'd wanted to cultivate her favor.

"They remained for the entire concert?"

"Indeed. The music ended about midnight. Trevisan led Gisela and his mother out and into his carriage, which quite blocked the road. It is a very narrow street. They clopped off home, and I went to a tavern and became rather drunk." His smile was rueful. "So you see, Trevisan has an alibi for that night, but I do not."

I shrugged. "He could have slipped away from home once he reached it and gone to de Luca's. Though I have to admit, I do not know *why* he should murder de Luca. They might have argued, but Trevisan is a very contained man. He'd more likely serve de Luca with a lawsuit than strike him while his back was turned."

"Yes, in all aspects, except for my daughter, Trevisan is very honorable," Proietti said bitterly. He lifted his glass. "Confusion to him."

As a watchful footman had already swept away my wine glass, I could not drink to his toast, but I said, "Hear, hear."

We watched Trevisan speak to the guests, coolly composed. He was well aware of the whispers, I could see, but he absorbed these without a qualm.

My wife was deep in conversation with the contessa, Gisela attending them both. If the other ladies felt snubbed by the contessa's lack of attention, they put their annoyance aside to enjoy watching the tableau. Tales of this musicale would be all over Rome by morning.

The contessa at last left the divan to stand before the

pianoforte. She clapped her hands for attention, and conversations tapered off.

Her voice, in its fluent Italian, held strength, though it was low and almost dulcet. From what I could understand, she thanked the guests for coming and spoke about the soprano, who had entered and stood a little way from the pianoforte. The pianist, a slim man, had quietly settled himself on the piano stool and sat waiting.

The contessa stood straight, no stooped posture for her, gestures calm and precise. She must have been a thoroughly beautiful woman in her youth, and I could still see that beauty in her.

The contessa ceased speaking, her audience applauded, and she glided back to her seat next to Donata. Gisela, who had taken an armless chair beside the contessa's sofa, made certain she was comfortable.

The soprano stepped forth, the pianist gently touched his keys, and the woman launched into song.

I grew instantly enchanted. The soprano's voice began in the softest of pianissimos, fluttering among the notes of the music. Then it began to swell, rising to the gilded arches of the ceiling, expanding to fill the room.

The audience was silent, entranced as I was. I could see nothing but the woman, hear nothing but her exquisite voice. She was rather plain, in fact, with golden brown hair straggling from pins around a sallow face. Her gown, while fashionable, did not fit her well, and one of her gloves sagged down her arm.

None of that mattered. Her voice transformed her into a goddess of beauty that could pierce the very soul. I would be a different man when I left this room, having been touched by this voice, this music.

The aria dipped in volume again then suddenly burst into fortissimo. The soprano sang on, her form becoming graceful and lithe, her arms lifting as the notes rose through the register, her hands outstretched in supplication.

I leaned forward in the chair I'd found at the edge of the crowd, Proietti next to me. The music swept into me, winding through my heart, my very fingers vibrating with it. I might have been alone in this salon, the others, even Donata, fading into swirls of color around me.

The soprano's voice climbed, found the highest pitch I'd ever heard a human being make, and held it. I expected the woman to sag or collapse, but she continued with the note, supporting it effortlessly.

When I thought I would hear nothing but that pitch for the rest of my life, the soprano suddenly swept her arms down, her voice going with it, and finished with a strong note in the middle of the register.

She ended as the piano did, but instead of falling to the ground in an exhausted heap, she smiled at us, relaxing into an ordinary woman once more.

I leapt to my feet and joined the room in wild applause, my *"Bravissima!"* melding with the cries of *"Brava! Brava! Voce bellissima!"*

The woman waited patiently, as if used to such accolades. She gestured to the pianist, who bowed slightly, knowing the applause was all for the soprano. He returned his fingers to the keys and began another soft introduction.

The soprano gave us two more pieces, each more extraordinary than the last. I understood why Italian opera in Napoli and Rome had become the rage in the last century, as it was in the north of Italy now. This soprano was but one performer in a local operatic company, I thought I understood from the contessa's introduction, not even a prima donna. And yet, her voice was one of the most beautiful things I'd ever heard.

At the end of the final aria, we were standing again, my hands tingling with my heavy applause. The soprano beamed at us and curtsied, hand to her heart, as though she was humbled by our admiration.

The pianist, who was quite good, also gained applause. I went to him as everyone streamed toward the soprano and shook his hand. I told him in fumbling Italian punctuated with English that I enjoyed his playing. Whether he understood me or not, he nodded and smiled, then departed quietly amidst the adulation for the soprano.

I knew I'd never get near the woman through the crowd, so I sought Donata, who stood next to the divan. The contessa remained in her seat, but by the small, satisfied smile she wore, she was pleased that her singer had been a success.

"If this is the sort of music one has in Rome, I will leave London and dwell here always," I declared.

"Sometimes we can find musicians to charm us in Rome," the contessa said dismissively. "I am a patron of La Fenice, which hosts the finest companies in the world."

"La Fenice," I repeated. "That is the opera house in Venice, is it not?"

"It is." The contessa's eyes flickered at my ignorance. "My son has many business affairs in Venice, as well as in Milan. His wife is Venetian, and I have adopted her city as my own."

Any other person would simply mean they'd found Venice captivating, but I suspected the contessa had elbowed her way into social life there and taken over. She was the sort who'd tell the Doge—if they'd had still had Doges—what to do.

The contessa did not speak of Trevisan's wife as though she

was on the verge of expiring. From the contessa's challenging stare, she dared me to mention Trevisan's wife at all.

"You seem to be fond of Signorina Proietti," I ventured. Gisela had moved to her father, I saw to my surprise, the two conversing somewhat awkwardly together.

The contessa scowled at me. "Why should I not be? She is a sweet, well-bred young lady."

Her eyes held steel. I decided, under Donata's and the contessa's steady gazes, that I should change the subject rather than pursue the matter.

"Thank you for allowing us to hear such exquisite music," I said. "It was kind of you."

The contessa nodded, nowhere near as humble in accepting praise as the soprano and the pianist had been. "It also gave you a chance to scrutinize us," she said with withering perception. "I hope we have been satisfactory."

With a sniff, she rose and stalked toward her guests, her walking stick tapping.

"She is an enigma," I said softly to Donata.

"Perhaps." Donata's tone told me I'd missed something. She patted my arm then slipped into the fray, soon engulfed by ladies who were fascinated with her.

Grenville too was surrounded where he spoke animatedly with the soprano, and she with him, like two cronies catching up on gossip.

Proietti remained in the corner with his daughter, and Trevisan circulated among the gentlemen. The guests were polite to Trevisan and he to them, but the way they held themselves with him shouted that they considered him an outsider.

As I turned my steps to Proietti and Gisela, a hand landed on my elbow.

"Captain Lacey. How splendid to meet you again."

I turned to see Signor Baldini, our guide through Herculaneum and Pompeii.

"Baldini," I said with pleasure. "Well met." I stuck out my
hand and shook his. "I am sorry we left you so churlishly."

"Not at all. I quite understood. Did you ever catch the
fellow trying to injure you and your party?"

"We did indeed. He was a fellow Englishman, and I am
happy to say it was a misunderstanding that we cleared up."

Baldini's eyes widened. "You are very forgiving. I'd have
given him over to the police."

"We settled the matter amongst ourselves." I had no intention of elaborating on Mr. Cockburn's troubles. Then a
thought struck me. "You are an expert in antiquities, Signor
Baldini. Perhaps you could help us with a problem."

"I have some knowledge," Baldini said modestly.

"I am going over the collection of the late Conte de Luca,
but I do not always know what I am looking at. Perhaps you
could see what we've turned up? We had questions about some
of it—the history of the pieces, I mean."

I did not like to say out loud among the aristocrats of Rome
that we now believed de Luca had acquired much of his objects
under not-so-legal circumstances.

Baldini flushed. "Yes, I heard of the conte's death. Quite a
tragedy. I will have to inquire of Conte Trevisan whether he
can spare me, but I would be pleased to assist."

"Excellent. Perhaps you could meet us at de Luca's house in
the morning, say at ten o'clock."

Baldini obviously wanted to ask more about it, but he
politely nodded and said that he would arrive punctually,
depending on what Conte Trevisan required.

"Conte Trevisan summoned you here?" I asked, as though
in idle curiosity. I recalled the Stanbridges telling me that

Baldini had gone off on an errand for Trevisan, and no longer could lead us through the ruins.

"Yes, he wished me to acquire some books for him. Ones on history and art that a young lady might find instructive." His mouth flattened in a thin line, his displeasure evident. It was clear that Trevisan had become involved with Gisela, and Baldini must have now realized his patron was not the paragon he'd believed.

To change the subject, I thanked him for his promise of help, and then we talked of Pompeii, Baldini relaxing enough to tell me bits of its history that intrigued me. He returned to the claim that his family could trace its line back to the Roman Republic, and I merely nodded. He could believe what he liked —Baldini did know quite a lot about Pompeii's history. He speculated that the ruins we saw were only one layer of the complicated story of the site, and I would not be surprised if he was correct.

He and I chattered about our interest, ignoring those around us, until the hour grew late. I glanced around with a start when Grenville drifted toward me to tell me we were departing.

Many of the guests had gone, moving on to whatever further entertainments they'd scheduled for the night. Much as in London, one went from musicales to the theatre or opera and finished the night at a supper ball.

Proietti, who'd also lingered, was reluctant to depart. "Many are congratulating me on making a fine match for my daughter," he told me as I broke away from Baldini to say good night to him. "They believe my wife and I should be pleased." Proietti sighed. "I would be if I could be assured Trevisan would make Gisela happy. But I fear he will deceive her."

From what I'd learned of Conte Trevisan, he might not

simply toss Gisela to the pavement after he ruined her, but even so, I sympathized with Proietti's position.

"Take heart," I said. "We will discover what he is truly about, and if he does love your daughter deeply, then his guests might be right that she makes a good match."

Proietti regarded me with skepticism. "No, you are correct that we do not know the entire story, but until we do, I will not trust him. *Buona notte*, Lacey, Grenville. And you, madame. I will arrive at Conte de Luca's to assist you tomorrow. As you English like to say—all hands to the pump."

He waved negligently and departed.

I told Grenville as we entered the hired carriage that Baldini had also agreed to assist us. Two men who spoke fluent Italian would be helpful in case we did find ledgers and papers at de Luca's home.

"Excellent. He is an intelligent man, is Baldini." Grenville sent me a pointed glance. "I know you like Proietti, Lacey, and he is a fellow soldier from the war and all, but I do wonder about his situation. A gentleman of somewhat reduced circumstances from what I can see, though his home is pleasant."

"Doing his best with what he has, I imagine." I recalled Proietti's admission that he'd been driven to near bankruptcy during the war, which was why he'd sold precious items to de Luca. He'd claimed to have recovered, but I could not verify the fact. "Not all of us are wise with income, as I well know." I cleared my throat as I finished. My own circumstances when I'd first met Grenville had been strained indeed.

"You were unlucky," Grenville said as the carriage wound through the narrow streets. "And your family had nothing to leave you. Proietti seems a bit feckless, if you'll forgive me. I do not say I trust Trevisan entirely, but Proietti is a bit obsessed."

"He is adamant, I agree, but I still find myself taking his side."

Grenville lifted an impeccably gloved hand. "I am not sneering at his objections to the arrangement, but he is rather letting his emotions run rampant."

I shrugged. "We *are* English."

"And therefore cold-blooded and stiff necked?" Grenville laughed. "People are people everywhere, Lacey, as you know. Some are cool like Trevisan, some hot-tempered like Proietti, and if you'll forgive me, yourself. Perhaps we were raised to place importance on different things, but once those things are put aside, we are much the same across the world."

"A true cosmopolitan, Grenville," Donata said in approval. "And a man of good sense. Now then, I have to say I rather like the contessa. She is a bit warmer than her son."

"Is she?" I hadn't thought her warm at all—I'd decided that coldness ran in the family. "I grant that she has excellent taste in music."

"Yes, I enjoyed the concert very much," Donata agreed. "But she did tell me why she is so fond of Gisela, and why she did not object in the slightest when Trevisan decided to bring the young woman into the house."

"Do enlighten us, dear lady," Grenville said with interest as I came alert

Donata went somber. "The contessa has become attached to the girl for a sad reason, I am sorry to relate. Trevisan and his wife had a daughter. She died, the poor thing, when she was but eighteen. Gisela reminds the contessa of her, and she is filling a hollow in the contessa's heart."

CHAPTER 21

*A*h." Grenville's syllable held much sympathy. "Was Trevisan's daughter ill?"

Every family had a brother, sister, aunt, cousin, who had died young of illness. My mother had been of a weak constitution, but I thanked God every day that my offspring and my wife were of the hearty sort.

"Not an illness." Donata broke off, the creak and bump of the carriage loud in the night. "When Bonaparte came into Italy, soldiers and men filled the streets of Milan. No, they did not attack Trevisan's daughter." Donata shook her head at me as I began to register horror. "It was an accident. There were wagons and carriages everywhere, and one morning, as she and her mother went out to shop, they both were struck down, trampled. Trevisan's wife survived. Their daughter did not."

Trevisan must have been devastated. I could imagine his anguish, his fear that he'd lost his entire family, his grief when his daughter was taken from him. He'd had no sons, I recalled Proietti telling me, only a daughter. I hadn't realized the daughter had been killed, and I inferred Proietti did not know this either.

"No wonder Trevisan became estranged from his wife," I said. "Poor lady."

"Tragedy can bring a family closer together, or it can break them apart," Donata said softly.

The Austrians had regained Lombardy five years ago, combining it with the Veneto to create the Venetian-Lombard state. Trevisan did not seem to be a man who'd bow his head to the Hapsburgs. His daughter's death and the constant change in political fortunes might be the entire reason he'd relocated to Rome.

"The contessa has taken in Gisela to replace her grand-daughter," I speculated. "No, *replace* is the wrong word. To console herself."

"I agree," Donata said. "She is a woman in pain. She must have loved her granddaughter very much. She will support her son's plans in order to keep Gisela with her."

When Trevisan and his mother had first seen Gisela, they must have been strongly reminded of the young woman they had lost, and both been drawn to her. They'd have realized that Gisela was *not* their daughter and granddaughter, but they must have glimpsed in her the girl that had been taken from them. A man could fall to pieces over a woman for many reasons.

"I do have sympathy," Grenville said. "But Conte Trevisan has been heavy-handed about it. The gossips of Rome's elite filled me in on the entire affair. They are scandalized that he has simply taken over the girl, but they enjoy the chance to gawp at him. Trevisan has given them much entertainment."

"At the Proietti family's expense," I said. "And I have had no satisfactory explanation about why Trevisan is so insistent that

I discover what happened to Conte de Luca. What is that connection?"

"That, I assume, we will discover as we continue to inventory the house." Grenville said. "I am happy that both Signor Baldini and Signor Proietti will assist us. Perhaps we can get through the lot much faster." He opened his hands, which was for Grenville a gesture of despair. "I am beginning to be baffled by this whole business. Surely Gian must have committed the crime. He stands to gain much if he is correct that de Luca willed his entire collection to him. De Luca trusted Gian, from what I observed. He'd have turned away without worry from his own son, fearing nothing."

"Perhaps." I'd had the ghost of an idea as I'd listened to the soprano tonight, though I needed time to think it through.

My greatest obstruction to learning the truth was deciding the reason why anyone who had access to the house would kill de Luca. Gian, of course, would inherit the priceless collection, but would he have murdered his father in so obvious and open a fashion? He'd be the first suspected, and indeed, he was even now in jail.

The cook had also had the opportunity. He was easily angered, and perhaps de Luca had said the wrong thing to him at the wrong time.

Why, then, had the cook turned up as usual the next morning? Why not flee rather than tamely wait to be arrested?

I hoped Bartholomew could find time to interview the maid and the neighbors. Someone must have seen *something*, or perhaps the maid had coshed de Luca when he'd made inappropriate advances.

Then there was the cousin, who'd not yet turned up—I would have to inquire about his whereabouts. Had the man been anywhere near Rome? Of course, he could have sent a confederate to do the deed, but how would that confederate have gained the house and made de Luca turn an unsuspecting back?

Then again, as Grenville had once stated, anyone in Rome could have murdered de Luca. The house was not well guarded, de Luca had been home alone, and a determined thief could have broken in. I made a note to ask Brewster how difficult it would be to gain entrance to the house, but I had the feeling it would not have been a monumental task.

The rest of the short ride was spent in silent contemplation, and I enjoyed Donata's warmth beside me, her hand on my arm.

We reached home and said our goodnights. Grenville, used to being up all hours, retired to his study. I expected Donata to return to her letters, but she followed me into my bedchamber, waving off her maid Jacinthe.

Bartholomew, who'd have been alerted by the arriving carriage, was ready with my night things. I dismissed him, perfectly able to undress myself, and closed the door, shutting out the world.

I expected that Donata and I would further discuss the Trevisans. Instead, Donata came to me and unbuttoned my coat and waistcoat, then proceeded to valet me. I became her lady's maid, and soon I had blown out the last candle, closing the curtains around our bed to shut us into a dark, private world that contained only the two of us.

———

IN THE MORNING, I LEFT DONATA SLEEPING, FETCHED Brewster and Grenville, and returned to de Luca's to continue our inventory. On our way we passed the Basilica

Sant'Andrea della Fratte, where Trevisan had listened to a concert the night of de Luca's death. I studied its rather plain façade, which had given Trevisan an alibi for de Luca's murder, but not, Proietti had been quick to point out, Proietti himself.

We arrived first, before our promised help, the police guards once more admitting us. Grenville and I continued with Brewster's method of listing the goods as we went, and we retreated to our parts of the house to work.

I found another painting, a miniature this time, on which I again asked for Grenville's opinion.

"Holbein," he said. "The Younger. I'm certain of it."

I touched the young woman with hair smoothed by a thick headband, her telltale Holbein features gazing serenely out at me.

"If it is genuine, where should it be?" I asked.

Grenville raised his quizzing glass to peer at it once more. "This one, I am not sure. But I am acquainted with a German prince who collects Holbein miniatures. He often badgers the Regent—excuse me, His Majesty—for pieces from his collection. Not successfully, I will add. Our new king likes to hold on to what he acquires."

"Perhaps you can write to your German prince friend to ask him."

The fact that Grenville could casually mention royal acquaintances with no intention at all of boasting both amused and amazed me. I often imagined that Grenville could stroll up to the emperor of China and say, *Good afternoon, old thing,* and the emperor would spring to his feet in joy to wring his hand.

"Of course," Grenville said, oblivious of my thoughts. "Note it on your sheet, and I will write him tonight."

As he turned to depart, the knocker struck the front door.

Brewster charged to it and pulled it open to reveal Signor
Baldini. The slim man bowed, his eyes betraying his eagerness.

"Good morning, gentlemen. Forgive my tardiness—I slept
poorly as always after a late night. I then did not wake until my
landlord's boy shook me hard. I apologize."

"Not at all," I said, gesturing him inside. "It is splendid of
you to help. I take it Conte Trevisan had no objection?"

Baldini frowned, as though the name of the conte
displeased him. "None." The syllable was short. Baldini shed
his greatcoat and hung it on a peg near the door. "I believe
Conte de Luca has some fascinating pieces?"

"As you will see," Grenville said. "Some excellent ones and
some that might be rubbish. He was an indiscriminate collec-
tor." He said this last with amusement, and Baldini unbent
enough to smile as though Grenville had made a good joke.

Grenville led Baldini toward the back of the house, and
Brewster jerked a thumb toward where they'd gone.

"You trust 'im not to nick anything?"

"He has had plenty of opportunity to do so in Herculaneum
and Pompeii but his views on those who do take things was
clear," I said. "His knowledge of art history, at least with the
ancients, is invaluable." I gazed about at the furniture and
objects we'd tidied in the foyer. "De Luca must have traveled
the world, picking up bits here and there from German
princes, Austrian emperors ..."

"Stealing 'em, you mean," Brewster rumbled. "A thief's a
thief, whether he's from the gutter of South London or the
highest of the high."

"I wonder *why* he stole them. And why some are carefully
displayed in well-organized rooms while others are in a jumble
in the attic."

Brewster shrugged. "No accounting for eccentrics."

"There is another possibility, you know. De Luca and his family might have purchased all these things legitimately. De Luca might have receipts hidden with these elusive lists Denis wants me to look for."

"If that's true, why stash all them bits upstairs? Why not bung them into a gallery and invite friends to see them? Or charge tuppence for the unwashed masses to parade through and have a look?"

"Discretion?" I suggested. "Sometimes a prince, emperor, or a pope doesn't wish to admit he needs funds, and sells a few family heirlooms to men like de Luca for the price they agree on." Proietti had done the same thing, on a smaller scale. "The transaction isn't public, and de Luca keeps the painting or sculpture tucked away until such time the prince or emperor can purchase it back."

Brewster's brows went up. "Like a pawnbroker to royalty?"

"Exactly. These princes of the dying Holy Roman Empire needed money to fight Bonaparte. He swept through the Continent like a devastating fire—a man like de Luca might have been a boon to them. They could raise extra funds and no one would be the wiser."

"Hmm." Brewster was not convinced, but I knew he'd think it through.

I peered out the front door once more, hoping to see Proietti also hurrying in, apologizing for his tardiness, but the courtyard remained empty. Outside the gate, the people of Rome went about their business as a light rain began to fall.

I wondered if Proietti had returned tamely home last evening or decided to force his point with Trevisan. Or perhaps Trevisan had at last held the promised meeting where they could discuss things. Thinking of the stubborn set to Trevisan's mouth and Donata's story that the contessa thought of Gisela as her lost grandchild, I had my doubts that Trevisan would loosen his hold.

Brewster shut the door and we continued to work, my list growing longer as the morning went on. I'd have to ask Baldini about most of the contents in one room, which was full of ancient Greek pottery. Real, forged, stolen?

A few hours ticked by, but Proietti did not appear. At the end of the third hour, Baldini gave an excited shout.

I hastened down the stairs to where we'd set him to work in some of the back rooms on the ground floor. These were not showpieces like the front rooms and contained boxes and trunks we'd hastily but not thoroughly gone through. We'd found no lists in them, in any case.

I reached the dim chamber first, Grenville and Brewster thumping down the stairs from above. I could not see Baldini when I peered inside, only dusty piles of old furniture and crates with their lids askew.

"Baldini?" I called.

"Here."

The muffled answer came from behind a pile of wooden boxes. I started around them, Brewster so close that his rough coat brushed my back.

A glimmer of light showed me where Baldini had got to. He'd lit a candle in the gloom, and a slit of light outlined a thin doorway where none had been before.

The paneling itself had pulled from the bricks to show an opening to another room. I had hunted for such hiding places as I'd searched, but we'd not yet examined this chamber carefully. It was in the very rear of the house, which backed onto the newer houses behind it, so the disparity in depth hadn't been noticeable.

The hidden space was about ten feet wide and many more

long, as it ran the entire length of the back of the building. My mouth hung open as Baldini flashed his candle around, and I heard Grenville's audible intake of breath.

"'Struth," Brewster said in reverence. "Never saw so many statues outside a gent's fancy garden."

They filled the space, carved stone, bronze, marble. Warriors, maidens, busts of Roman emperors—I noted the distinctive features of Vespasian, Augustus, and Hadrian—Apollo clutching Daphne as she began to morph into a laurel tree, a muscular David pulling back his sling as he eyed an unseen Goliath, a regal marble lady reclining on an equally regal marble couch, an onyx chubby Cupid, asleep, and various other large statues to grace a Roman villa or an emperor's palace.

"Good Lord," Grenville said softly. "Canova, if I'm not mistaken." He stepped reverently to the reclining marble woman, who was near to life-sized. "And Bernini." He glanced at Apollo and Daphne. "What the devil are these doing here?"

"Copies?" I asked, though I didn't truly believe this explanation.

"Could be," Grenville conceded.

"No," Brewster said at once. "The real thing has a feel, don't it?" He touched Apollo's marble shoulder. "Smooth as anything. Only time does that."

I took the expert's word for it.

"Could this be important?" Baldini bent over a trunk he'd opened, one filled with enough ledgers and papers to make both Denis and Trevisan happy.

I lifted a long ledger and opened it. Inside, in a barely legible scrawl, were notes and numbers, words crossed out and others added in margins. It would take a long while to go through it, but I had a feeling that we'd find gold among this dross.

"It could be," I said cautiously. "It could also be the conte's expense reports for his kitchen for the last fifty years. Grenville and I will lug these home and pore over them."

"I'll have a go, if you like," Baldini offered.

He spoke politely, but there was a light in his eyes that was too cajoling, too eager. He might be trying to be helpful, but I was suddenly certain of nothing.

"No need," I replied. "Grenville, Brewster, and I are old hands at going over art inventories. We will get through this lot in a trice."

Grenville said nothing about my optimistic boast, his face a careful blank.

"Right." Brewster shouldered his way forward. "I know who'll be the one doing the hauling. Mind your feet, Signor Baldini."

He all but shoved Baldini out of the way, his hobnailed soles in true danger of squashing Baldini's trim boots. Brewster put his arms around the trunk and lifted it as though it weighed nothing.

"Just pop that on the top, guv."

I relinquished the ledger and let Brewster carry the entire box out of the room. Baldini watched after him with some trepidation. "Are you certain ...?"

"Brewster is quite loyal to me," I assured him. "I would trust him with my life. Have, on several occasions."

Baldini gazed longingly at the items in the room, especially those that were ancient rather than from the Baroque or more modern eras. The Roman emperors eyed him back, chipped marble attesting to centuries of wear.

"Best we shut this up," I said. "Until we know to whom

these belong." I herded Baldini out of the room after Grenville and then shut the paneling. "How did you find this?"

"Entirely by accident." Baldini bounced on his toes. "I had backed up to study this exquisite vase." He indicated a red pot with black athletic figures charging around its circumference. "And bumped into the wall. I was astonished to feel it give way, and the paneling popped out."

He demonstrated how a hidden knob on the wood separated it from the wall.

"Well, thank you for that," I said. "This has been of immeasurable help."

Baldini flushed. "I am happy to be of service."

"Right." I clapped my palms together. "Shall we continue, gentlemen?"

Grenville and I trudged out of the chamber, leaving the Greek vases to Baldini.

Another hour passed without any more revelations. I tediously wrote down what I found in my rooms—even if the ledgers did tell us what everything in this house was, it would be best to compare the two lists.

I had to wonder who we could trust to return the objects or discreetly inquire whether these princes wanted them back. I imagined the cardinals who ran the Papal States, if they learned about this lot, rubbing their hands and lugging everything back to the Vatican. Or the Austrian emperor sending someone like Metternich to retrieve not only the emperor's belongings but the rest of the treasure as well.

If Denis learned of the cache we'd just unearthed, he might decide to keep it for himself. And Trevisan? Was he principled enough to help return the things or did he too have an ulterior motive?

As I wrote an entry on my list for an elegant bronze athlete, the knocker thudded once more. I left the athlete poised to begin his race and tapped my way to the door. Brewster hurtled down from the top floor, but I reached the front door before he did.

I opened it to find, as I'd hoped, Proietti. He was breathless, as though he'd run all the way from his home. He was also smiling.

I hadn't seen the man smile except for an ironic grin here and there, but now he was positively beaming.

"Captain," he said, giving me a truncated bow. "My apologies for my late arrival. My wife, she returned home today. She very much would like to meet you and Mr. Grenville. Can you come with me now?"

CHAPTER 22

*G*renville and I followed Proietti through the wet afternoon streets, Brewster coming behind us. Baldini had offered to stay at the house and keep working, and we could think of no excuse to deter him. Brewster had stashed the ledgers somewhere, and I trusted him to have found a safe and well-hidden place.

We entered the narrow lane that led to Proietti's home. A woman sweeping a doorstep called a greeting to him, and porters who delivered goods raised caps or nodded. A young lady, her mother, and their maid all smiled at Proietti when he tipped his hat to them. They exchanged good afternoons, and the ladies watched interestedly as Proietti hurried past toward his front door. The entire street apparently knew that the signora was home.

Proietti's door opened, his retainer's expression sunnier than I'd ever seen as he ushered us in with the sweep of an arm. I heard voices as soon as we entered, the house no longer dark and silent.

A woman's tones floated down the stairs, firm though not

strident. A man answered deferentially as did another woman. Proietti took the stairs buoyantly, his stride swift. Grenville and I followed, though Brewster hung behind, speaking to the retainer as he faded into the shadows.

Upstairs, we entered a large sitting room we hadn't seen before. The shutters were open, and though the gray day outside was gloomy, this chamber was airy and light.

A woman in a dark burgundy gown stood in the middle of the room giving orders to a maid who plumped pillows on the sofa, while a manservant busily lit candles in newly polished candlesticks.

The woman turned abruptly as we entered. "Alessandro," she said to Proietti and continued in Italian before she swept her gaze to us.

Signora Proietti had very dark hair and animated dark eyes —she was nowhere near the delicate creature I'd imagined who'd fled Rome with a broken heart.

"Captain Lacey, thank you for attending." Signora Proietti's voice was a pleasing alto, her accent charming. "Mr. Grenville. I am very pleased to meet you."

Grenville, a master of courtesy, bowed. "Enchanté, Madame. It is good of you to admit us to your abode. Shall you sit?" He gestured to the sofa, the maid having finished straightening its cushions.

"I have heard of your pleasing manners," Signora Proietti said. "Paola will bring coffee."

The maid at once scuttled away while the footman took our wraps. The footman departed, closing the door carefully behind him.

"Captain Lacey, my husband has written to me about how you have stayed at his side." Signora Proietti sank to the sofa, and Proietti waved Grenville and me to chairs. He settled in next to his wife, his entire being radiating gladness.

"I was pleased to help," I said. "Though I have not done much."

"You have kept him from despair," Signora Proietti corrected me. "I could not sit idly. Once I knew my daughter was determined to be with Conte Trevisan, I traveled north to visit friends and find out about him. I disliked to leave Alessandro alone, but I knew he would be well."

"The house is empty without you, Lucia," Proietti said with all sincerity. "And with Gisela gone too ..." He spread his fingers, a man hopeless.

"You found these companions to guide you. I discovered many things as well."

Signora Proietti turned to us, her eyes alight. Unlike Contessa Trevisan, who was a faded beauty, Lucia Proietti was robust and lively.

"Do tell, dearest lady," Grenville said. "You have us on tenterhooks."

Her brow creased in bewilderment. "Excuse me? What is a tenterhook?"

"Dashed if I know," Grenville returned. "But it's what one says when one is in a state of quivering suspense."

"I shall have to remember. The English language is a bizarre one, is it not?"

"Lucia," Proietti said gently, but I could see he was on tenterhooks as well.

"Forgive me. I am being rude." Signora Proietti straightened her hands on her lap. "My friends in Venice are acquainted with Contessa Trevisan, the wife of the conte here. She is forty but her hair is already gray, poor lamb."

"She is ill?" I asked.

"Not at all. She is in quite good health but low spirits. Mourning the daughter she lost, though I see that news is not a surprise."

"Conte Trevisan's mother told my wife the story," I explained. "How Trevisan's wife and daughter were run down in the street in Milan."

"Yes, it was sad, and I quite sympathize. His wife has not recovered from this, nor do I believe she will. My friends say she is angry she has survived and that her body has healed."

"A sad state," I said with compassion.

"I also learned she knows full well what the conte is doing. He writes her every day, it seems. She declares she knows what he is about."

I listened in surprise. A man writing his wife every day did not indicate he was tiring of her. By all accounts, Trevisan had done nothing untoward with Gisela—she was not his lover, at least not yet. Gisela herself had been shocked that anyone should imply so. It was all very strange.

"Do you know if Trevisan's wife knew Conte de Luca?" I asked. "Trevisan is very interested in him."

"My friends mentioned nothing of this," Signora Proietti said. "They had heard of Conte de Luca's death, as he was almost as well known in Venice as he is here. But I am afraid they said it was what happened in a violent city like Rome." She smiled a little, a woman amused at her friends' misperceptions.

The maid returned with coffee, which she set out with competence. Once the maid had departed, Signora Proietti poured coffee in demitasse cups for us all.

Our saucers also each bore a little cake, which Proietti dunked into his coffee before eating. I did the same, and found a spicy, delicate biscuit, complemented by the flavor of the coffee. Excellent.

Proietti turned to his wife. "I am hoping now that you are home, Lucia, we can persuade Gisela to return to us."

Signora Proietti's eyes dimmed. "I believe we might not prevail, Alessandro. The Trevisans are powerful, and Gisela, from what she writes to me, is happy. I will hope that Trevisan's wife puts a stop to all this soon, and when she does, we will welcome Gisela home."

"That we will." Proietti's voice grew sad, and he drew a breath. "But we must not trouble the captain and Mr. Grenville with our difficulties. They have been finding unusual things at de Luca's house, have you not? No one is certain who killed him, either. An interesting problem."

I took the cue to change the subject. Without betraying too much about our speculations on the collection, we told Signora Proietti about some of the odd things we'd found in the back room.

"Conte de Luca did travel widely," Signora Proietti said. "Was famous for it. But how did he move such large pieces into the house without anyone knowing? Neighbors in Rome are inquisitive, Captain. We cannot mind our own business."

She made a very good point. De Luca's house was relatively isolated behind its gate, but at the same time, people would notice large wagons full of massive statues being unloaded into the courtyard. They'd stare and discuss it, even if it happened in the middle of the night. I had to wonder how de Luca had hidden them away with no one being the wiser.

We chatted a while longer, then Grenville and I departed. Proietti reminded us he'd promised to help, but I waved him off. His wife's arrival took precedence, and he seemed happy to remain with her.

"The downstairs is pleased the mistress is home," Brewster said as we walked back toward de Luca's house. "They're certain she'll put everything right, and that the young miss will come back without fuss."

"We shall see," I said. "The Trevisans are certainly an eccentric family, though tragedy can mar one."

"It can indeed," Grenville agreed. "De Luca was yet another eccentric, if a more congenial one. I am itching to get at those papers. I take it you hesitate to trust Baldini with them, Lacey."

"Yet, I don't know why," I said. "He is a scholar, with a scholar's curiosity. His is also quite disapproving of treasure hunters, not to mention kings who take whatever they fancy."

"Unless he fancies them for himself," Brewster said.

"True, but does he strike you as a thief?" I asked him.

"Naw." Brewster tugged his hat straight in the lightly falling rain. "He's more the sort that would wag his finger at a robber and probably get knifed for his pains."

I had to agree. "He did seem very interested in the ledgers, though."

"I put 'em where he won't find 'em," Brewster assured us. "Trust me, guv."

I did. Brewster knew how to hide things he wanted no one to find.

By the time we reached de Luca's, the sun was fading, late winter darkness nearing. Baldini was still there, fervently writing up what he'd found in the back chamber. He was using a large book from a shelf as a desk.

"Ah." He raised his gaze from where he hunched over. "There you are. I have found Michelangelo's head."

As alarming as that sounded, he reached down and lifted a lump of stone with the beginnings of a face in it.

"One of his abandoned carvings," Grenville exclaimed.

"How astonishing." He hefted the stone to study the chiseled beauty of the partial face. "Michelangelo had several commissions going when he was instructed to drop everything and begin work on the ceiling of the Sistine Chapel." He admired the half sculpture a moment longer before he carefully set it down. "This should be in Florence, I think," he murmured.

"Shall we call it a day?" I asked when Grenville straightened up. "It is growing late, and Signor Baldini will want his supper."

Baldini glanced at me in surprise, as though food was the furthest thing from his thoughts. "I do not mind staying. The dark does not bother me."

"Perhaps, but I do not want the police marching in and arresting you," I said. "We will begin again in the morning."

Baldini reluctantly set aside his pen and stoppered the ink bottle he'd left on a nearby table. "What will happen to all this?" He waved a hand at the cache.

"Truthfully, I do not know," I answered. "We will have to decide who it all belongs to, I suppose, and whether de Luca purchased it rightly."

"If he didn't, everything will return to its original owners?" Baldini inquired.

Grenville answered, "Only fair, isn't it? If I found one of my artworks in this pile, I'd certainly want it back."

Baldini gazed at him with an expression of disappointment. "It would be better that these pieces remain together, I think. To be put into a museum and studied by scholars."

"Not our decision to make," Grenville said mildly, brows lifting.

"No." Baldini's scowl darkened his face. "Conte Trevisan and men like him will send the items back to those who will hide them away from all but a few privileged pairs of eyes.

They have no idea what these things would mean to scholars who'd truly treasure them—they will be no better than those who have robbed Herculaneum down to its bedrock."

I broke in. "So, you would shovel these treasures into some-place like the Louvre, as Napoleon wished to with his spoils of war?"

"No," Baldini snapped. "He was wrong to loot all he did. But Conte Trevisan is equally wrong. He is—"

He stopped abruptly, as though he'd said more than he meant. He'd obviously changed his opinion about the benevo-lence of his sponsor. I wondered if the two men had quarreled, and about what? Gisella? Or about Trevisan's interest in de Luca's collection.

"Quite," Grenville said. "Shall we, gentlemen?"

Once Baldini realized we'd stand over him until he left the house, he conceded to depart with us. We exited through the courtyard, and one of the patrollers locked the door and then the gate behind us.

Baldini he left us with a subdued goodnight, walking north while we made our way south through darkness to Grenville's home and a meal. Brewster carried the box under his good arm and steadied it with the other hand, still bandaged.

Donata had gone out, Bartholomew told me when we arrived, to the opera with ladies she'd met the previous evening. Donata was a social butterfly, and she'd enjoy herself.

For myself, I itched to begin with the contents of the trunk. Grenville did as well, and after we shoveled down our meal, we each took an armful of papers and retired to separate rooms so we could pore over them in silence.

Bartholomew brought me coffee and set it gently on the writing table as I spread out the first sheets.

"I spoke this afternoon to the Conte de Luca's neighbors, as you suggested, Captain," he said.

I looked up from the first sheet covered in illegible handwriting. Bartholomew stood with his usual confidence, his blue eyes clear.

"Thank you, Bartholomew," I said in sincerity. "What did you discover?"

"They were happy to talk to me," Bartholomew said. "Found me intriguing, I think. The neighbors say Conte de Luca was a generous man, always giving people coin for assisting him or tossing it to beggars on the street. He went in and out quite a lot and traveled to the ends of the earth—so they said. Never had many visitors, though. Kept himself to himself. Even bought up the properties around him so his house would be more quiet."

"Did he, now?" A man who owned the houses adjacent to his—say the ones that backed onto it—could build private rooms and take large artworks in through those abodes. Probably another secret door connected the long room with the house behind him, and who knew what would be found in *those* houses? I made a mental note to gain entry and see what we could discover.

"Mirela Floris is the name of the maid," Bartholomew continued. "His neighbors gave me the name of her street, so I went 'round to her lodgings. They're across the river and a bit south, kind of a warren there. I told her—and her very large husband—that I had a lady friend looking for work, and I heard she charred for a conte who paid well. Now that the conte was dead, would his heir hire more maids? Mirela and her husband were congenial to me, but said they didn't know. Mirela only went in one day a week to sweep floors and tidy. One week's worth of dust would be on all the things, which were never moved and never looked at as far as she knew. She wasn't allowed up past the third floor, so she had no idea what was up in the attics. New things did come in, she said, but she never saw them arrive. They were just there to be dusted the next week."

Intriguing. "What did she think of the conte himself?"

Bartholomew shrugged broad shoulders. "She didn't see much of him but said he was kind enough. Never any sordid goings-on that she saw. If he had a mistress, he kept it quiet, and said mistress never came to the house. He gave Mirela a decent wage, and she asked no questions. She's sorry he's dead, and hopes his cousin keeps her on in the house."

She had not told him much that we did not already know, but a confirmation was helpful. "Thank you, Bartholomew. Your assistance is always valuable."

"I keep my eyes open, Captain," Bartholomew replied modestly. He straightened the coffee pot on the tray. "Will that be all, sir?"

"Of course, Bartholomew. When her ladyship returns, please tell her I am in here, will you?"

"I will, sir. You want any more coffee, you just ring."

Bartholomew breezed away with his youthful energy, and I returned to my puzzle.

If I'd hoped to find an orderly inventory of all goods in de Luca's house as well as the neatly laid out list of de Luca's contacts James Denis sought, I was disappointed.

The ledgers were filled with scrawls of barely readable handwriting. Each item—I assumed—was listed on the left, with notes and symbols to the right. I was reminded of the catalog done of the Prince Regent's collection by Mr. Higgs, his librarian, which had led us to stolen objects.

But while those lists had been neat and methodical, I struggled to understand these numbers and letters and even to read what objects were listed.

Not until I'd gone through several pages and growled over them, did I realize that the language de Luca had used was not Italian, but French.

Once I saw that, my eyes were opened a bit. I sprang up, clutching a page, dashed to Grenville's room, declared, "They're in French!" and dashed away again.

Grenville's "Ah, of course," floated triumphantly behind me.

That a Roman man wrote in French was not surprising. It was a language spoken over much of the Continent, and de Luca and his confederates, whoever they were, must have found using it more convenient.

I returned to my room, certain I'd cleared up everything, but of course I hadn't. I could read the lists better now and went back to the beginning, but they were still a mess.

De Luca hadn't documented anything in a straightforward fashion. He'd list tables from the court of Louis the Fourteenth of France next to ancient Greek vases and Roman statuary, then a bronze by an eighteenth-century artist. Comparing his lists to mine, I saw that he hadn't even divided up the things by room.

The annotations were likewise puzzling. For example, one next to an Etruscan vase read *PVI, V, 04*. A Roman statue, *UVII, PBar, 07*.

I threw my pen down after a time, rubbing my eyes. Nowhere had we found a list of de Luca's contacts, though I consoled myself that it might still be in the trunk. Brewster was also leafing through a pile, and I hoped he'd be better at breaking codes than I was.

A scent of night air mixed with perfume wafted over me, and a soft kiss landed on the top of my head.

"I heard you snarling all the way up the stairs," Donata said in her soothing voice.

"It is impossible." I turned in my chair and took her hands, my fingers cramped. My wife was a much better thing to study than de Luca's scrawled code. "I am ready to throw it all in the river and retire to Grenville's villa. I miss the children."

Donata squeezed my hands. "You will prevail," she said with far more confidence than I felt. "You have despaired plenty of times before."

This was not much comfort. "Are you fatigued?" I asked. "Or will you sit with me for a while? Your logical mind might help."

"Heaven forbid you state this before members of the *haut ton*." Donata pressed her hand to her silk-clad bosom in mock horror. "A lady with a logical mind is an oddity, a bluestocking, much to be pitied."

"I am sorry to learn this." I gave her a little smile. "I hoped my daughters would have greatly logical minds, but I see that they must be featherheads or be condemned."

"I will teach them to hide it." Donata's eyes sparkled. "Now, let us employ my logic."

We sat side-by-side, and between us, a pattern emerged. Most of the codes were a mystery, but I deciphered a few of them and began to form a hazy idea about what the lists told us.

I wasn't certain and wanted to ponder it and discuss it with Grenville and Donata, but if I was right, this was an amazing case of theft, larger than any I'd ever heard of before. All parties to this theft—most of them, anyway—were now dead. Trevisan's interest became almost, though not quite, clear.

Before I could voice my speculations to Donata, Bartholomew interrupted us.

"Begging your pardon, Captain, your ladyship. His lordship, Conte Trevisan, is asking for you—he's in the downstairs hall." Bartholomew's brows pinched into a frown. "He is greatly agitated and told me to say it was very urgent. I almost couldn't stop him charging up here after me, except that I said your ladyship mustn't be disturbed."

Donata rose. "You'd better go down, Gabriel," she said decidedly. "Call for me if I might assist."

I reluctantly left her and the task that had suddenly grown very interesting, but I did need to ask Trevisan a few questions.

Trevisan forestalled any greeting by rushing to me as soon as I came off the stairs. He was indeed agitated, his color high, his breath quick.

"You must come, Captain. They've taken her. Dear God, they've taken her."

My heart dropped. "Gisela?" I demanded. "Who has?"

Trevisan blinked, then stared at me as though I were a madman. "No, no, not Signorina Proietti. The contessa. My mother." He seized the lapels of my coat. "She has been kidnapped, and you must bring her back to me."

CHAPTER 23

I did not need to ask Trevisan if he was certain. The anguish and fear in his eyes told me of his conviction. I pried his hands from me and waved off Brewster, who'd charged in as soon as Trevisan had come at me.

The two of us succeeded in getting him to sit on a padded bench against the wall, Bartholomew materializing with brandy. Both Donata and Grenville emerged into the gallery above and stared down at us, Donata's gown rippling like water.

"Who has taken her?" I asked Trevisan as I sat down next to him.

Trevisan gulped the brandy Bartholomew shoved at him and drew a shaking breath. "They sent me this."

I took the paper from his trembling fingers. It was written in Latin, in capitals, rather like an inscription on an ancient tomb.

Bring the evidence of the crimes to the ancient palace of the people. No vigiles.

The palace of the people. Insurrectionist speech, but that,

coupled with the mock inscription made me suspect that we were to take the lists we'd uncovered at de Luca's. *Vigiles* was the ancient Roman word for their watchmen, further cementing in my mind who had written the note.

I tucked the paper into my pocket. "Who would know your mother's routine and how to get to her?"

Trevisan swallowed another gulp of brandy, draining the glass. He seemed grateful for my questions.

"She had gone to evening mass. She goes always on Sunday night—she has not lost faith as I have."

"Because of what happened to your daughter," I stated.

His startled glance, full of pain, told me I was correct. "Yes," Trevisan said bitterly. "Where was God then?"

I too hadn't had much use for God when my wife had left me, taking Gabriella with her. I had begun to be more grateful once I'd found Gabriella again.

"Sant'Agnese en Agone?" I asked, naming the church in which he'd first met Gisela. "Did she go there tonight?"

Trevisan's nod wrenched my heart. His eyes were full, his fears tearing down the walls of his reserve.

"Who would have known this?" I asked again.

He shrugged. "So many. Her maid, all the servants, Gisela, Signor Baldini…"

"Lacey," Grenville exclaimed over the railing, but I remained composed.

"Signor Baldini was angry with you today," I stated. "When we first met him, he could not sing your praises enough, but today he said your name with bitterness. What had changed?"

"Gisela," Trevisan whispered. "He was so very outraged."

I knew, things having straightened in my head as I'd worked on the lists tonight, that Gisela was merely the catalyst that had begun Baldini's anger. His paragon, Trevisan, hadn't been a paragon after all, he'd discovered. Baldini's manner about him when we'd discussed what would happen to de Luca's hidden cache of artworks had been one of disgust. And he'd been so very interested in the lists.

"How long has your mother been gone?" I asked.

"Several hours. She did not return from mass for supper, as she always does. She had taken a sedan chair—her maid walked and lost her in the crowd. I have been searching the streets … "

"The contessa entered a sedan chair, but it did not carry her home," I said. "Your mother does not strike me as one to blithely go along with such things, so I will assume she was given something to keep her quiet."

Trevisan covered his face with a trembling hand. "This is my fault. I ought to have stayed in Milan, minded my business …"

"You could not have. What you are doing is important."

He glanced at me in surprise. "How do you know?"

I rose. "I'm not the bumbling English soldier you take me for. I know where the things in de Luca's house came from and that you are trying to put things right. Baldini is furious about that, isn't he?"

"Yes." The answer was breathy.

"He's taken her, the nearest and dearest person to you, as your wife is in Venice, out of reach. I know what he will want for her safe return."

Trevisan stared at me. "You do? This note means nothing to me."

"We found inventories, of a sort, to de Luca's collection. I believe he would very much like to get his hands on them before you do."

Trevisan shot to his feet. "We cannot give them to him."

I held up a hand. "I did not say we would give up every-thing, only that he will wish it. We will bring the contessa back safely without compromising your mission. I do not think Baldini is the sort who would hurt a woman."

Trevisan shook his head. "I do not know anymore. He was so enraged at me."

I turned from Trevisan and his anguish, pacing the hall, my walking stick tapping, though I scarcely felt my stiff knee as I thought rapidly.

Baldini had taken the contessa a few hours ago—that is, if we were right that it was Baldini behind the deed, though I knew in my bones that this was the case. He'd been disillusioned, and such men acted irrationally. He must have been quite frustrated when we'd rushed away to see Proietti and he hadn't been able to discover where Brewster had hidden the box of papers.

He'd not have gotten far in a few hours. Baldini was happiest in the world of the past, as he'd showed when he'd ecstatically taken us through the long-buried worlds of Pompeii and Herculaneum.

I considered the idea that he'd take the contessa all the way to Herculaneum, to hide her in the long, dark tunnels he knew so well. But it was a more than a hundred miles there and even in a fast coach, it was a few days' journey. He'd want to meet with us sooner than that.

I went through the words on the note again, and chose the site it had to be.

"Where is Gisela?" I asked sharply.

"She went home this evening," Trevisan said, his voice tired. "Her mother has returned—she wanted to see her."

"You are certain she is there?"

Trevisan's trepidation returned, but he nodded, grasping

his own arm as though trying to reassure himself. "I took her there myself, saw her enter the house."

"Good." Proietti would keep her safe. I imagined Baldini had decided to take the contessa, because Gisela had gone to her family where she'd be well protected.

"Grenville will return you home," I said. "And stay with you. Brewster and I will find your mother."

Grenville gave me a nod as though he approved of my choice. If Baldini contacted Trevisan at his house, Grenville had the skills to deal with him or any ransom demand.

"I too will accompany the conte," Donata announced. Her fierce gaze down at me dared me to argue.

I did not. She could keep Trevisan calm and also help his mother when she was returned.

Brewster said nothing at all, which meant he approved of my plans. He'd not have hidden his opinions if he'd objected.

Donata withdrew to fetch warm wraps against the continuing rain, then she descended to the ground floor with Grenville. She squeezed my hand on her way past me, Trevisan's carriage glistening outside the now-open door.

Trevisan did not look at me, only followed Grenville, who took on his calming tones as he guided Trevisan and Donata into the coach. Grenville raised a hand to me and leapt in after them, and then the carriage clattered away.

Brewster, who'd disappeared while I saw the others off, returned with lanterns which he set on one of the stone benches. Next, he stuffed rope, extra candles, flint boxes, a small axe, and various knives into two leather bags. He quietly handed me one bag, which I slung over my shoulder before I lifted a lantern.

I considered recruiting reinforcements—Bartholomew and Matthias specifically—but decided against it. Brewster and I knew about skulking in the dark, and we were both trained fighters. While the brothers were robust and had proved their might more than once, I did not want to risk Baldini stabbing or shooting them in the dark.

Brewster and I stepped into the night. This street was murky, though there were lights in the wider squares. As I led Brewster south, the lights faded, and soon we walked through needles of rain from the inky black sky. Our covered lanterns helped us not trip on the cobbles but did not provide much more illumination.

"Where we going, guv?" Brewster asked as we marched along.

"To the ruins."

"Very amusing. This whole city is tumbling with them."

"The place built by emperors to win the loyalty of the plebeians. The ruins in this city that are most difficult to miss."

As I spoke, we skirted columns half-buried in muck where it was said Julius Caesar himself had been assassinated. After that, we plunged into narrow lanes, houses rising around us. Several churches emerged from the dark, silent now, their large doors closed.

I knew this route—at least, I hoped so—as it had been one I had explored when I'd first reached Rome. Brewster, who'd accompanied me on these walks, soon understood where I meant to go.

We emerged from the streets on the edge of a hill, damp air wafting upward. A path led down to the excavations, the track difficult to find in the dark, but at last, I located it.

Brewster went first, testing the ground, and I came behind him, tapping with my walking stick before I put each foot down. Pale columns thrust themselves skyward in the moonlight, though most of the ancient pillars lay on their sides or broken into pieces. I'd reveled walking where Augustus and Marc Antony had roamed, yet been saddened that the great Forum Romano had been reduced to a pile of rubble.

The Romans had used the road we picked our way down to begin their triumphal processions, making their way from the Capitoline and through various roads to the Via Sacra. Giant arches dotted the way, where Caesars through the ages had erected monuments to adorn the route.

When I'd explored a few weeks ago, with a trusty book to tell me what the various piles of stones were, I'd found the foundations of the temple to Julius Caesar, where passersby had left flowers; the Rostra, from which the speeches I'd learned in my youth had been given; and various temples to Saturn, Castor and Pollux, and Vespasian and Titus.

At the end of the ancient forums, rising in weighty might, was the Colosseum.

The Flavian Amphitheatre was now known as the Colosseum, the name taken from the immense statue of himself Nero had had erected near the great lake of his pleasure garden. The Flavian emperors, Vespasian and Titus, had drained the lake and used the treasure they'd looted from Judea to fund the vast amphitheatre, a temple to entertainment for the people of Rome.

Earthquakes had toppled a large portion of an outer wall, but the towering immensity was still impressive. That much survived intact was amazing, but various popes had named this a sacred space, believing Christians possibly had been martyred there, and in the last century had begun restoring it. Indeed, brick bracing had been put up not many years ago to keep the walls from falling completely. The original stones were pockmarked with holes from where people of the past had dug out the iron pins that held the edifice together.

The place had been captivating to me when I'd wandered about with Brewster in our first days in Rome. Tonight, I saw only darkness and danger.

As Brewster and I ducked under an archway and cool, dank air floated around us, I wondered if I'd guessed correctly. Baldini loved Colosseum, yes, and had even offered to take Grenville and I over it. But did he perhaps have a favorite place other than this he went to try to connect with his ancestors? Rubble of Augustine's house on the Palatine hill? Ruins of the Theatre of Marcellas? A deep niche inside the Circus Maximus? Those could also, at a stretch, be called palaces of the people.

However, as a hiding place, the Colosseum was a good one. Corridors ringed the building, stairs leading upward to more hidden places, and perils wherever one turned. We might search for hours and find nothing.

I swallowed my qualms and followed Brewster through a vaulted opening to a long corridor that led around the lower floor.

The candle in Brewster's lantern was a pinprick that floated right and left as he moved ahead of me. I listened for voices as we walked, but heard only the tramp of our boots, the occasional rustle of a night creature, and the wind and rain outside.

If the contessa was here, she'd be cold in this dampness. I did not know her age, but she could so easily take sick, especially in Rome, which was notorious for its fever-laced airs.

Brewster halted and motioned to an opening to our left. It led to a stair that went down toward the cells where the gladiators and wild animals had been kept for the games. The lower levels were more stable than the upper, a guide who'd lingered here had told me on my first exploration, and would provide perfect places to stash a person.

The trouble with the Colosseum, this late at night, was that it was more than simply a good place to hide. It was riddled with vermin, some of the human kind.

As I trundled down toward the Colosseum floor, a man stepped out from behind me. He must have silently followed us in or come at us from a cross-passage, because Brewster would not have missed him.

I turned to see a long knife gleaming in his hand. The man spoke in Italian, but I understood his gist as his grin flashed.

I dropped the lantern, and my sword rang from my walking stick. The ruffian took an uncertain step back, surprised to find me armed, but he wasn't deterred for long.

His boot slid on gravel as he struck, but he regained his balance quickly. I sidestepped onto my good leg and smacked him with the blunt of my blade, trying to drive him back rather than commit murder.

He snarled in rage and rushed me. My assailant was practiced, but I could see—and smell—that he was also inebriated. Good thing, because he was fit and lithe, his knife darting about with skill.

A sound like a stampede came at us. In an instant Brewster was bowling me out of the way and landing on my attacker. The fight became brutal and swift, and I heard the attacker yelp in pain. Then more footsteps echoed as others raced toward us.

I pushed myself from the wall Brewster had shoved me into, stepped forward to go to his aid … and the floor opened under my feet. I must have found a hole between the stones, or a weak point in the bricks, because the next moment I, along with mortar and rubble, slithered down, down, down a long chute until I fetched up on hard floor somewhere below the earth.

My bad leg bent beneath me, and I groaned, but a quick assessment showed I'd only pulled it, not broken any bones.

"Brewster!" I shouted upward.

My voice fell flat against closed-in walls. Brewster either could not hear me or was too busy fighting, because no answering shout followed.

A watery sensation of panic flitted through me. I had been walled into a tomb in Egypt, an experience I hardly cared to repeat. My heart pounded, and I suddenly found it difficult to breathe.

This was not a tomb, I reminded myself, but a building that had been full of passageways, stairs, ramps, and even lifts for hauling men or beasts up into the arena.

I'd dropped my lantern, but not my sword and sheath, nor my bag, which had been slung over my shoulder. I fished in this last for a candle, thanking Brewster's foresight. He too had not forgotten being buried in the dark.

My hands were shaking as I brought out the flint box and tried to strike a spark. I had to make several attempts, but at last one caught on the candle's wick, and I blew gently to coax a flame. The wax hissed as it melted, then the candle flared. The still air around me helped the flame become steady.

I was in a tunnel under a barrel-vaulted ceiling, its stones much rougher than those of the passageways above. There would be stairs somewhere, as the fighters would have had to enter and—those who survived—exit the arena. I'd also read of tunnels that had led from the gladiators' cells underground back to their *ludus*, or school, so that they would not have to dash across the street, and possibly run for freedom, to reach the amphitheatre.

I simply had to wander this place until I found my way up

again or until Brewster, who would be certain to fight off any assailant, came to help.

"Baldini!" I shouted. My voice bounced from the narrow walls. "I have what you want."

No answer. I shouldered my bag, restored the sword to my walking stick, and trudged through the tunnel, holding my candle carefully. Stinging hot wax dripped to my hand but I refused to let that small pain make me drop my only light.

I called out at intervals as I went, but heard no reply. I might be wrong and Baldini and the contessa could be high up in the stone seats, but he'd certainly been at home in the underground places in Herculaneum. I'd be foolish not to explore all levels of this place, but as it was, I had to make a start here.

The passage led through the cool darkness which was much more comfortable than the rainy streets outside. It curved to the left slightly, following the contours of the building.

Not long later, I came across the cells. Openings in the walls, the wooden doors long rotted away, showed the tiny spaces where the gladiators had awaited their fate. I lifted my candle and peered into one, finding only a stone bench built into the back wall. The gladiator would have had that to rest on and nothing else.

I lumbered onward. More cells, some with bits of iron clinging to the door frames and no beds inside them. These might have been for the animals—leopards, lions, and the like —captured in Africa and brought here to be killed for entertainment. I had a soft spot for animals and hoped they'd shed plenty of their hunters' blood before they'd died.

I was convinced I'd made a full circle of the Colosseum without finding any sort of stairway, intact or in pieces, when I heard a faint cry.

Anything could have made it, a stray cat, a child far away outside, or the contessa in pain. I quickened my steps, but the sound was not repeated.

I heard nothing at all, in fact. No sign of Brewster climbing down to rescue me, no Baldini gloating that he'd lured me here, no toughs coming after me to rob me and leave me for dead. No sound but my own footsteps and labored breath.

My candle, spent, sputtered and went out. The darkness pressed on me, and I drew a sharp breath. I had more candles in the bag, which reassured me, but the sudden darkness was unnerving.

I unslung the bag from my shoulder. It slid out of my cramped hand, hitting the stones with a loud clank. The cry, startled now, came again.

I quickly fumbled with a new candle and the flint and steel. The voice, a woman's, floated to me once more as I struggled to make a light.

At last, a flame danced high, just in time to illuminate Signor Baldini's mad eyes as he slammed a heavy stone into my face.

CHAPTER 24

J woke, groaning, in a cell. This one was lit by several ancient-style oil lamps, and it was occupied.

Trevisan's mother sat on a stone bench that had once been a gladiator's bed. Her wrists and ankles were bound, and there were bruises on her face, but her eyes were open and sparkling with fury.

I fumbled my way toward the shut door, my knee protesting. Baldini had taken my bag of helpful items and my walking stick, though I was not very surprised about that.

"Locked," Contessa Trevisan informed me in her imperious manner.

I pressed on the door, which had no handle, and confirmed her statement. It was a fairly new wooden door—all the ancient ones had long since rotted away or been taken for their parts. The lamps, which I guessed were in fact from the ancient world, flickered over the rough walls, bathing us with the faint odor of olive oil.

"Is he mad?" I asked in general.

"He told me he believes he descends from Scipio Africanus," the contessa said in clipped tones.

"The general who defeated the Carthaginians," I finished. I gestured to the thick ceiling above me. Baldini had liked to go on about his family's ties to the ancients, but I'd first thought him merely fanciful and perhaps teasing foreign tourists. "And this is the palace of the people."

"Bread and circuses." The contessa settled her mantle as though she were in her drawing room at home. "Those in charge should give the masses food and entertainment."

"And art?" I asked, thinking of Baldini's anger that princes and kings would have their artwork returned, instead of scholars being able to study it.

"Certainly, that too. Conte de Luca amassed quite a lot of it."

"It was not his to amass," I said. "I know that."

"Good." The contessa gave me a nod. "Then you understand."

I thought I did. Some bits of the puzzle I did not like, but I knew de Luca had been audacious. I wondered if he'd agreed to the plan in order to save his own skin, or because he, like Baldini, cared about where the artworks would end up. Most likely, my cynical self told me, he'd been promised a lot of money.

A man who lived these days with only a few servants was either a bachelor without many needs, a man who practiced simple living, or a man in straitened circumstances. I guessed the latter in de Luca's case. I imagined the promised money had made him willingly hide the treasures.

Any rumination was cut short by the door grinding open. I straightened, ready to fight, though I was aching and tired. My head throbbed.

Baldini stood in the doorway. Behind him was a large man, one of the ruffians who'd attacked Brewster and me.

"You didn't bring the trunk," Baldini said accusingly.

I leaned on one hand against the wall, trying to behave as though I was in no pain whatsoever. "We could hardly deliver a thing like that, Signor Baldini. But this lady should go home and rest. You have me, and I presume Mr. Brewster. Grenville will negotiate for our release."

"And let Conte Trevisan do as he pleases?" Baldini spluttered. "He has *betrayed* me. He has betrayed us all."

The lamp Baldini held was also an ancient sort, a bowl with a protruding spout, rather like a teapot without a handle. The oil went into the bowl, and the wick in the spout gave off the light. De Luca had showed us some in which the spout was the shape of a man's penis, but this lamp was more decorous.

"How has he betrayed you?" I asked. "Trevisan's goal is to return all the things Bonaparte stole to their rightful owners, is it not?"

Baldini's eyes widened as though he'd thought me, all this time, an ignorant lout of an Englishman.

"How do you know about that?"

"It is quite obvious." It was nothing of the sort, but I mimicked Grenville's trick of behaving as though one had more knowledge than whomever one addressed. "De Luca was storing the items for Bonaparte, which were destined for the Louvre in Paris. Nothing as large as the horses of St. Mark's in Venice, but smaller pieces that were not as obvious."

"Yes." Baldini's scowl was dark. "Conte de Luca was a traitor."

"An opportunist, rather." De Luca had told Grenville and me that Bonaparte had called on him and threatened to take everything in his house. De Luca had put him off, he'd declared, promising that Bonaparte could return once he was done conquering half the world and have what he liked.

Perhaps their association indeed had begun that way. But more and more artwork turned up in de Luca's house as Bonaparte fought his way south and French agents helped themselves to paintings, sculptures, tapestries—all the great art from monasteries, cathedrals, and palaces. Bonaparte, as Brewster might say, was a dab hand at nicking.

I'd started to realize what some of the codes meant. *PVI* could mean Pius the VI, the name of a pope; *V*, the Vatican, and *04*, 1804, the year the item was taken. *UVII*, could be Urban the VII, though I wasn't certain what *PBar* was. *Palazzo s*omething, perhaps.

"De Luca likely had no choice but to let his home be turned into a storeroom for the pieces that fit into it," I finished. "Maybe that was the price he paid for keeping his own collection from Bonaparte's hands."

"And then the Corsican was defeated." Baldini stated this with great satisfaction.

"He was defeated, and artwork began to be sent back to where it belonged. But no one came for de Luca's store, at least not right away. He managed to keep the secret of what was hidden there."

"He wanted to sell it all." The contessa's clear voice cut through our discussion, her words holding derision. "He had no interest in provenances and the value each piece had for its owner, just in the money he could make from them."

"Because he had little money of his own," I said. He might have lost his fortune, like Proietti had, when the French took over, or perhaps de Luca's family, like mine, had spent all their money before de Luca had come into the title. "His own heirlooms he possibly could not or did not want to sell," I went on, "but the extra loot Bonaparte's agents had left—that was fair game. A friend told me that de Luca had been acting as an agent to procure art for others, which can be a lucrative business, especially as he now had a storeroom of art at home."

"No one forgot about anything." Baldini's eyes flashed rage in the dim light. "All the princes and archbishops knew their pieces were still missing and wanted them back. They sent—"

"Conte Trevisan," I finished. "He came to Rome to pick over de Luca's collection and return the things to their rightful owners. *Everything.* Which is why he insisted nothing be moved from de Luca's house. Whether Trevisan means to give those who might have already bought stolen pieces a fair price or simply browbeat them into returning them, I do not know."

Had Trevisan confronted de Luca? And had de Luca declared he would not relinquish what he had? What had Trevisan done then? He was a cold man, but even cool men could lose their tempers. And when they did ...

"How do you know all this, Captain?" the countess asked.

Again, I was struck with how poised she was, but concluded this was simply her character.

"I did not for a long time." I cleared my throat, the damp air making it sore. "But your son, Contessa, if you'll forgive me, seemed to be several different men, which confounded me. Was he a libertine who coerced a young lady to live with him while making plans to put his wife aside? Or a devoted husband kind to a young woman simply because she reminded him of his lost daughter? He seemed determined to find the truth of de Luca's death, which tells me he's a man who wishes rules to be followed. Then he was adamant that *no one* entered the house but me and those I trusted. We had no stake in this game, you see. I should be flattered he had faith in me, but I rather think he counted on my ignorance."

I finished this speech and drew a breath, longing for a drink of water.

Baldini's lips had parted while I'd spoken. "You have the right of it, Captain." His voice was quiet in the muffled room. "Conte Trevisan is now determined to return all the stolen art to their owners."

"Why does this upset you?" I asked. "You have no love for Bonaparte and the manner in which he took over your world."

Baldini shook his head. "The monasteries, churches, and kings robbed us all through the centuries," he said with conviction. "They had the power, the wealth, and the art, hidden away for themselves to enjoy. Finally, we have a chance to make it ours. What Bonaparte stole and de Luca kept should be *ours*. For scholars to study and others to view. And Trevisan, a man I thought was civilized, who promised me he wanted to do what is right—he wants *to give it all back to them.*"

"And you must stop him," I said as though in understanding.

"This is why you will give me the lists of the stolen artwork, Captain, and keep them from Conte Trevisan's hands. If he lets me give those artworks to those who deserve them, then I will return the contessa to him."

"How do you intend to find those who deserve them?" I asked. "Start your own museum for scholars and charge pennies for admission?"

"You mock me." Baldini's rage returned. "I thought you of all people, a poor man dependent on his wealthy friends, would see. They will be available to anyone who will treasure and study them."

Any man down-at-heel given a miniature by Holbein would likely sell it quickly for food to fill his belly, not prop it on his mantelpiece and admire it. I supposed Baldini meant they'd go to scholars as he'd mentioned before, who would lock the things away to study them as earnestly as the despised popes and kings.

Baldini was a dreamer. The pieces had been stolen from men powerful enough to end his lofty ideas and simply take what they wanted, arresting Baldini for kidnapping the contessa into the bargain.

"Is this why you killed de Luca?" I asked. "Because he sought to profit from his luck?"

Baldini's dark eyes widened. "You think *I* committed murder? I never laid a hand on Conte de Luca. I am not a man of violence."

Yet he held us captive here with a hired tough ready to beat us down if we tried to flee. The guard was a mountain of muscle, rather like the man in Denis's house, with a knife held in a competent hand.

"Perhaps de Luca's refusal to see your side of things infuriated you so much that you struck out," I suggested. "Not meaning to kill, but that was the consequence."

I saw the contessa flinch, her hands tighten on her mantle. I wanted to reassure her I'd let no such thing happen to her, but I had to keep my gaze on Baldini and the man behind him.

"*No.*" Baldini's adamance made me start to believe him. "I would never kill another." He wet his lips. "Besides, I met you in Herculaneum two mornings after Conte de Luca meet his death. I could not have traveled from Rome to Herculaneum so quickly."

I did not have to ask how he knew exactly which day de Luca had been killed—Trevisan would have told him if it had not already been common knowledge.

"It could be done," I said.

"Not by me." Baldini began to splutter. "I am not a skilled rider, nor do I have the stamina to ride so quickly."

"Very well," I said. "I will concede the point. But what will you, a man who does not like violence, do now? I have no intention of letting you steal that which was already stolen. Also, you are endangering the contessa's life." I adopted the tones of the stern commander I once was. "Let her go home."

"I cannot." Baldini sounded both sorrowful and desperate. "I must keep Trevisan from those lists."

"Your idea is laudable," I said. "I would like to see such beautiful things in a museum for all to admire and available for historians to study. But you have not planned well. Even if I do have Grenville hand you the lists, you will have to flee a long way from here, and the items themselves are locked into de Luca's house, the keys with the police. You'll have no way to carry out your scheme."

"I will if great men help me."

I was skeptical about what great men would come to Baldini's aid. I thought about Grenville's friends in Rome—well-connected, well-traveled, well-read, somewhat reformist minded if their conversation was anything to go by—as well as the Stanbridges, living in Napoli for its beauty, dependent on that country for allowing them to stay.

These ex-patriates would, I think, happily return the stolen items to their rightful owners, believing themselves honorable for thwarting Bonaparte's plans to take the best art on the Continent for himself.

I did not tell Baldini my speculations. I had no intention of letting him coerce me into returning the lists, even if I partly agreed with him that the wealthy of Europe would simply shut the artworks away into their private homes, never to be seen again. James Denis had once told me that all art was in fact stolen—the artists themselves were often cheated of their fees.

In truth, I was conflicted in the matter, but as Baldini had locked the contessa and me into this cell, I wasn't very sympathetic to him at the moment.

"The contessa is ill," I stated. She was wan and shaking, and I had no wish to see her harmed by this encounter.

Baldini drew himself up. "She will return home when the artwork is safely dispersed, away from Count Trevisan—and *you*."

He stepped back into the corridor, and the tough slammed the door. I threw my weight against it, trying to shove it open, but the man outside was strong. I heard an iron bolt slide into a slot, and then the grating of a piece of stone moved to block the door.

The flickering lamps were feeble against the blackness. When the oil burned out, we would be in darkness itself.

"Do not worry," I told the contessa. "I have dug my way out of such places before. I once even set fire to a door to get out of a locked room."

"Let it not come to that," the contessa said severely.

I admired her bravery. She ought to be terrified, but instead, she sat in ice-cold rage.

I refused to give way to despair. Brewster would prevail and find us. Trevisan would give up trying to be discreet and scour the city for his mother. And if he did not, Donata would.

As soon as I could no longer hear footsteps in the distance, I studied the door. I wondered if Baldini had caused it to be made, or perhaps someone had stored something down here, and Baldini, exploring, had found it and decided to use it to his advantage.

The door was by no means a masterwork of carpentry.

Wood easily rots and molds, and this door wasn't reinforced by any metal. I hurled myself into it, shoulder first, but that, unfortunately, did little but hurt my shoulder.

"A board is loose on this end." The contessa pointed to where the edge of the door met the wall on the bolt end. "I pried at it, but it was too much for me."

My admiration for her increased. She'd not only weathered her abduction but had tried to work her way out.

I found the board she indicated, braced myself on the wall, and began to kick it. The wood bowed a little, but did not break.

"You are courageous, contessa," I said, continuing my assault on the board. "You remind me of my wife."

"Ah, the Lady Donata," the contessa said. "She is a woman of much sadness, I think."

I paused to glance at her. "Did she say that?" I asked in surprise.

"She did not, but I saw it in her. She has suffered loss. She was a widow, was she not?"

"Yes, but her husband wasn't much of a catch. Donata had no love for him."

"She was young when she married, she told me. I imagine she was in love, as ridiculously as one can love at such an age. Her husband broke her heart."

My boot on the door told the room what I thought of the late Lord Breckenridge. "He did cause her pain. I haven't forgiven him for that."

"Has she lost a child?"

"She nearly did." I recalled the horrible night when Donata lay in great pain trying to bring in Anne, and I'd known with certainly she would die. Only the surgeon, the strange man employed by Denis, had saved her life. "Our daughter Anne is right as rain, thank God, but Donata can bear no more children."

"Perhaps that is it. She has the look of one whose hope was taken from her. I have seen it on my own face." The contessa smoothed her skirt, fingers trembling. "I did manage to bear two healthy children in the end. Vittore, my son, and Paolina, my daughter. She married an Austrian." Her lip curled. "But she is happy, and I do not begrudge her."

I continued thumping on the door. "My wife told me about your granddaughter. I was sorry to hear it. A terrible thing."

"It was." The contessa's voice grew subdued. "She was a beautiful child, with a full life before her. Taken because a clumsy Frenchman could not control his horses. Bonaparte has much to answer for in her death."

I reflected that the Corsican should bless his luck that he was safe on Saint Helena and out of the contessa's reach.

"I did not mean that your wife is unhappy now," the contessa went on as I renewed my determination to beat my way out of here. "She has a contentedness about her. She has learned to shut out pain and embrace life once again. I envy her this."

I halted my battering, first to catch my breath and secondly to send her a look of compassion. "Perhaps one day, you will too."

The contessa gave me a faint smile. "No, Captain. That will not happen."

She said nothing more, and I went back to work, unable to think of words to comfort her. Perhaps there were none, only platitudes to half patch the wound that would never close.

The board finally gave. I pulled it off, nails groaning as they popped out and clinked onto the wall, dangerously close to my face. On the other side of the hole I'd made, the bolt held the door firmly. I wriggled my fingers through the gap, but the opening was too small for me to grasp the bolt.

"Contessa," I said. "Might I borrow your hand a moment?"

She gracefully rose without question and joined me at the door. The contessa's hand did fit through the gap, but the bolt was stiff.

However, her resolution could have brought an army to a halt. The contessa pried and jiggled the piece of iron until finally, long after I'd have given up, the bolt slipped free of its setting and the door creaked open.

It was stopped, of course, by the chunk of stone the ruffian had shoved in front of it. The block was large, and I was running short of energy, but I threw myself at the door once again.

The light of the oil lamps behind us flared in one dying gasp, and then went out, both of them together, enclosing us in darkness. The stone slid agonizingly back inch by inch, until there was enough of an opening to admit my body—that is, if I went sideways, didn't breathe, and left many of the threads of my coat and trousers behind.

The contessa, a far slimmer person than I, slipped through when I reached for her without even rending her mantle.

We were free. I took her hand to lead her on, when two of the ruffians stepped out in front of us.

CHAPTER 25

The men were silhouetted in light that leaked from somewhere above, more holes in the ancient building. It was dawn, the night drawing to an end.

I was exhausted, sore, downcast, and very thirsty, but I let my famous temper overcome me at the sight of them. I roared, rushing at the men, no weapon handy but my own fists.

The men hesitated in sheer surprise, hardly expecting me to charge them. The yell from my throat was the same as when I'd ridden at the French lines, our screams meant to put fear into those hardened soldiers.

The assailants halted only a second or two, then came at me, ready to cut me down with wicked-looking knives. I dove under one's reach, the aching shoulder I'd used to break down the door slamming into his rather softer body.

My knee was in agony as I pummeled him, but I knew that if I backed away, he'd stick his knife into me. I jabbed my hand at his throat, every desperate fighting method I'd learned rising without my mind consciously directing it. The second man hovered, trying to get in a blow, but I continued to swing around with the man I fought to confound the second man's aim.

The contessa, not being a fool, used the opportunity to scurry away from the cell. I hoped she'd not encounter another tough before she discovered the way out and found help.

Out of the corner of my eye I saw the contessa stop. She lifted a rock from the floor of the corridor, staggering under its weight, and brought it down on the neck of the second assailant.

He did not obligingly drop to the floor, but he howled and stumbled, leaving me only one man to fight. I could not bellow at the contessa to run as she lingered, as though trying to get in another blow, because I had no breath, and my throat was parched.

The second man, rubbing the back of his head, snarled an invective and started for the contessa, knife firmly in hand.

I threw the man I wrestled into him. I shoved the contessa away from the fray, but that was all I managed before both men closed on me, fists and boots landing blows. The blade came for my face.

The cry of a banshee—those wailing spirits that foretell a death—sailed down the corridor. A whirlwind followed, but it was truly a man, one who'd fought like a demon in the night near the ruins of Herculaneum, the only person I'd ever seen able to best the rock of Brewster.

The two men swung to face this new menace, but he gave them no chance to regroup. Whatever rage existed in Mr. Cockburn, from the taunts of boys when he'd been a youth to the loss of his beloved brother, poured from him now.

He spun and kicked, whirling a dagger in patterns that made me dizzy. I attempted to assist him by landing a roundhouse blow on one of my opponents, but then I had to back away and let him work.

Cockburn would have put the champion pugilists Jackson and Mendoza to shame. He quickly had both men groaning on the ground and holding various limbs, one weeping softly. Cockburn rapidly stripped them of their weapons, tucking them into various parts of his clothing.

"Thank you," I said to him, my voice a rasp. "How did you know we were down here?"

Cockburn shook his head, pointing to his ear and waving at the air around us. I understood that he could not read my lips well in the semi-dark. I experienced a moment of chagrin for forgetting he was deaf but hid it by taking the contessa's hand.

She was shaking all over, the rock she'd held now falling from her grasp and rattling on the ground. I gently tugged her to follow me, but I'd carry her if need be.

Cockburn was none the worse the wear after the fight, and he led us through the vaulted corridor. He took us unerringly to a set of steep stairs that the contessa could never climb—I had doubts about my ability as well. I lifted her slight body into my arms, ignoring her protests, and proceeded to carry her upward. My leg hurt like the devil, and I had to go slowly, but I gained the top and set her gently on her feet.

"My apologies for the indignity, madame," I told her as she shook out her gown and shot me a glare. "But we must make haste."

Cockburn, unwinded, took us once again through the maze of passageways, up another ramp past the newer brick walls, and finally out into the damp morning.

Brewster ran toward us, and behind him came Grenville. A carriage had halted beyond them, its gleaming coach lights cutting through the rain.

The congenial Grenville came for the contessa, assisting her to the carriage as though he'd arrived to convey her to a supper ball. I, the ragged soldier, limped heavily to it, with Brewster behind me to shove me in. I saw Cockburn watching anxiously, before he vanished behind the door Brewster slammed.

My ears buzzed as I landed on my seat, darkness dancing before my eyes. I was gone to a dreamlike place, scarcely noticing when the carriage jerked forward into the Roman dawn.

———

WHEN I RETURNED TO MYSELF, I WAS RECLINING IN A comfortable chair next to a warm porcelain stove, rugs on my legs and a blanket around my shoulders. My wife reposed on a sofa near me, and the contessa, as upright as ever, sat next to her, her thin hand between Donata's softer ones. We were alone in the room, no servants hovering.

I vaguely remembered arriving at Trevisan's house, Brewster hauling me from the carriage like a sack of grain and trundling me inside. Various maids and footmen peered uncertainly at me, and at one point I thought I saw Proietti's daughter, but she dissolved into mist. I had no idea how long I'd been here, but the sun was well up, I assumed on the same day.

I must have made some sound, because Donata was next to me, a cool hand on my face. Her lips pressed mine a moment later. I longed to be alone with her, to cradle her body next to me and kiss her hair, drowsing in her warmth, but she withdrew, leaving me bereft.

"I am alive," I croaked, my throat still dry as a desert. "Barely. Is there any water?"

A clink and a trickle sounded and soon Donata handed me a blissfully cool glass beaded with moisture. I drank the cool Roman water that had poured through aqueducts for centuries, soothing my parched mouth and easing my throat.

The contessa looked weary but far better than I must. From her poise, she might have simply gone for a long ride in the country instead of being abducted and locked into a gladiator's cell.

"Brewster did not perish, obviously," I said to Donata as she returned to her place beside the contessa. "Is he unhurt?"

"He is faring far better than you. The contessa told me what happened, so do not strain yourself. She has been most worried about you, as have I. You were raving by the time you arrived here this morning and we felt you ought to remain until you were well. I had to explain who Mr. Cockburn was. Apparently, he was quite the rescuer."

"He should go on the pugilists' circuit with his technique," I tried to speak lightly but my voice was scratchy. "I must put Pierce Egan on to him." Egan was a journalist who loved all things boxing and wrote eloquently about it.

"Mr. Baldini has been arrested," Donata said. "While you were pummeling your way out of the cell, Mr. Brewster encountered him. As you might imagine, Mr. Brewster was quite furious with him. Mr. Cockburn turned up and helped him subdue the man. The watchmen couldn't ignore what was going on, and Brewster convinced them Mr. Baldini was a dangerous madman. The police hauled him away before Brewster could explain that he'd lost you in the dark, but Mr. Cockburn went searching. A mercy he did."

"Poor Baldini," I said. "I am not happy with him, but perhaps he should be looked after. Lent a solicitor if nothing else."

The contessa's eyes were flinty. "No. I'll not forgive him for what he did to me—and to you—this night, trying to make my son bow to his wishes. He is mad. He murdered Conte de Luca, did he not?"

"No," I said. In the cell and during the fight outside, my mind had showed me the incident in stark clarity. "You did."

The room went silent, save for the steady pop of the fire inside the stove. Donata's lips parted, but the contessa did not move.

"I began to realize it after the musicale," I said when neither woman spoke. My throat was still parched, and I took another sip of the beautiful water. "When I listened to the soprano— one of the best I've ever heard, by the way—I was enraptured. All others could have vanished from the room, and I'd never have known until she finished." I lifted my hand but barely had the strength to gesture. "You went with your son and Gisela to a concert at a church the night de Luca died. Proietti saw you there. He told me that you sat with friends. His eyes were for his daughter, and Gisela and your son were focused on the music, which I imagine was as fine as what we heard at your musicale. Neither Proietti nor the conte nor Gisela would have noticed you slip from that church—the Basilica Sant'Andrea della Fratte. Conte de Luca's house is just around the corner from it."

The contessa closed her eyes once. When she opened them, her defiance had gone, and I saw only resignation.

"He conspired with Bonaparte," she said. "For *money*. De Luca was always a greedy man. Yes, I went to speak with him. My son had asked him to give back what the Corsican stole, and de Luca refused him. Laughed. I went that night to beg him to reconsider, to tell him that my son would shame him to no end if he did not. He dismissed me. He said he'd sell the things on to the highest bidder. He even told me that he'd met you and Mr. Grenville, and that Mr. Grenville had the wealth to purchase whatever he wished. De Luca wanted my praise for being so clever as to find an English buyer for his stolen things."

"You are a strong and courageous woman," I said. "You had no qualms last night about picking up a stone and striking a man attacking me. De Luca would not have feared you—he'd have turned his back on you without worry. Did he admit you to the house himself?"

"He did. No one else was there—he answered my ring at the gate."

"And saw no reason not to speak to you in one of his well-furnished rooms on the ground floor. Where there were many heavy vases standing at the ready."

The contessa listened without blinking. "I did not know he would die."

"You likely did not," I agreed. "You were angry and wanted to hurt him. He refused to cooperate with your son, and you picked up a vase and hit him."

The contessa smoothed her skirt. "So you say."

Donata did not leap to her defense. She listened quietly, her face still.

"You are also cool-headed," I went on. "You wiped your hands of any blood, laid down the vase, and walked out of the empty house, closing the door and gate behind you. You went back to the concert so you would be sitting in the enclosed pew with your acquaintances when it finished. I imagine you had some excuse for them for stepping out a few minutes, that you'd needed air shut up in the crowded church, or the like."

"I am elderly," the contessa said, pride in her voice. "Sitting for long periods is difficult for me."

"I am sorry to hear this," I said. "But now your son will have de Luca's inventory—Grenville and I are happy to hand over his records, and Conte Trevisan may continue with his mission."

The contessa studied me, not making any attempt to excuse her actions. "And me? Will you be pleased to give me to the police captain?"

I sank back into the chair, more weary than I'd been in a long while. "I do not work for them. But even if I did tell the captain the truth, I doubt you'd be convicted, or even arrested."

The contessa was too well connected, Trevisan too respected. The law worked differently for aristocrats, and de Luca, after all, had been in coercion with Bonaparte.

The contessa rose. She was every inch a great lady and had experienced both joy and deep sorrow in her life.

"It will not matter," she said to me. "I am an ill woman and will not live past six months. I know this because I watched the same thing happen to my mother. God will be my judge for my crime. Good day, Captain. Lady Donata."

She gave us each a stiff nod, then she turned and stalked from the room. The door opened as a footman on the other side hastened to let her out. Her skirts swished, her heels clicked, and she was gone.

Donata let out her breath. "Well." She rose and reached for my hand, but said nothing more.

"She and her son would suffer if I told the police captain what truly happened," I said. "Even if I am right that she would never be convicted. I could not bring more tragedy into their lives."

Donata brought my hot, cracked hand to her cool lips and kissed it. "No, of course you could not." Her voice was soft, tender, and I recalled what the contessa had told me about the loss she'd seen in her eyes.

When she'd thought Peter had been taken from her a few months ago, Donata had been in deep anguish, followed by towering rage. I wondered if that was all that the contessa had sensed.

Now was not the time to pursue it. I tugged Donata closer until she sat on my lap, her head on my shoulder. I touched her cheek, soft as silk.

"Thank you," I said, and then we spoke no more about it.

———

I HAD BEEN CORRECT WHEN I'D MUSED THAT ROME WAS A PLACE of fevers, because one took me. I was laid up for days in Grenville's house while Bartholomew, Matthias, and Gautier ministered to me. I made Donata stay away from me, not wanting to risk contagion. She chafed but satisfied herself with giving me strict orders through Gautier, who delivered her instructions to rest, keep warm, and swallow Gautier's concoctions with cool authority.

I was wretched for a while, my head pounding, my throat aching, congestion stuffing my head. Gautier's potions, which I manfully drank while he stood over me, saved my life, I was certain of it.

Once I was able to rise from my bed and move about in a somewhat normal fashion, Mr. Cockburn came to visit.

CHAPTER 26

*M*r. Cockburn was dressed in a well-tailored suit, more resembling a gentleman of the City than the tough who'd once attacked me in the dark and fought like a madman against the men who'd imprisoned me. As I watched him accept a cup of coffee from Gautier, I'd swear he was nothing more than a genteel man of business.

Donata joined us for this meeting, serenely sipping coffee while she observed Mr. Cockburn. Grenville was the most relaxed of us, leaning back in his chair, cup balanced in his hand.

"You look in fine spirits, if I may say, Mr. Cockburn," Grenville remarked.

"I am returning to London," Cockburn said. "I mean to prove my brother was an innocent man, give him a proper burial under his own name, and put things right." A flush touched his cheek. "Mr. Denis has been of great help."

Denis had written me, while I lay in my sickbed, that he'd managed to find witnesses to Leonard Cockburn's death, witnesses who were willing to swear they'd seen Broadhurst

stab the man, then disfigure him. Denis had taken the precaution of having his men detain Broadhurst and they would
trundle him back to London. I had already written to Sir
Montague Harris about the situation, and I had faith that Sir
Montague would see that justice was done.

"Mr. Denis can be very helpful," I said, fixing Cockburn
with a stern gaze. "Be careful of his, assistance, though."

Cockburn nodded, innocence in his eyes. "I am grateful. He
has also offered me employment."

"Doing what?" I asked in alarm.

Cockburn shrugged. "Travel, discover things, help people
who have been captured." His glance at me was wry. "Not in
return for his help with Broadhurst," he continued quickly. "I
mean a proper job."

With Denis, nothing was as it seemed, but Cockburn would
have to find that out for himself.

"Speaking of which," I said. "I have not had the opportunity
until now to thank you for my timely rescue, Mr. Cockburn.
How did you happen to be on hand?"

"I saw you," Cockburn said simply. "I do not sleep well of
nights, and so I walk. I board near the Colosseum, as I told
you. You passed me, you and your man, both looking grim, and
I followed you. I lost you in the dark once you were inside the
Colosseum, but I came upon Mr. Brewster fighting for his life.
I joined in." He shrugged as though he'd merely picked up
something Brewster had dropped.

"I must thank you." Sincerity rang in my voice. "I don't
think I could have held on before Brewster reached me."

Another shrug. "You did me a good turn after I tried to do
you a very bad one."

"Still." I finished, and we let the subject rest before we grew
embarrassed at too much praise or gratitude.

"Bartholomew told me this morning that Gian and the cook have been released from jail," I said to Grenville as the awkward pause continued.

"Indeed," Grenville sat up straight, interest taking him. "I went to the house and spoke to Gian, to congratulate him and make certain all was well. The police captain has decided it was a passing thief. Gian has admitted he does not remember clearly whether he locked the door and perhaps did leave it open. The thief thought himself lucky, did not realize the master was at home, then knocked him on the head, and fled, too terrified to steal anything. This happens, apparently."

"Apparently," I said.

Donata looked me full in the eyes before she resumed her quiet calmness. An astute lady, she discerned that I'd had more of a hand in this imagined scenario than I let on.

Grenville did not notice our silent exchange. "The cook is once more ensconced in de Luca's kitchen, making wonderful meals."

"Surprising he doesn't seek another house to work in," I said relaxing back into my chair.

Grenville shrugged. "It might be difficult for him to find other employment. Even proved innocent, an arrest stains one."

That was true. I hoped de Luca's cousin simply accepted the cook as part of the house and carried on.

"Gian will also help Trevisan in his task," Grenville went on. "I suspect Gian of being completely hand in glove with de Luca, but he makes out that he is genuinely shocked and of course wants to return all the items to where they belong."

Gian could play both sides of the coin—the lackey who had no idea what his master had been up to, and the heir who would receive what part of the collection de Luca and his family legitimately owned. I silently wished him well.

The rest of the visit was a bit more relaxed, Cockburn returning to the theme of traveling to London and working to remove the taint from his brother's name. He planned to make certain the investors were paid back for Broadhurst's sins, using the money Broadhurst had managed to smuggle out of the country. I had the feeling that here, Denis would be of the most help.

When Cockburn departed, I returned to my chair after our farewells, still tired from my illness. I did not have much time to rest, however, because Gautier ushered in more visitors—Proietti and his wife—and vanished to bring more coffee.

After the lengthy greetings inquiring about my health and Signora Proietti advising me on remedies sure to bring back my strength—one involving raw eggs, hot peppers, and plenty of brandy—we settled into conversation.

My wife was taken with Signora Proietti and she with her. Signora Proietti tried to be very deferential to her until Donata firmly tucked her hand through Signora Proietti's arm and pulled her to sit on the sofa.

"Conte Trevisan has asked me to help him go through Conte de Luca's collection," Proietti said as soon as the polite greetings were finished. "He found even more in the houses behind de Luca's, vast statues from palazzos all over the peninsula. He is pleased—as much as Trevisan can be said to be pleased."

"Ah," I said. "Then he has warmed to you. I am glad."

Proietti made a self-deprecating chuckle. "*Warm* is not the word I would choose. He continues to believe I am an ineffectual father but has said that if I prove myself in his task, he believes he can procure employment for me. He has many friends, all of them quite wealthy."

"Which will be a boon," Signora Proietti broke in. "We cannot pretend otherwise."

"I also think my daughter has put in a good word for me." Proietti's smile turned rueful. "When Trevisan is finished here, he will be going back to Milan. His mother is not well, he tells me, and she wishes to be among her friends and family ... when the time comes."

The contessa had been very certain her end was near. I hoped for her sake it would be a peaceful one.

"Will your daughter ...?"

I could not finish the question, but Signora Proietti beamed at me.

"Gisela will be coming home to us once the conte has gone. She is staying only to tend the contessa."

"No more charade about Trevisan marrying her?" I asked.

"No," Proietti answered. "Though I know he was tempted to make her a permanent part of his family." He grew pensive. "Gisela vows that she knew the conte and contessa were fond of her only because she reminded them of the conte's daughter. But the situation was not so simple, and I know this. So does Gisela. Trevisan is a complicated man. Gisela is prepared to return home, but I see the pain in her eyes. I believe she truly fell in love with him."

"She is a brave lass and tenderhearted," her mother finished softly. "If romantic. I hope that we can find someone worthy of her."

"She will mend," Donata said with conviction. "In time, she will speak of it as a whim of youth." Her voice softened. "The Trevisans, I think, will not mend."

"Yes, the poor things," Signora Proietti said. "The contessa pretends to be so arrogant, but her heart was broken."

As my wife and the Proiettis continued to converse, I faded a bit, recalling how Trevisan had come to speak to me before I'd left his house, as the fever had begun to seize me. He'd waited until I was alone then had stood before me.

"I thank you, Captain Lacey," Trevisan had said stiffly. "For what you have done for my mother."

I tried to laugh. "If anything, I served as a post for men to hit, so that they would not strike her. My rescue attempt was feeble."

Trevisan's mouth quirked into a thin smile, the first softness I'd seen on his face. "But successful." He swallowed. "I meant, I am grateful for letting her die in peace."

"She has suffered quite a lot," I said quietly. "I do not say that de Luca deserved death, but she struck out in anger and never meant to kill him."

Trevisan huffed, his smile deserting him. He drew a breath as though to correct me, then released it. "As you say. I will finish as quickly as I can here and take her home."

"I will need a culprit to give the police captain to satisfy him," I said. "Gian and de Luca's cook are innocent and should be set free." I paused, sifting through an idea I'd had while resting in this chamber with Donata. "Gian knows that house better than any you will ever find. Let him help you sort through the things. The job will go faster, I imagine."

Trevisan's face pinched, but he nodded. He wasn't a fool. "It will be as you say. I have no small influence in Rome. I will make certain the men are released."

"It would have been so easy for a passing thief to find his way into the house, especially if Gian had forgotten to lock the door," I said pointedly. "He found it open in the morning, he said. Perhaps he could be persuaded to be uncertain whether he'd locked it before he departed to visit his friends."

Trevisan only stared at me, but I thought I saw a modicum of respect flicker in his eyes. "This is what must have happened. I will explain to the police captain."

He began to bow as though ready to depart, but I cleared my throat. "One more thing, if you please."

Trevisan's good will was quickly evaporating. "What is that?"

"The Proiettis," I said. "They would feel the loss of their daughter if you took Gisela with you. I believe you have had a similar experience."

"It was not the same," Trevisan's voice went icy, he the chilly aristocrat once more.

"I know it was not. Gisela would be alive and well but so far away from them. They are a close family."

Trevisan's brows drew down, his mouth a sour line. I would never know if Trevisan had meant to marry Gisela, or only adopt her, or merely have her become a companion to his mother. His grief was deep, and he might have wanted to sink himself into her sunny nature and try to find healing.

My idea that he'd taken her in to cloud the real reason he'd come to Rome was a wrong one. Trevisan had needed Gisela to ease him, and I imagined he'd decided to damn the scandal. Pain made one's judgment murky.

"I will think on it," Trevisan said, shutting himself off from me. "Your man wishes to remove you now. I think you must go."

"Yes." I struggled to my feet, shaky and weakening. "That would be best. Good night, Conte Trevisan."

"Goodbye," he'd said firmly, and then left me. I'd not seen him from that day to this.

I swam back to the present to rejoin the discussion. "I am pleased that you and Gisela are reunited," I said to the Proiettis.

"And I." Proietti rose. "I came to thank you, Captain Lacey. If I had not run straight into you in the street that morning, I might be without my daughter forever. Instead, she is coming home to me, and I have employment so that I can pay my loyal servants' wages."

I met him in the middle of the room and shook his hand. I worried that he would embrace and kiss my cheeks as his countrymen did, but he seemed to remember that I was an awkward Englishman and contented himself with the handshake.

Signora Proietti also regarded me with admiration. Behind her, Donata smiled wisely and kept her silence.

———

THE MORNING AFTER THE PROIETTI'S VISIT, DENIS SUMMONED me. Grenville and Donata were busying themselves packing— Grenville would shut up this house, and we'd return to the villa two days hence, which suited me.

Grenville and Donata held the opinion that I was not quite healed and should rest, and truth to tell, I longed to cease my adventures. While I was interested in what would happen to the contents of de Luca's house and the fates of Gian and the cook, I knew they were in good hands with Proietti and Trevisan. I wanted the peaceful spring I'd come to Rome for, and to spend time with my daughters and my son.

Denis's note was as brief as always.

Bring the statue to me, and I will reimburse your expense. Denis.

I retrieved the alabaster Cupid in its leather bag from my

wardrobe and strode north through the streets to Denis's large, hired house. I walked because the day was sunny yet pleasantly cool, and in spite of Donata's and Grenville's beliefs, I felt quite well, better than I had in a long while.

Once I'd learned of Gian's freedom, I'd instructed Bartholomew to hie to de Luca's house and give Gian the equivalent in *scudos* of one hundred guineas. I also made certain Bartholomew brought back a receipt of the transaction. The Cupid statue had not been part of what Bonaparte had stolen. According to Gian, Bartholomew said, de Luca had spoken the truth that it had been in the family for a long while.

Armed with the statue, I headed north. Brewster, as always, was my shadow.

"You're chuffed today, guv."

"I am." I swung the bag a little. "Illness makes me realize what a blessing is good health, and the city today is beautiful in the sunshine. A villain will pay for his crimes, and innocents are freed. This does make me chuffed."

"No more running around ruins then?" Brewster sniffed. "'Tis dangerous to this good health you love so much."

"Nonsense. I will take Peter and Gabriella to see Pompeii, but this time, I will be the guide."

Brewster muttered something in reply, but I ignored him.

Denis's retainer—one of his regular men, not the granite-faced Luigi—opened the door before I could raise my hand to knock on it. Brewster strolled in behind me, staying by my side instead of seeking the kitchens or his fellow bodyguards.

I was led upstairs, Brewster at my heels, to the library where I'd met with Denis on my last visit. As before, he was perusing a book when we entered. He continued to read from it for a moment before he carefully placed a slip of paper in the crease to mark his place and laid the book aside.

"The statue?" he asked by way of greeting.

Used to his abrupt ways, I placed the bag on the wide library table in front of the bookshelves and pulled it open.

"The receipt for the equivalent of one hundred guineas." I laid the paper on the table. "And a statue of Cupid, or Eros, a known forgery."

I lifted the alabaster carving from the bag and set it gently next to the paper. Denis came to it at once, a spark of excitement lighting his dark blue eyes. He shielded those eyes from me and bent over the statue, turning it from side to side to examine it.

His shoulders relaxed as though he'd feared I'd brought him the wrong piece. "Excellent." His voice held emotion—for Denis. "Most excellent."

"The lists of agents you asked for." I dug those from the bottom of the bag and set the sheaf of papers next to the receipt. "They were found among the trunk of papers hidden in the back room. Trevisan was happy to send them to me—or rather, to Grenville." Trevisan was cutting me out of his life, but I imagined he wasn't happy I knew too many of his secrets.

Denis barely glanced at the list. His rapt attention was all for the statue in front of him.

"At one time, I fancied that the lists had been concealed inside this," I said, touching Eros's broken wing. "I wondered if that was why you wanted the thing. I thought to break it open and discover if this was the case."

Denis straightened up in a rush, alarm flashing across his face before he guarded his expression once more.

"You did not, did you?"

"No, no. I came to my senses."

Denis lifted the statue to scan it, as though searching for new cracks, then satisfied I'd not harmed it, he set it down and stepped back to admire it. No invitation for me to sit, no lackey gliding in to serve us brandy or coffee.

I had no intention of scuttling away like a hired man, my errand done. "For my troubles, please tell me why," I said. "You stated that you knew this statue was a forgery, but you wanted it anyway. There must be a reason."

"There is." Denis faced me. I thought for a moment he would not answer but he looked directly into my eyes, his holding a flicker of triumph.

"It is indeed a forgery of an ancient Roman statue. A forgery ... made by Michelangelo Buonarroti. I thank you for retrieving it for me. Good day, Captain."

CHAPTER 27

*M*ichelangelo?" Grenville exclaimed as we sat in his drawing room that evening. "Good Lord. What bloody cheek."

"It is rumored he sculpted forgeries," Donata said serenely. She sat close by my side on the settee, as though making up for the days when my illness kept us apart. "When he was young and destitute and trying to make his name."

"A hundred guineas." I leaned back, sipping the rich coffee I'd miss when we returned to London. "I thought him a fool to pay so much. Now I realize he paid far too little."

"I wonder if Conte de Luca knew its true worth," Grenville mused. "He scoffed at it."

"Yes." I swirled the dregs in my cup. "I believe de Luca was the sort who understood price but not value. Bonaparte found a good ally in him."

"Which cost him his life," Donata said. She did not sound as sympathetic as she might. She squeezed my arm. "And nearly cost you yours."

I met her gaze, my body warming. I'd missed her while I'd

lain alone, swallowing Gautier's concoctions and trying to read while my fever ran its course.

Grenville cleared his throat. "I must get on with my packing. I am always certain I will forget something vital." He clattered down his cup and departed from the room, closing the door firmly behind him.

Donata moved still closer to me, taking both my hands. "Soon we will be strolling the gardens, enjoying the sunshine. And the moonlight." Her thumb traced the backs of my fingers.

"Love," I said softly. "The contessa said something to me when we were trapped in that cell." I hesitated, while Donata studied me, mystified. "She told me you had lost a child, that she could see it in you."

I expected Donata to be surprised, to say she must mean nearly losing Anne and then Peter, but her cheeks reddened, and she looked away from me.

"Donata?" She tried to withdraw her hands, but I held them fast. "The contessa was correct?"

"Yes." The word was so quiet I almost did not hear it. "I never like to think about it."

"I would like to know."

Donata had always been a private person, but I was a great believer in the idea that a burden shared was a burden halved —not that I always followed my own convictions.

"So you should." Donata drew a breath, as though steeling herself for an ordeal. "She was my first child, Breckenridge's, when we were newly married. I was young and full of hope, though I'd already realized some of Breckenridge's character. I was certain he'd change as we grew together, certain he'd change when I presented him with his firstborn. But carrying the child was difficult. One day ..." Her eyes clouded. "It happened quickly, and I still do not know why. But it was done. She was so very tiny."

I rose to my feet and tugged Donata to me, my arms going around her. "Love. I am so sorry."

"Breckenridge never forgave me." Her words were muffled, her cheek on my chest. "Not even when I gave him Peter."

I held her tightly, my lips in her hair. Donata had always been a fond mother, solicitous toward her son and now her daughter. Part of the reason must be this—she'd known what it was to lose a child, to have that hole in her life.

I did not berate her for not telling me. It must have hurt for her to even think about it, let alone find the words to share the tale. I knew she'd wanted to close off every part of her life with Breckenridge and live only in the present moment.

I had sometimes wondered why Peter had been born nearly seven years into Donata's marriage. Breckenridge had been on campaign in the Peninsula for much of their wedded life, but even so it might have taken Donata that long to be able to carry a child to term.

Her loss had happened about fifteen years ago now, but I was certain that this was not long enough to ease the pain. She would have told me, I knew, eventually, as she unfolded more of herself as our years together slid by.

I held her closer, my love for this woman overwhelming me. Outside in the street, vendors cried their wares, their musical voices surrounding us in this marvelous, teeming, uncompromising city that had survived war and earthquake and fire, from the ancient world to this day.

Inside, I soothed my wife, who had hurt more than I could understand, when I'd thought my own pain too much to bear. We held each other, her heartbeat against my chest, and knew each other a little better than we had even an hour before.

———

BEFORE WE LEFT ROME, I VISITED MR. BROADHURST, WHERE HE waited his return to London in lodgings behind the church of Sant'Agnese en Agone, guarded by several of Denis's largest men.

"You said you'd help me," Broadhurst bleated at me after I convinced the guards to let me in.

He regarded me in hurt outrage, and I eyed him severely. "I have met men who killed and stole for many reasons." My mouth firmed. "I have liked only a few of them less than you."

"I trusted you," he began.

"And many trusted you." I lost my temper. My reason for coming here had been to finish with him, to put an end to the matter in my mind. I thought of Joseph Cockburn, alone and unable to hear in an unforgiving world, who'd had to learn to defend himself at a young age. Of Leonard Cockburn, murdered because he'd wanted to return what he and Broadhurst had stolen, even if it destroyed the pair of them. Of the many men and women Broadhurst had cheated out of money that they could not afford to lose.

"You are a sordid and pathetic man," I snapped. "Sir Montague Harris is a just magistrate, and he will see to it that you receive what you deserve. Nothing more, nothing less."

Broadhurst only stared at me. His expression held some shame for his past deeds, but also a gleam of cunning. He was a swindler, one who'd persuaded many he had their best interests at heart. No doubt he told himself he could talk or buy his way out of Denis's clutches.

He would hope in vain. Denis would ignore any attempt Broadhurst made to cajole him into letting him go. Denis owed me a favor, and he'd use Broadhurst to pay it. Denis disliked obligating himself to anyone, and though Broadhurst might wheedle all he wished, I knew Denis would remain steadfast.

He'd take Broadhurst to London and hand him over without fuss to Sir Montague. Denis no doubt would use the situation to assuage the magistrates and with an eye to keeping them from interfering too much in his business, not that Sir Montague could be coerced.

I could almost pity Broadhurst. Almost. I gave him a cold nod, worthy of Conte Trevisan, and left him, Broadhurst's cunning look dissolving in a wave of trepidation.

————

Two days later, I scarcely waited until Grenville's coach had halted before I was throwing open its door and descending as quickly as I was able to the drive in front of his villa.

Three stories of stone rose from the surrounding garden that the coach had reached via an iron gate and a curved drive, a grand sweep of staircase leading to the front door. Through this door poured a dozen people, some in servants' garb, some in dresses floating as they hastened down the stairs, one small boy in a coat that was already awry, his boots coated with mud.

They flowed toward the carriage, the servants to welcome Donata and their master, Marianne heading straight for Grenville. The two connected, Grenville's arm firmly linking with Marianne's as they moved off into the garden. Grenville for once forgot his politeness in his need to be with his wife.

Marianne's son had come, she not wanting to leave him behind in England, and he dashed straight to Bartholomew, who was hauling down valises, to show him whatever he'd stuffed his pockets with. Bartholomew paused in his duties to admire rocks and insects and declared he wanted to see David's entire collection.

Peter hurled himself at me, his cries of *Papa!* ones of a strong lad ready for antics. A nurse held Anne, who was shouting as heartily as her brother. Anne reached arms out and was rewarded by Donata sweeping her up.

"Here's my little angel," Donata announced. The little angel shrieked in delight and smacked a sticky kiss against her mother's cheek.

I greeted Peter, pulling him into an exuberant hug before we then manfully shook hands. Released, Peter ran to join David and Bartholomew. Peter, though a year or so younger than David, had become the lad's protector.

My gaze had already locked to the young woman in ivory skirts who attempted to descend the stairs with more dignity than had her brother.

"Father," she said to me. She gave me a practiced curtsy, which I ruined by embracing her tightly.

"I missed you, daughter," I said, my voice breaking.

"And I you." Gabriella smiled at me when we parted, showing the truthfulness of her sedate words. "I want to hear all about your exploits in the Colosseum and the gladiator cells."

"Very bloodthirsty of you." I had written her a truncated version of events, making light of them, though she must know there was more to the story.

"Not at all. I am very interested in history." Gabriella took my arm. "I have read much, though Mama disapproves."

She meant her true mother, my former wife, who now lived in France with the man who'd taken her from me. Carlotta had been raised to believe that a woman with any sort of learning had little chance of marrying or being respected. That Gabriella had decided to be unconventional was heartening.

"Emile is interested in history as well," Gabriella went on. "We study it together."

"Is he? Well done." I said this distractedly, still uncertain of this young Frenchman who'd won Gabriella's heart. I'd been reminded in the last weeks how fragile and easily crushed was first love.

"He is here, Father. He arrived yesterday. Isn't that a delightful surprise?"

Emile had been due at the end of this week. Before I could register whether the surprise was delightful or not, Gabriella pulled from me and held out her hand to a young man I'd not noticed in the crowd.

He had brown hair pushed awry by the light breeze, a round face, brown eyes that were rather too wide, but perhaps that was his nervousness. His coat and trousers were subdued black, his cravat loosely tied, his boots serviceable.

He stumbled a little on the bottom step but caught himself as he landed by Gabriella's side.

"Father," Gabriella said happily, "may I present Emile Devere? Emile, my father, Captain Gabriel Lacey."

"Sir." Emile made me a tense bow. "I am pleased to make your acquaintance." His English was flawless though accented, a man who rarely spoke anything but his own tongue.

He gazed intently at me, his eyes full of so much hope and worry, that for a moment, I softened to him. But only for a moment.

This was the young man who wished to marry Gabriella, to make a home with her, to have children with her, to care for her the rest of her life. This was the man who would either cherish her or make her miserable.

I held out my hand, and Emile took it. If my handshake was a bit too firm, Emile bore it, his mouth tightening only a little as he assessed my strength.

"Mr. Devere," I said. "Well met. I will be pleased to make your acquaintance during the remainder of our stay."

Gabriella's smile widened with some relief, but Emile remained uneasy and flexed his hand when I released it.

When I sent him a grin, was I reminding him that I'd fought many a man in my day and bested most of them? Or simply that I was pleased at last to meet the lad Gabriella had told me about?

Time, conversations, and circumstances would tell.

For now, I tucked Gabriella's hand under my arm, reached the other for Donata and Anne, and called to Peter, who raced to join us, and led my family up the stairs and into the cool and welcoming house.

AUTHOR'S NOTE

Thank you for reading! I enjoyed exploring the Rome of the early nineteenth century in Captain Lacey's footsteps. The time between Napoleon's invasion and the Risorgimento in the 1860s is an interesting one, and an era of great change. In Captain Lacey's time, Italy was a series of independent states, many ruled by foreign powers, the Kingdom of Italy not created until 1861. Napoleon had attempted to unify the peninsula (with himself in charge, of course), but at his defeat, Italy fragmented again, many of his reforms set aside. The seeds had begun, however, for the Italian states to join, rid themselves of foreign kings, and become one country.

Rome is an amazing city, as Donata calls it "vibrant and robust. So many eras in history, and yet the people here live firmly in the present."

I found that to be true. I was enchanted with Rome, astonished by it. It was nothing at all what I expected, and at the same time, everything I'd hoped for. If you go, prepare to spend time there, a week at the very least, to absorb all you can. I recommend visiting in September or October—the weather is excellent and the huge crowds have mostly dispersed. (It will still be crowded, but less so.)

I have stayed near the Piazza Navona, and so set the story in and around that area, as I came to know it well. The Piazza itself is a beautiful space to simply spend time in, watching Rome go by. And of course, the ancient ruins are not to be missed. I highly recommend a tour of the Colosseum that allows you to go underneath it, into the corridors and cells in which the gladiators, prisoners, and animals were kept.

If you enjoy stories set in Rome, please have a look at my series set there in the time of Nero, featuring Leonidas, a freed gladiator. The first book is **Blood of a Gladiator**, in which Leonidas, finding himself freed from the games, searches for a way to keep himself. He's given a slave, Cassia, who is a scribe, to help him, and together they find themselves embroiled in murder and intrigue, as well as coming under the scrutiny of Nero himself.

Captain Lacey will now return to London for more adventures with his family and friends.

Best wishes,

Ashley Gardner

ALSO BY ASHLEY GARDNER

Leonidas the Gladiator Mysteries
Blood of a Gladiator
Blood Debts
A Gladiator's Tale
The Ring that Caesar Wore

Captain Lacey Regency Mystery Series
The Hanover Square Affair
A Regimental Murder
The Glass House
The Sudbury School Murders
The Necklace Affair
A Body in Berkeley Square
A Covent Garden Mystery
A Death in Norfolk
A Disappearance in Drury Lane
Murder in Grosvenor Square
The Thames River Murders
The Alexandria Affair

A Mystery at Carlton House
Murder in St. Giles
Death at Brighton Pavilion
The Custom House Murders
Murder in the Eternal City

The Gentleman's Walking Stick
(short stories: in print in
The Necklace Affair and Other Stories)

Kat Holloway "Below Stairs" Victorian Mysteries
(writing as Jennifer Ashley)
A Soupçon of Poison
Death Below Stairs
Scandal Above Stairs
Death in Kew Gardens
Murder in the East End
Death at the Crystal Palace
The Secret of Bow Lane
Speculations in Sin

Mystery Anthologies
Past Crimes

ABOUT THE AUTHOR

USA Today Bestselling author Ashley Gardner is a pseudonym for *New York Times* bestselling author Jennifer Ashley. Under both names—and a third, Allyson James—Ashley has written more than 100 published novels and novellas in mystery, romance, fantasy, and historical fiction. Ashley's books have been translated into more than a dozen different languages and have earned starred reviews in *Publisher's Weekly* and *Booklist*. The Below Stairs Mystery series, which she writes as Ashley Gardner, has been optioned for television.

When she isn't writing, Ashley indulges her love for history by researching and building miniature houses and furniture from many periods, and playing classical guitar and piano.

More about the Captain Lacey series can be found at the website:

www.gardnermysteries.com.

Stay up to date on new releases by joining her email alerts here:

http://eepurl.com/5n7rz

CPSIA information can be obtained
at www.ICGtesting.com
Printed in the USA
LVHW110603030123
736323LV00005B/346

9 781958 798003